It was uncomfortable and it was lovely.

She, Christopher and Patrick looked so much like a real family that Mallory's heart yearned to make it so. Which was impossible.

Was she falling in love with him? No, she'd passed that stage—she *was* in love with Patrick Lonergan.

If only he would return the sentiment.

Which he wouldn't.

Patrick had been quite up-front about his feelings. He wanted her. But that was sex, not love. Not a happily ever after.

Accept and enjoy, Mallory lectured herself. But throughout it all, her mind kept chanting a litany: *If only he would love me. If only he would love us.*

Dear Reader,

Welcome to Silhouette **Special Edition**...welcome to romance. Our New Year's resolution is to continue bringing you romantic, emotional stories you'll be sure to love!

And this month we're sure fulfilling that promise as Marie Ferrarella returns with our THAT SPECIAL WOMAN! title for January, *Husband: Some Assembly Required*. Dr. Shawna Saunders has trouble resisting the irresistible charms of Murphy Pendleton!

THIS TIME, FOREVER, a wonderful new series by Andrea Edwards, begins this month with *A Ring and a Promise*. Jake O'Neill and Kate O'Malley don't believe in destiny, until a legend of ancestral passion pledged with a ring and an unfulfilled promise show them the way.

Also in January, Susan Mallery introduces the first of her two HOMETOWN HEARTBREAKERS. Was sexy Sheriff Travis Haynes the town lady-killer—or a knight in shining armor? Elizabeth Abbott finds out in *The Best Bride*. Diana Whitney brings you *The Adventurer*—the first book in THE BLACKTHORN BROTHERHOOD. Don't miss Devon Monroe's story—and his secret.

The wonders of love in 1995 continue as opposites attract in Elizabeth Lane's *Wild Wings, Wild Heart*, and Beth Henderson's *New Year's Eve* keeps the holiday spirit going.

Hope this New Year shapes up to be the best ever! Enjoy this book and all the books to come!

Sincerely,

Tara Gavin
Senior Editor

Please address questions and book requests to:
Silhouette Reader Service
U.S.: 3010 Walden Ave., P.O. Box 1325, Buffalo, NY 14269
Canadian: P.O. Box 609, Fort Erie, Ont. L2A 5X3

BETH
HENDERSON

NEW YEAR'S EVE

Silhouette®

SPECIAL EDITION®

Published by Silhouette Books
America's Publisher of Contemporary Romance

To Mom and Dad,
my rescue squad

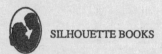 SILHOUETTE BOOKS

ISBN 0-373-09935-5

NEW YEAR'S EVE

Copyright © 1995 by Beth Henderson

This edition published by arrangement with Harlequin Enterprises B.V.

® and TM are trademarks of Harlequin Enterprises B.V., used under license. Trademarks indicated with ® are registered in the United States Patent and Trademark Office, the Canadian Trade Marks Office and in other countries.

Printed in U.S.A.

BETH HENDERSON

began writing when she was in the seventh grade and ran out of Nancy Drew books to read. It took another couple of decades, and a lot of distractions and procrastination, before her first book appeared in print.

Although a Buckeye by birth, Beth spent twenty years in the West, living in Tucson, Arizona, and in Las Vegas, Nevada. During that time she sampled a number of professions and has been a copywriter and traffic director in radio, done print display advertising, and has been a retail department manager. Now returned to her hometown in Ohio, she is completing a master's degree in English at Wright State University.

Her first love has always been scribbling stories. Writing also under the pen names Elizabeth Daniels and Lisa Dane, she has had a total of nine novels, both historical and contemporary romances, published. *New Year's Eve* is her first book for Silhouette and is her tenth story...to date.

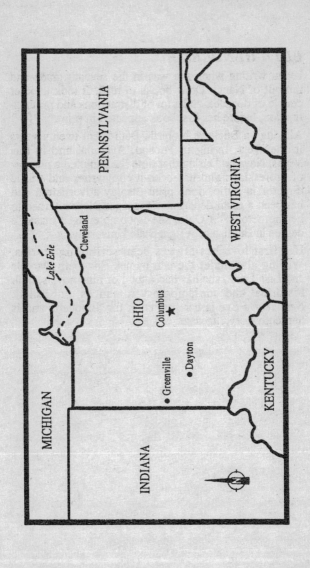

Chapter One

The sounds of laughter and music floated out to Mallory Meyers in her tiny kitchen. She hummed along with the softly playing background of holiday melodies on the stereo. The selection was her aunt's favorite, "Oh, Come All Ye Faithful." Aunt Anita had always preferred to sing it as "Adestes Fideles," the Latin words giving the song a haunting, mystical flavor.

It meant the same in either language, and the crowd of adults that had recently filled Mallory's front room had appeared to have answered that call. Now only two remained to work their way through her dwindling supply of Christmas cookies.

This was the second year running that Mallory had chaired the St. Edmund's holiday bazaar. When kidded about it, she claimed Pastor Kevin Lonergan had caught her at a weak moment and charmed her into doing it.

Charm was one thing everyone agreed their minister had in abundance.

Kevin had wheedled the first year. "Come on, Mal. Your expertise will be the making of us. Who knows how to empty a shopper's purse better than a professional retailer?"

Truth was, Mallory couldn't resist any suggestion the man made when he smiled at her.

But this year he hadn't had to push her. She had volunteered.

She really should have her head examined, Mallory decided, placing a star-shaped cookie on her tray. As a newly created general manager of softlines at the Rittenhouse Department Store, she had an overly full schedule just keeping her sales floor running smoothly, now that the Christmas shopping season was in full swing. And she still had to oversee the ordering of merchandise to sell six months down the road.

It wasn't even that she was an overly religious woman. She belonged to St. Edmund's Church because she felt it was a necessary part of her son Christopher's socialization, of his education. One that was far more comfortable than the one her parents had given her. They had belonged to a small fundamentalist sect. There was nothing gentle about the teachings in their church. When she had discovered that she was carrying Dirk's child, and that Dirk was married, her parents had cast her out, disowned her. She hadn't seen them in seven years.

Anita Quillan, her maternal aunt, had been much more understanding. She had taken Mallory in, offered the unquestioning love that her niece so desperately needed, and rejoiced with Mallory at the birth of her beautiful son. In gratitude, Mallory had granted her aunt's dearest wish and joined Anita's church.

It hadn't been a leap of faith. It hadn't really been a demonstration of love for Anita, either. Mallory knew that her decision to convert had been made for the benefit of her son's future, rather than her own.

Perhaps that was what she liked about Kevin. He understood her reasoning and didn't push her into delving into theology as some well-meaning ministers had done in the past. He merely used her talents to work God's will. That was what Kevin called cleaning out his parishioners' pockets at the annual Christmas bazaar.

Knowing her remaining committee members had a weakness for sweets, Mallory emptied the cookie jar, piling the last of the fir-shaped cookies on the plate.

Chris had helped decorate the cookies again this year. He was generous with the green and red sprinkles. A good many stuck to Mallory's fingers. She licked the sugar off absentmindedly.

Her little boy was growing up. It seemed impossible that he was already six and dazzling her with his first-grade knowledge. Soon he'd shun helping make cookies, finding junior high football practice more important. After that, it would be a quick jump to wanting to drive the car and impress girls. Any day now he'd reach the age where he wanted to know more about the man who had sired him.

What could she say about Dirk Segal that didn't sound contemptuous?

Nothing. The man had lied to her, seduced her, then left when she needed him the most.

Chris didn't need that kind of male influence in his young life. And, after her ordeal with Dirk, there was little chance of Mallory ever fully trusting another man. She'd made a mistake. She wouldn't repeat it.

There was no reason to take a chance and get romantically involved with anyone, when there was already a man well-suited as a role model for Chris. He was a good friend, a very decent and honorable man. Mallory didn't fool herself, though. The real reason she was so fond of Pastor Lonergan was that, being recently widowed and grieving deeply for his lost bride, Kevin was a man with whom she felt safe. Friendship was as far as either of them would allow their relationship to go.

"Mallory!" a woman's voice called from the front room. "Come talk some sense into Rosemary."

Mallory hefted her tray of cookies. "Coming!" she called.

As she stepped through the kitchen doorway, she caught a movement near the glittering, lighted Christmas tree. Chris ducked back into the hallway, but she'd seen him investigating the large box Aunt Anita had left for him earlier. It was most definitely the racetrack set he'd drooled over each Saturday morning during his cartoon marathon. Remembering his tastes, Anita had wrapped it in paper that was covered with drawings of his favorite cartoon tiger cat, each figure either sporting a Santa costume or bearing a red-and-green package. Probably of lasagna, Mallory mused. Like their cartoon hero, Chris and Anita also loved the pasta dish.

And so did Kevin. Maybe one of these days she would learn to make it, rather than just buy frozen lasagna when she invited her aunt and the minister for dinner.

Mallory pretended she hadn't seen Chris. He would soon tire of staring at his first present of the season and crawl back into bed. He was a good child, warm, loving and handsome. Everything a mother could wish. He had inherited her coloring, his hair a soft brown, his eyes a muted gray. She was pleased his features showed no sign of becoming like his father's. She hoped they never would.

"You wouldn't believe this woman," Frances Hutchins declared as Mallory slid the newly filled tray of cookies on the coffee table. Fran gestured at Rosemary Bittner, across from her, and reached for an angel-shaped cookie. "She thinks you should ask that new doctor to be your date at the store manager's holiday party." Fran settled back into the tweed cushions of the sofa and bit off part of the angel's wing. "Set her straight," she urged, her mouth full as she signaled Mallory with the cookie.

Mallory dropped onto a floor cushion near the remains of the wood fire in her fireplace and rested her chin on her updrawn knees. It hadn't snowed yet, but there was a strong wind blowing outside. She had dressed warmly, shedding her business suit for a heavy bright red sweater, snug jeans and thick red slouch socks. Since all the women on her committee were friends, Mallory hadn't bothered with putting on shoes or doing more than tying her dark hair back from her face.

Rosemary didn't give Mallory a chance to respond to Fran's challenge. She leaned forward in the rocking chair she'd commandeered earlier, and took a cookie, as well. "What's wrong with Dr. Williams? He's a very nice man, nice-looking, and divorced. More important, he's just the right age for you, Mallory."

"It's sweet of you—" Mallory began.

Fran cut her off. "He's got to be ten, fifteen years older than Mal," she said. "Plus, he's got teenagers. Rather brainless girls, from what I've seen."

"You only think so because they giggle a lot," Rosemary explained kindly. As the pastor's housekeeper, Rosemary Bittner kept abreast of the doings of many of the parishioners. She always looked for the best in each of them. Mallory often thought Rosemary had missed her calling by not becoming a minister herself. At the same time, she was very glad that Rosemary was available to baby-sit at strange hours. With her hectic retail schedule, Mallory frequently was forced to turn Chris over to Rosemary's care in the evenings and on weekends as well as after school.

She could do without the well-meaning woman's constant efforts at matchmaking, though.

"Dr. Williams is too staid for Mal," Fran continued. "She needs a man who can perk up her life. Add some excitement to it."

"I like my life," Mallory said.

"Only because you don't know what you're missing," Fran declared. Rosemary nodded in agreement. "I'm not just talking passion, Mal—I'm talking love, giving, taking, sharing."

"All that just for Mr. Rittenhouse's party?" Mallory protested, her eyes twinkling with humor. "I don't even think I really need a date, Fran. I haven't had one other years."

"You were just a department manager then. You weren't a big shot," Fran said.

"I'm still not a big shot."

"You are to us, dear," Rosemary insisted, "and to all those little people who work for you."

Mallory wasn't sure the employees of the jewelry, cosmetics, and various clothing departments would care to be designated "little people," but she knew what Rosemary meant. As a member of upper management, she needed to do some things differently now. But did that necessarily mean she needed an escort to the holiday party?

"Well, I disagree that Dr. Williams should be a candidate," Fran said. "Who else is available, Rosemary? You know everybody in the parish. There has got to be more than one single man available."

Rosemary nibbled on her cookie angel's other wing. "I'm thinking," she assured the two younger women.

"Personally, I've been driving Larry crazy, asking about the guys he works with. He claims they are all too flaky to foist on Mal," Fran confessed.

Although she had met Fran's husband only a few times, Mallory decided she liked Larry Hutchins quite well. Someone, at least, was displaying good sense.

"There's that nice Mr. Titus," Rosemary said.

Fran axed the idea before Mallory could protest. "He's bald and overweight. Who else?"

Mallory sighed silently and turned toward the fireplace. It looked as if she would have visitors for a good while longer. Perhaps she should add another log or two.

"You know, Mal," Fran mused, reaching for another cookie, "we've been wondering what to get you this year. Something special, because of all the hours you put in on the bazaar. But if we can come up with a date for you for this party, you can consider him as wrapped, tied, tagged and under your tree this year."

The rocking chair creaked as Rosemary set it in motion again. "What about George Erwin?"

Fran choked on a crumb. "Erwin! Give me a break!"

Mallory sighed out loud this time and picked up the fireplace poker to stir the embers. It was going to be a long night.

Christopher Meyers pressed back against the wall and thought about what he'd just heard. He knew he should be in bed, but the lure of the package his great-aunt had left earlier in the day was hard to resist. He'd been crossing off the days on his calendar, and still the days until Christmas dragged.

His flannel pajamas didn't keep him very warm outside his covers, but he hadn't remembered to put on his robe or slippers. Heck, he knew he wasn't supposed to be out of bed! He had promised himself one last look at the present with his favorite cartoon character on the paper, and then he'd realized what his mother's friends were talking about. They wanted her to have a date.

Chris pondered the matter. He could see the flickering colored shadows made by the lights on the Christmas tree. They made pretty patterns on the wall. Usually he liked watching them, imagining himself into a world of adventure like the heroes in his favorite comic books and cartoons. But he barely noticed the designs. His mind was too busy turning over the novel idea of his mother going on a date. Wasn't that what his friend Jeff's older sister did? Jeff hadn't thought much of her boyfriends. Not until one had given him a dollar to get lost. Jeff liked that guy a lot.

But Mom?

Chris took one last look around the corner, this time homing in on where his mother sat on the floor near the fireplace. She looked pretty tonight, he thought. She always did to him. He was fairly sure other guys liked looking at her, too. Like that Dr. Williams that Mrs. Rosemary was talking about. Mom probably didn't even know Dr. Williams watched her, but Chris knew. He agreed with Mrs. Hutchins. Dr. Williams wasn't right for his mom.

Which led him to the realization that other guys' moms did have grown men around. Sometimes they were his friends' fathers, sometimes just their moms' boyfriends. He'd even seen Jeff's mom and dad kissing in their kitchen before breakfast one morning. It had been sort of embarrassing, until Jeff said they kissed each other a lot, that that was how he had gotten his little sister. You got babies when your mom and dad loved each other. Or at least that was what Jeff said.

Since he didn't have a dad, it was just him and Mom. No babies. He kind of liked Jeff's new baby sister. She was pink and still pretty bald, but she always smiled when she saw him. He liked the way she smelled. Not neat, like Mom, but different, and nice.

It might be cool to have a baby sister of his own. He could be a big brother and teach her things, like Jeff did. 'Cept it meant he had to have a dad, as well as a mom, to get one.

And a dad would get to kiss Mom in the kitchen. Would that mean she wouldn't have as many kisses for him, then? He'd have to ask Jeff tomorrow, Chris decided, and crawled back down the hall carefully, so as not to arouse suspicion in the adults in the outer room.

Before he got back in bed, Chris crossed the room and took a bedraggled stuffed cat from the top of his dresser. Once it had been fat and fluffy, but duty as his protector at night when he was little had turned it into a soft orange lump with only one eye. There had been some mighty battles with monsters in the night, but his cat had kept him safe. That had been when he was a baby, of course. The cat had retired when he started school. He was a big boy now. The idea of having to share his mother wasn't something to ponder alone, though. It felt good to have an old friend with him. He'd ask Jeff about dads tomorrow, Chris promised himself, just before his eyes drooped closed. Or maybe Pastor Kevin. He would know.

She was gone. Funny how he had to keep reminding himself of that, Patrick Lonergan thought. You'd think when you'd lived with a woman for seven years that you'd miss her. Miss something about her—her scent, her sound, her essence. Her passion. But there was nothing. Sunshine St. John had breezed out of his life as easily as she had breezed in.

Seven years. A long time. In some ways, a lifetime.

Hell, he should miss her! Why in Sam Hill didn't he?

Pat slammed a fist against the open barn door, startling one of the hens that had chosen to roost in the upper loft. He didn't notice when the perturbed bird fluttered back to earth and stalked past him. Pat stared out at the house he had shared with Sunshine, the house in which he and his twin brother, Kevin, had grown up.

It was empty. Had been even when Sun lived there with him. What it was missing was the laughter of his late parents, Marie and Michael Lonergan, the gibes of Kevin as they sparred with each other. Sun had just marked time in the same rooms. She'd made no changes in his mother's decorating, she'd made no lasting mark on his soul.

Even Kevin had found Sunshine harmless. Embarrassing to have around, but still harmless.

It had been hard for the minister to accept his twin's live-in girlfriend. It had kept Kevin away from the family homestead for a long time. Pat didn't blame his brother. He knew it was impossible for Kev to accept what he preached against to his congregation.

Kev lived his life the way he wanted. Fortunately, without a holier-than-thou approach. But the restrictions of Kevin's choice had no appeal for Patrick. There had been those in the past who thought that for each good deed Kev did, Pat went out of his way to counter with an evil one. They had been known as the Angel and the Devil at school, Kevin winning citizenship awards, Patrick spending time in detention.

When their parents died suddenly, within a few weeks of each other, it had been Patrick who returned to the farm, who picked up his father's dream and continued to care for the land.

Such beautiful land.

Pat turned away from the house, forcing his gaze to roam over the one thing that meant something in his life. His land.

It spread out toward the horizon, as flat and even as if Mother Nature had taken a rolling pin to it. With the harvest long finished, it was empty, only the distant copse of ancient hardwood trees breaking his line of sight. He'd visited Kansas in his travels before coming back to western Ohio, but the vistas had been different. The prairies hadn't called to him the way this soil did. He hadn't even known he missed it until the farm had come under his care.

And now even the land couldn't cure the emptiness he felt. It wasn't just Sunshine's abrupt departure. She'd left nearly six months ago. He'd just been too busy running his farm-management cum stockbroker business to really miss her. Sun was a free spirit. She hadn't believed in cooking much, or breeding animals, or growing crops. Sun existed on her own plane and had met him on the only level they both understood—the softly welcoming surface of a bed. Even the pleasures to be shared there had begun to pale in the last year. For a man who had one hell of a reputation among the local women, many of whom he'd chased and caught during his teens, losing interest in his lusty bed partner was entirely out of character.

So why had he lost interest in bedroom aerobics? Was he getting that old?

Pat ran a hand through his hair. He didn't feel old. The mirror told him his hair was just as dark a brown as it had always been, and burnished with a hint of copper, rather than silver. There were deep lines around his eyes, but they could be attributed to the sun. He spent so much time outdoors that even in December, his skin was a warm toasted brown. He was only thirty-five, or would be on Thursday, he thought ruefully. There wasn't an inch of fat on his lean body, and since he'd been reduced to eating his own cooking, it didn't look as if there ever would be.

The idea of adding another year was depressing, though. His investments were flourishing, his other business interests were holding their own nicely, and until the holidays were over he really didn't have one heck of a lot to do with himself. If Sunshine were still around, he might be tempted to take a vacation. Go someplace where thoughts of grain prices and pork futures didn't even enter a man's mind. A tropical paradise, perhaps. But without an equally warm companion to share it, there didn't seem to be much use in going.

Patrick hunched his shoulders against a particularly wicked draft and pulled the collar of his fleece-lined bomber jacket higher. Maybe he was getting old, to feel the cold this sharply. Kev would probably tell him something profound about the emptiness of his soul. Just the thought made Pat smile. Damned if he didn't miss his brother. Shoot, Kev was getting just as old as he was. Older! By fourteen minutes.

Pat shoved at the barn door, drawing it closed and securing it. He felt revitalized just at the idea of going into town. All it took was a couple of calls, and the kids from the neighboring farms would see to the few chickens he kept for old times' sake. Since Sunshine was a vegetarian, chickens lived to an old age on the Lonergan Farm. They'd survive a little longer without him around, Pat decided. He was overdue for some quality time with his sibling. He hoped Kevin hadn't lost his taste for fine whiskey. Kev had renounced a lot in joining the ministry, but he still had Irish blood running through his veins.

There were just some things a true Lonergan shouldn't have to give up.

Chapter Two

Kevin Lonergan glanced up from his notepad when his housekeeper tapped lightly on the door of his office. His hand moved quickly to the reading glasses that perched precariously low on his nose. The spectacles disappeared before Rosemary eased the door open.

Ah, vanity, thy name is Kevin, he thought, then wondered fleetingly if his twin had succumbed to the demands of their advancing years. It would make it much easier to bear his failing eyesight if he knew Pat suffered from it, as well.

"Pastor? Do you have a moment to speak to a troubled parishioner?" Rosemary asked. The smile on her lips jarred with the serious tone of her voice until he spotted the troubled soul in question. Christopher Meyers was fidgeting from one foot to the other, his small face screwed into an expression of unease.

Kevin grinned widely and got to his feet. "It's no problem at all, Mrs. Bittner," he said. And it wasn't. He'd been hoping for an interruption that would take him away from the necessary evil of composing a sermon for his Sunday services. The boy was the answer to his prayers.

Rosemary stepped back and pushed the door wider. "You can go right in, Chris," she murmured. "When you're finished talking, come sample my new batch of cookies in the kitchen."

When Chris merely nodded, Kevin decided the boy's problem was more serious than a bad grade in math. Math was the bane of Chris's existence. He'd come to Kevin for help before, which had amused the minister. If Chris only knew how he'd struggled through arithmetic himself! Patrick had always been a whiz at it, had even made a career out of figures.

The situation took on enormous proportions when Chris waited for the housekeeper to leave, then softly closed the office door. The boy had never felt the need for secrecy before. What could be disturbing him? And to such a degree that Chris didn't feel comfortable discussing it with his mother?

Kevin knew more about what made Christopher Meyers tick than he could even guess about the foibles of his other parishioners, no matter what their ages. Since Kevin was comfortable around children, Chris was often underfoot at the church office. Rosemary Bittner watched him after school, and on other occasions when Mallory's schedule kept her at the store. When Rosemary's housekeeping duties at the church and Kevin's adjacent home coincided with the hours she watched Chris, the boy tagged along with her. Although there were some who would find it strange to hear the echo of a child's laughter in his now bachelor quarters, the sound of Chris's

giggle chased away some of the gloom that had shadowed his life since he'd lost his beloved wife, Beverly, a
few months earlier.

There wasn't another child of his acquaintance who
radiated love and contentment as much as Chris did.
Mallory's efforts were superhuman, indeed, to supply her
son with the confidence to be himself, to feel special and
yet remain unspoiled.

Kevin moved around the side of the desk. "Chris, my
man!" he said. "What's the hitch today? Two and two
not making five?"

"Two and two are four," Christopher said. He brightened briefly. "I got an A on my last test, so I'm sure that's
right now."

"An A! Congratulations! Knew you could do it, sport.
So what's the problem today?" Kevin gestured for his
visitor to take one of the straight-backed chairs in front of
his desk. Rather than settle officially behind the desk, as
he would have with an adult visitor, Kevin spun the other
guest chair around and straddled it. "We're not talking
the difference between an adverb and an adjective, are
we? 'Cause I've got to confess, Chris, I was never too sure
on that myself when I was your age." *Or any other,* he
added silently. Not knowing hadn't affected the content
of his sermons. You didn't have to know a part of speech
to use it, after all. Details like that had always been Pat's
specialty, while metaphysics had appealed more to him.

Chris wiggled up onto the chair, his short legs dangling
as he perched on the edge, his toes just clearing the carpet. He cleared his throat. "It's Mom," he said.

"Your mother?" Kevin echoed, mystified.

"Sorta," Chris said. "I want ta get her a really neat
present for Christmas."

Kevin relaxed. His collar didn't feel quite as tight as it had a moment ago. "Any ideas?"

Chris stared at the scuffed toes of his athletic shoes. One of them was untied, the laces dangling loosely. "She needs a date," the boy mumbled, and glanced up to meet the minister's eyes, his own pleading. "Just for some party she has to go to," he rushed on. "Could you go with her, Pastor Kev?"

The request stunned Kevin. "I don't think—"

Chris hurried into speech again, cutting him off. "Some of the guys have got dads that do things like that with their moms. You know, go to parties and stuff. Jeff says they kiss and have babies, too, but you don't have ta do that. Just go to the party. They'll probably have cookies and cake and candy and punch and—"

"Chris..."

"Please!"

The entreaty in the boy's gray eyes was heartbreaking.

"I can't do it, Chris," Kevin said quietly.

"But..."

Kevin sighed deeply. "Listen to me just a minute, Chris. You know how you love your mother?"

"Uh-huh."

"Well, when you get married, you love your wife just as much as that." *Sometimes even more,* he added to himself.

It had been nearly three months since Beverly's sudden passing. Kevin knew she would have wanted him to go on with his life, to find another woman with whom to share his ministry. But not yet. Not for a good long while yet.

Chris's gray eyes regarded him solemnly. "You miss Mrs. Lonergan, huh?" the boy said.

"Yes, I miss Mrs. Lonergan," Kevin admitted.

"Mom says that she's with the angels now, and you can talk to her, and she'll hear you, even if she can't talk to you."

Kevin smiled wanly. From the mouths of babes, he mused. "Your mother is absolutely right," he agreed. "So, you see, I can't go to the party with your mother."

"'Cause Mrs. Lonergan would get jealous," Chris agreed. "Like Jeff's sister did when her boyfriend asked some other girl out."

If it made sense to Christopher, he'd go with that explanation himself. Although he was out of the running, that didn't mean he couldn't help the boy with his problem. "I think I can help you find a present for your mother, though."

"You won't get in trouble?" Chris asked. "Jeff's sister sure didn't like..."

Apparently all Chris's knowledge concerning the continuing give-and-take between the sexes was based on his friend Jeff's sister's love life.

"Mrs. Lonergan is very understanding about letting me help a man in need," Kevin said. He glanced at his watch. "In fact, if it's all right with Mrs. Bittner, perhaps we could hit the mall before you go home to dinner."

Chris's feet began swinging back and forth, the dangling laces of his untied shoe swishing gently. "But she doesn't need anything from the mall," he whined. "Just a date."

"Perfume," Kevin offered.

"She's 'lergic ta it."

"Jewelry."

"Got lots."

"A sweater." Although how he was supposed to guess Mallory's size was beyond him, Kevin thought. Perhaps Rosemary could help.

"Nope." Chris was becoming inflexible, the set of his small chin tilted stubbornly. He reminded Kevin of Mallory when she was displeased with the look of a booth at the bazaar.

Kevin took a last, desperate stab. "A pretty nightgown," he offered. And heaven help him if one of his parishioners caught him in a lingerie department, choosing something lacy for Mallory Meyers!

Chris sighed deeply. "She needs a date, not a nightgown. Maybe Mrs. Rosemary can talk ta Dr. Williams or Mr. Titus."

Kevin flashed on the pompous figure of Dr. Williams, then on the ridiculous form of Mr. Titus. They were members of his congregation, and he knew they had good qualities, even if they hid them quite well. But the idea of either of the men in question as Mallory's escort was enough to curdle a strong man's stomach.

There were some things that even a man of God couldn't condone, although he'd had to swallow some bitter pills in his life as a minister. Like Sunshine St. John. Thank goodness that woman was out of his brother's life. Now, if only...

The idea bloomed in glorious, unusually clear detail in his mind. It was so brilliantly logical, Kevin wondered why the solution hadn't occurred to him sooner.

"Let's leave Mrs. Bittner to her cookies a while longer. I might have an idea," Kevin said.

He reached over to the desk top and picked up a small picture frame. The photograph showed two tall young men wearing plain white T-shirts, tight, worn jeans and scuffed, muddy boots. Identical mops of dark hair, green eyes and roguish smiles made the two nearly indistinguishable. He'd been on a brief visit home from theological school when it was taken, while Pat had already been a successful stockbroker in the Big Apple. Their once-yearly swings through the home farm had coincided that year, much to the delight of their fond parents.

"You remember this?" Kevin asked, passing the photograph to his young friend.

"Yeah." Chris held the frame carefully between his small hands. "That's your brother." He pointed to the figure on the left unerringly, which surprised Kevin, since he didn't remember ever pointing out which of the pictured men was Patrick.

"I know because he has more muscles than you do," Chris explained guilelessly.

Kevin glanced at his forearm. Although the fabric of his shirt covered it, he had to agree with the boy. Patrick always had been more physically active than he, and thus more visually pumped. He'd worked out regularly at a gym when he worked in New York City. Now that he labored daily on the farm, the difference between them was probably no longer slight.

There was only one snag in his solution to Chris's problem. Its name was Patrick.

Chris gazed at the picture a moment longer. "Is he married to anybody?" he asked, his finger still on Pat's photo.

"Nope," Kevin said, pleased that Chris had caught on already.

"Do you think maybe—?"

Kevin smiled warmly at his young parishioner. "I think it's time I gave Pat a call and invited him for a visit. Think you could get me a picture of your mom?" *To use as bait,* he added silently.

Chris nodded. "She looks real pretty in the one Aunt E'ta took."

Kevin translated the slurred name to indicate Mallory's Aunt Anita.

"That's when we went to the beach last year," Chris continued. "Aunt E'ta told her she looked sexy in her swimsuit."

Better and better. Kevin's grin widened. If there was anything he knew about his brother, it was Patrick's weakness for good-looking women. And Mallory Meyers qualified for that designation with great distinction. A photograph of her in a bathing suit would definitely lure Pat into his trap.

Make that a double trap, Kevin revised quickly. As nice as it was to have Mallory available for charity duty at St. Edmund's, she needed more to her life than good works and her career. And so did Christopher.

With three wandering souls under his care, it was only natural for him to try his hand at matching them. Pat needed a family of his own, Chris needed a father, and Mallory, self-sufficient as she was, needed a husband.

Feeling distinctly as if he were a spider inviting a group of flies to tea, Kevin leaned forward and fondly tousled Chris's unruly brown hair. "That picture sounds like just the ticket, sport," he agreed. "Think you can bring it by tomorrow?"

Mallory tucked the phone between her cheek and one hunched shoulder. She ticked off the items on an order form for men's ties while listening to her caller's panicked voice. "Just finish crocheting as many pot holders as is physically possible, Fran," she said, and reached for her adding machine. Her fingers flew over the keys by touch as she double-checked the totals of both cost and retail on the form before scribbling her signature at the bottom of the page, okaying the order. "It doesn't mat-

ter if we've got an even hundred or not. The idea is to
make money for the church, not to balance out an inventory."

After running the holiday bazaar two years in a row,
Mallory was sure she'd heard all the stories a dozen times.
In some ways, guiding the parish volunteers through the
process of gathering goods, creating appropriate crafts
and planning the layout of their booths was easier than
managing the softlines departments at Rittenhouse. In
others, it was more complicated. At St. Edmund's there
weren't hard-and-fast rules to follow, the committee was
made up of amateurs who hadn't the least idea of what
they were doing, and procrastination abounded. They
were a week away from the bazaar now, and nearly all the
craftspeople were calling in with half-baked reasons why
they wouldn't be able to supply the total number of items
they had promised while in the grip of the planning frenzy.

Little did they know that she had mentally cut each
amount in half on her own charts. Experience did count
when you got down to the wire.

It was another reason why she could listen to St. Edmund's frantic flock and process the summer orders for
Rittenhouse at the same time. Fran, Rosemary and the
others still had Christmas foremost in their minds, but, of
necessity, Mallory's priorities had moved on to resort wear
and back-to-school clothing. If the orders didn't go in
now, her departments would be empty when the seasons
changed. And that wasn't good for sales.

Trouble was, she enjoyed the frenzy of the bazaar far
more than the power of her new management job. But to
give Chris a stable home, she needed a regular, decent
salary. She could consider free-lance charity-event supervision once he was grown and on his own. Until then, it
could be little more than a pleasant fantasy.

Fran babbled on some more. Mallory studied an order for junior swimsuits and jotted a note to the merchandiser in charge of that department. "Percentage of two-piece suits too high," she wrote. "Refigure within same allowance with more one-pieces. How many high-cut leg styles?"

"Fred Woods says he'll make up some of his special barbecue sauce and bottle it," Fran said.

Great! Mallory thought sarcastically. How many jars did the elderly man think he could turn out in a week's time? Rosemary had spent a couple weeks canning her peach preserves in a decent quantity. Mr. Woods had demonstrated a short attention span in the past. Still, it was sweet of him to offer, Mallory reminded herself. Chances were Fred would turn over the time-consuming task to Kevin, anyway.

The idea brought a mischievous smile to Mallory's face. It had probably been at Kevin's urging that Fred had come up with the idea in the first place. It would serve Kevin right for interfering, if he ended up with the job himself.

Perhaps she'd soften the blow and invite him for dinner the night before Christmas. With Aunt Anita and Harvey Vinson, her new husband, off on a visit to Harvey's daughter in California, it would seem very quiet this year. And there would be all that lasagna to eat. It had become traditional to have Christopher's favorite that evening. Mostly because she always ended up stuck at the store until the doors closed at six o'clock. There were always a few stragglers, customers who felt Rittenhouse should stay open longer for their last-minute convenience. Popping frozen pasta in the microwave was the perfect answer.

Before she could begin planning her holiday meals, though, there was the annual Rittenhouse party to live through, the St. Edmund's bazaar to orchestrate and her own holiday shopping for Christopher and her friends. Fortunately, she'd seen Anita eyeing a particularly dashing powder-blue suit, and had snapped it up early. A last-minute trip to the toy store would refresh her mind about the games Chris felt he couldn't live without this year. She always got Rosemary something special for her gourmet-equipped kitchen. And Chris always gave his baby-sitter a box of her favorite chocolates, so that he could share in the bounty. Fran was easy. All Mallory had to do was breeze through the lingerie department and find the most ridiculous confection of lace and little else. As for Kevin, Beverly Lonergan had once told her he had a weakness for candied fruits. Maybe she could accomplish some shopping on her lunch hour. If she managed to get away for one, that is. Some days that was nearly impossible.

"Oh, by the way—" Fran's voice purred over the telephone receiver, "—just what are you planning to wear to the Rittenhouse holiday bash?"

Somehow *bash* didn't describe the elegant, sedate dinner and cocktails that Albert Rittenhouse hosted at his country-club home each year. The guests were a select group, only members of the management team and the three top sales producers in the store. It was held on the Sunday evening a week before Christmas, a time when most of the guests would have willingly exchanged the hours spent at Rittenhouse's home for hours in sweet slumber. Sleep was a luxury during the hectic weeks of the holiday shopping season.

"Probably just my black suit," Mallory answered. The same thing she wore each year. It was basic, had satin lapels and could be dressed up easily if she ended up with floor duty before joining the festivities.

"Oh, Mal!" Fran wailed. "Not again! You need something snazzier this year. Something in berry red or gold lamé."

Mallory wrinkled her nose. "The suit will be fine," she said.

"Hmm... Maybe if you bought a bustier with jet beading and lace..."

Well, what did she expect from someone who drooled over racy lingerie catalogs? Mallory mused. She hoped Fran didn't decide to give her a sleazy looking bustier for Christmas. Fran was just the type to insist Mallory wear it somewhere.

"Not my style, Fran," Mallory hastened to point out, and moved on to her next order form, this one dealing with infant wear.

"At least get a silk camisole."

Mallory crossed her fingers. "I'll think about it," she lied. "This doesn't mean you're still determined to get me a date, does it?"

Fran sighed theatrically. "The matter's been taken out of my hands," she announced. "Probably for the best, since I wasn't even batting .500 on suitable men. All I can say is, you won't be going alone."

Now what did that mean? Automatically Mallory reached toward the adding machine, set to run a new check on the order figures. "I didn't invite anyone, Fran."

"You didn't have to, Mal. Chris took care of that little matter."

"Chris? You mean *my* Chris?" Mallory's hand froze over the ten-key; she dropped her pen and forgot about the toddler dresses on the order form.

"Gotta hand it to the kid, Mal. He's one smart cookie. Must get that from you."

Mallory wasn't open to compliments on her son at the moment. "What's Christopher done?" she demanded.

"Found you a date, of course. Although if I'd known Pastor Lonergan had the answer, I wouldn't have . . ."

Mallory leaned forward in her chair, put her elbows on the desk top and rested her brow against her hand wearily. Mentally she went through all the available men in the parish. If Kevin was involved, the man had to be known to her already. Who would they foist on her? Hopefully not Phil Williams. The good doctor had a lecher's eye, and absolutely no interest in his pretty teenage daughters. In many ways he reminded her of Dirk Segal, Chris's biological father.

Could it be Marcus Titus? His name alone was enough to make an intelligent woman go into hysterics—it sounded as if he belonged to a Roman legion. On Halloween, did he dress up like a centurion, complete with bowed legs and bony knees to go with the balding pate and beer belly?

Who else was there? The parish was so nicely filled with married couples. That was something she liked about St. Edmund's.

Dear Lord, who would Kevin pull out of his hat?

"Fran," Mallory said, cutting across her friend's ramblings. "Why in the world would you want me to dress up for a blind date?" Especially in the sexy suggestions Fran had been throwing out.

"I just want you to make a good impression, Mal." The sincerity in Fran's voice had an unfamiliar edge of excitement to it.

"Who is he, Fran?"

Fran wasn't giving anything more away, though. "If you want, I could help you shop for something appropriate. You really should retire that black suit, Mal. It was all right to wear when you were a struggling department manager, but now that you're a top dog at Rittenhouse, you need to have something more stunning."

Stunning. The word and Fran's tastes didn't mesh. "Fran . . ." Mallory's voice held a threat now. But what was she going to do to punish Frances? Buy her flannel pajamas instead of a transparent teddy? The idea had definite appeal, but Mallory had a sneaking suspicion that Fran's husband, Larry, looked forward to the erotic lingerie his wife adored receiving. Well, she'd have to think of something else. Maybe put Fran in charge of the bazaar's fish pond. Or suggest her friend be drafted for duty in the dunk tank at the festival that summer.

"I can't tell you who he is, Mal," Fran insisted. "He's Chris's present to you. You have to be surprised. Just take my advice to heart, and buy a new dress. Spaghetti straps, maybe, or something backless."

Where did Fran think they lived? The tropics? It was December, for heaven's sake!

"Sequins," Fran added hopefully. "Believe me, you'll be glad you did. I know what the guy looks like, Mal. This is definitely one man you want to impress."

"But, Fran—"

"Gosh! Look at the time!" Fran groaned. "I've got a roast burning in the oven. Gotta go. Just don't forget to get a new dress."

Mallory stared at the phone, listening to the dial tone buzzing. Just what she needed. A new headache to worry about this holiday season.

She supposed it was sweet of her son to make the effort to get her a date. He'd obviously overheard Fran and Rosemary talking about it. But to ask Kevin to help him find this paragon! The way Fran was going on, the man could be nothing less.

Who in the world had Kevin Lonergan dug up? And, more important, *why* had he?

Chapter Three

Patrick sat slumped and at his ease in the padded arm-chair, his stockinged feet crossed at the ankle and propped on his brother's desk. He was still dressed in the clothes he'd arrived in, nearly new jeans and a heavy navy cable-knit sweater. He cradled a tumbler of Kevin's carefully hoarded Irish whiskey in his hand, a look of pure satisfaction on his face.

The dinner they'd shared had melted on his tongue: tender tips of beef in a savory sauce, over homemade noodles, a vegetable and cheese casserole, flaky rolls, a crisp tossed salad with Mrs. Bittner's own herb dressing, and a shared bottle of Chablis. He hadn't had a meal like that since…well, since he'd left home. Their mother had been a great cook.

Apparently Kevin felt the same way, for he had re-moved his tie, loosened his belt, and kicked off his shoes, as well. Although his stance mirrored that of his brother, feet up, shoulders pressed back into the cushions of his chair, Kevin wore a striped dress shirt, a tan sweater vest and granite-gray wool trousers.

"Tell me again what you gave up in joining the ministry," Pat urged.

"Material things," Kevin answered, his voice drugged with contentment.

"Yeah, sure," Pat said. "Like your Oldsmobile."

"I saved for it."

"And the state-of-the-art stereo."

"I'm frugal, my needs simple."

"Wide-screen TV."

"So, okay, there are some material things I didn't give up. I'm a widowed parson, not a monk in a monastery."

Pat grinned and sipped his whiskey, letting the bite ease down the back of his throat. "Did you give up anything?"

"Chasing women," Kevin said.

"Ah, yes."

"You were handling my share of them pretty well, in addition to your own," Kevin reminded his brother.

"My sad reputation," Pat murmured. "Actually, I tarnished your name, as well, you know. When a girl wasn't interested in me, I told her I was you."

Kevin's head rolled against the cushions. "I was afraid of that."

"Rumor got back to you, huh?"

"Sally Pellegrini," Kevin said.

Pat chuckled. "Oh, Lord. She really had the hots for you, Kev."

"So you fulfilled her dreams."

"What can I say? I'm incredibly human. We still had drive-in movie theaters in abundance back then. As I recall, all that happened was that the windows got steamed up.''

Kevin smiled, his gaze on the ceiling. "So she says."

Patrick's left eyebrow arched a quarter of an inch higher. "Don't tell me. She's a parishioner now, right?"

"Married Carl Mayhew and moved into town. They've got four children, three boys and a girl."

The brothers were quiet, content to enjoy each other's company and savor their whiskey. Pat was very glad his twin's taste in fine liquor hadn't changed. And that his visit merited the unearthing of Kevin's carefully hoarded imported whiskey.

Kevin was the first to break the silence. "So what have you been doing since Sunshine left?"

Pat's smile grew wicked. He'd known Kevin would bring Sun up at some point. "Same as you since Bev's passing, bro."

Kevin nodded. "Cold showers when the occasion merits."

"You got it."

Kevin sipped thoughtfully at his own glass of whiskey. "Miss her?"

"Bev? Oh, Sun. Strangely enough, no."

"Any new, uh, girlfriends?"

Pat gave a bark of laughter. "Don't you mean lovers? Been too busy."

Once again silence fell between them. Pat watched his twin closely. It was eerie the way they could catch each other's thoughts after all this time. He'd been looking up Kevin's phone number when his brother called and invited him to spend the holidays in the city. At the time, he hadn't put the coincidence down to their twin bond, but to the simple fact that for the first time in years they were both alone for the holidays. Their parents had thrived on celebrating Christmas, throwing their home open to friends and family alike. Now that the elder Lonergans were gone, Bev had died and Sun had left, there was a poignant emptiness to the winter months.

The twin link was rusty from disuse, Pat decided, or else his brother was hatching something. Strange that everyone had always thought he was the more mischievous of the two. Kevin could plot circles around him.

"Feeling full of brotherly love?" Kevin asked lazily.

Oh, something was definitely up. Pat knew better than to trust that tone of voice.

"In what way?"

Kevin leaned farther back, continuing to stare up at the ceiling. "I have a parishioner who needs a favor."

Pat pitched his voice to match Kevin's, keeping it light and free of suspicion. "What sort of favor?"

"Does it matter? It is the season . . ."

"What sort of favor?" Pat repeated.

"He wants . . ."

"He?" Pat grinned. "We have been away from each other a long time. I could have sworn your parishioner was female."

"Well, actually, you did pick that up right," Kevin admitted. "It's complicated."

Pat took a healthy gulp of his whiskey this time. He was going to need it. "I'm listening."

He was still rather dumbfounded when Kevin had finished his explanation. "So the boy is buying me as his mother's Christmas present."

Kevin wrinkled his nose. "You make it sound as if I were pimping for God. You were procured with the best of intentions. And a heartfelt donation of Chris's time to the church, in the matter of raking leaves."

"No mean feat," Pat agreed. St. Edmund was one of the older churches in town. It had none of the sleek lines seen in new buildings. The grounds were also filled with a good number of mature shade trees.

He definitely felt sympathy for the boy who'd done duty with a long-handled rake to buy his services. "So all I'm supposed to do is go to some party with this woman? What's the matter with her that she couldn't get her own date?"

"Mallory Meyers is a busy woman," Kevin said.

"A dog, huh?"

"See for yourself," Kevin offered, and tossed a snapshot across the desk.

Pat picked it up and leaned back into his chair to study it. A wide expanse of beach with white-tipped waves filled the background. The sky was a perfect blue. The foreground showed a sandy beach and a nearly finished sand castle. The boy in the photograph showed signs of an earlier sunburn, his narrow little shoulders peeling, part white, part brown, part a glowing new pink. His smile was wide and showed empty spaces where his front teeth had once been. The woman wore a one-piece swimsuit with electric slashes of color crossing it. A straw hat dangled down her back from tied ribbons. Her soft brown hair was a little longer than shoulder length, and was straight and wind-tossed. Her smile was as bright as that of the boy next to her, all warm and loving.

Okay, so Mallory Meyers wasn't a dog. That streamlined length of leg would have been envied by a good many showgirls. And her figure was everything a man fantasized about. Her face was a perfect oval of female loveliness. Lips that pouted slightly, eyes that crinkled with laughter, skin that looked as warm and inviting as satin.

There was something else about her that cheered him. Thinking about escorting this beauty was conjuring all sorts of interesting images in his head. His interest in the fair sex wasn't as dead as he'd feared.

Since the relationship was supposed to remain platonic, there was going to be a cold shower in his very near future.

"You think I can do this, huh?" he asked, still staring at Mallory's picture.

"Oh, I think taking a pretty girl to a party is right up your alley, Pat," Kevin murmured.

But could he keep his hands off her? Especially a woman who looked like Mallory? "Tell me about her," Pat urged.

Kevin swung around in his chair, letting his feet drop to the floor, leaning forward, his forearms on the desk top. "She's had some tough times, Patrick. Got mixed up with the wrong guy when she was in college, and got pregnant."

"The kid's handsome. Looks a lot like her," Pat said.

"Yeah, he does. You'll probably meet him tomorrow. He runs tame around here."

He does? Pat mused. Maybe there was more here than Kev was letting on. After all, how many ministers had at hand photographs of their female parishioners in bathing suits?

"Be careful with that picture. Chris will want it back. It's his favorite. He hated to give it up, even for an evening," Kevin said.

Perhaps he was reading too much into the situation, Pat mused and tossed the snapshot back on the desk. "She's one good-looking woman. How come she's unattached? I would think she'd have men camped on her doorstep."

"Apparently Christopher's father was a..." Kevin paused, searching for the appropriate word, one that carried at least a hint of Christian charity in it.

Pat had no such restraint binding him, and offered a few colorful suggestions.

"Well, yes, I think any one of those would fit," Kevin admitted. "Mallory's gun-shy when it comes to men. She's wonderful with groups of people. Well liked by everyone in the parish. Since she took charge of the holiday bazaar, it's been running like a smoothly oiled machine. We used to have it early in December, but she pushed the date back to a few days before Christmas. So we can grab shoppers when they are desperate, she claims. We even combine it with a fish fry, to make it convenient for our people."

Pat wondered if there was a burnished halo around Mallory Meyers's pretty brown locks. They'd sure picked the wrong guy to escort her!

"You're sure you want *me* to come within a mile of this paragon?" Pat asked.

Kevin was still quite serious. His tone was soft when he answered. "I wouldn't trust her with any other man, Patrick."

"Hell of a vote of confidence." Pat swore and tossed off the rest of his whiskey. He sat his empty tumbler on the desk. "Pour me another finger or so of that stuff, Kev. I have a feeling I'm going to need all the false courage I can muster."

Rosemary stood in the doorway of Mallory's kitchen, her hands folded complacently over her apron. "How pretty you look," she told Mallory.

Christopher rolled on his side, taking a quick break from watching "How the Grinch Stole Christmas" on

television. "Real pretty," he said, adding a bit more em-
phasis.

"Same old suit," Mallory pointed out, but she did stop
by the mirror over the mantelpiece to check her reflection
once more. She had bought a new blouse to go with it, but
not one of the sexy little nothings that Fran had suggested. Her new blouse was of old lace over a sculptured
bodice of creamy satin. It had a Victorian waist, with the
neckline high at the throat, the sleeves full at the top and
secured at the wrist with a satin cuff four inches wide. The
buttons were tiny pearls that ran in tight precision down
the front. Mallory had swept her dark hair up, letting a
few tendrils dangle free at the nape of her neck and
around her ears. She'd worn the simple pearl earrings
Chris had given her last year for Christmas, and had
pinned an antique locket on her black satin lapel. Her
aunt Anita had presented the pin to her on the day Chris
was born. It still held his infant portrait inside.

Mallory felt she looked dignified and sufficiently elegant for the ordeal of Mr. Rittenhouse's party. She knew
the direction the evening would take by rote. Mr. and Mrs.
Rittenhouse would greet their guests in the large tiled entryway to their home. Mrs. Rittenhouse would wear a silver dress of designer make, smile a thin, insincere smile
and wave her guests on to the living room, where a bar was
set up. The store managers would stand around, com-
menting on the lovely decorations, and the store display
manager would glow, since he'd been in charge of trim-
ming the Rittenhouse's private tree, as well as those in the
store. After a few minutes, they'd all be discussing sales
in their departments, troublesome customers, the flu ep-
idemic that felled sales associates each holiday season, and
the upcoming horror of year-end inventory. Once everyone had arrived and mingled, the dining room doors

would be flung open and the group would troop to their appointed places, politely eat whatever delicacy the Rittenhouses offered, murmur thanks over the bonus checks Mr. Rittenhouse presented and listen to his long-winded speech of appreciation when he received the silver token of the season from the store employees.

Why did the gift always have to be silver? Mallory wondered. Mr. Rittenhouse had a case full of useless silver gifts: plates, bowls, trophies, statues.

Well, hers was not to wonder why, but to pitch in her share of the cost on the dratted thing.

The smell of freshly baking cookies wafted from the kitchen, the aroma curling around her. Rosemary was restocking their supply. How nice it would be to just stay home with Christopher, watch the Dr. Seuss story and eat warm cookies.

It wasn't just the idea of enduring the annual holiday party that bugged her, it was the idea that she had to endure it all with a stranger at her side.

Who was this blind date? Her Christmas present from Chris. Everyone was being very closemouthed about his identity. Even her son! Which was very curious. Chris had never kept a secret from her before. He'd always been too excited to keep it to himself.

Not this time, though. Chris's eyes glowed with pride when she questioned him, but he refused to name names. All he would say was that he liked the man a lot.

Which was the same thing Rosemary said. Fran, of course, so far forgot herself—and the era—as to declare Mallory's blind date was, in her own words, "to-die-for dreamy." Mallory had asked if Fran had been indulging in any Gidget-movie marathons recently.

The clock on the mantelpiece chimed the quarter hour. Mallory fidgeted with the back of one of her earrings.

"You did tell my present what time he needed to be here, didn't you, Chris?" she asked, and hoped her voice sounded calm. Inside, she was a mass of quivering nerves. Her stomach was churning, and her hands were wet with anticipation. And dread.

A commercial replaced the Grinch on the screen. Chris got to his feet. He was already in his pajamas and robe. His slippers lay forgotten on the rug before the television. "Yep," he answered. "You'll like him, Mommy," he assured her. "He's a real nice man."

Mallory gave him a brave smile. "Of course he is, darling. I know you have excellent taste. You picked these out for me, didn't you?" She fingered her earring again.

The sound of a car in the driveway wiped the smile from her face. Chris didn't notice. His nose was already pressed to the front window. "He's here!" he announced in ringing tones, and sped to the front door.

"Slippers!" Mallory reminded him sharply.

"Oh, yeah," Chris mumbled, and stopped barely long enough to pull them on. He still beat the man outside to the door.

Mallory stood with her back to the fireplace, her hands pressed together. Who was he? It had to be someone she knew. Didn't it? *Don't be a fool, Mal,* she lectured herself. *You're pressing thirty, you're a grown woman, a mother, you have a successful career. You can't be afraid of a man. Can't be.*

Her heart wasn't paying attention to the lecture. It was pumping a mile a minute, making it difficult for her to breathe normally.

There was the murmur of a deep male voice in the hall, and the bright chatter of her son's welcome. She heard footsteps.

Get a grip, Mallory!

Then he was there, his hand in Christopher's as he allowed the boy to pull him into the room.

He looked a veritable giant, with the bulk of his suit coat and overcoat building his shoulders to monstrous proportions. His hair was tousled from the wind, and his cheeks were reddened from the cold. A large gift tag was pinned to his coat. Even from a distance she recognized Christopher's uneven printing. To Mommy With Love From Chris, it read.

The man smiled ruefully and flicked the tag with one finger. "Hi," he said. "I think you were expecting me."

Mallory relaxed. "Kevin," she said.

Chris giggled, hiding his mouth behind his hand. "No, he ain't," he said.

"Isn't," Mallory and the man wearing the gift tag said in unison.

"I'm Patrick Lonergan, Kevin's brother," the man explained.

"Pat's Pastor Kev's *twin* brother," Christopher crowed.

"As if you couldn't guess," Pat added, and gave her a genuine smile. It was the same combination of devilry and charm that she'd come to know on Kevin's familiar face. "You must be Mallory," Pat said, and held out his hand.

Mallory moved in a daze. She shook Patrick Lonergan's hand and tried to find something to say. Her mind was a blank.

"Actually, Kev would have come along to perform the introductions," Pat continued, "but since I was making off with his car tonight, and he isn't fond of my truck, he opted to stay home and finish off the latest batch of Mrs. Bittner's cookies."

"Mrs. Rosemary makes the best cookies," Chris said. "Mom, can I stay up late tonight? There's no school tomorrow," he reminded her hopefully.

Mallory folded under her son's wide-eyed plea. "Just until nine. And no more than four cookies with your milk."

Christopher's smile of delight was all the reward she needed. "It's getting late. I'd better get my coat," Mallory said.

The commercial break was over on TV, but Chris had lost interest in the Grinch for the moment. "First Pat's gotta see my room," he insisted, and took the man's hand once more.

Patrick flashed another of his special smiles Mallory's way. "Slight detour. Be back in a minute or two." Then he allowed Chris to lead him past the Christmas tree and down the hall.

Mallory stared after them, still numb over the identity of her date. She looked over at Rosemary. "Am I going nuts, or is Kevin playing a game?" she asked.

The older woman chuckled in understanding. "No, he's really Kevin's brother. You need to see them together, I suppose. Patrick's been with us a couple days now, and he's turned the place topsy-turvy. Christopher dotes on the man. They've been playing go fish, if you can believe it." She patted Mallory's arm in an effort to soothe the young woman. "He really is a very nice man, Mallory. How could Kevin's brother be anything else?"

He could be an ax murderer for all they knew, Mallory thought. But any man who would play cards with Chris day after day couldn't be all bad. Her son was nuts about go fish.

Besides, Fran had been right. Although his features were similar to Kevin's, there was something about Patrick Lonergan that made him "to-die-for dreamy." Bringing him along would certainly give the Rittenhouse crowd something to talk about other than the dreaded inventory.

"I'd better be ready to leave when he escapes Chris's clutches," Mallory said.

Apparently Rosemary felt she still needed some reassurance. She followed Mallory to the hall closet. Even held Mallory's coat while she slipped into it. "Everything will be fine, dear," Rosemary murmured. "You'll see."

"Of course it will," Mallory answered. *Like hell,* she thought. Rosemary had absolutely no idea what a bad idea this was.

Christopher led the way back down the hall, cheerfully pointing out the highlights to Patrick. "That's the bathroom, that's the guest room, and that's Mom's room."

"Very interesting," Pat agreed. "Now I'd better get your mom to her party. After all, that's what you bought me for, isn't it, sport?" He turned to Mallory, inspecting her in an all-encompassing sweep, from the upturned collar of her camel-hair coat to the black silk stockings and two-inch black heels. His smile took on a more rakish edge.

Mallory's heart began doing strange things. *Oh, no,* she thought in dismay. *Don't let this happen, don't let me feel this way.* But breathing was difficult when she was this close to him. She tingled.

"Looks like she's rarin' to go," Pat said to Chris. His voice seemed deeper, more intimate, than it had earlier.

No, no, no! She didn't feel this aware when she was with Kevin. Perhaps if she kept the pastor firmly in mind, this madness would disappear.

"Have a good time, Mallory," Rosemary said.

Chris hugged her tightly. "Yeah, have lots of fun, Mom. I won't eat more than six cookies."

"I thought I heard the number *four* mentioned," Pat murmured.

"Oh, yeah." Chris looked unabashed. "I'm not so good at numbers."

"Too bad for you," Pat said, and ruffled the boy's hair. "I am."

Patrick turned back to Mallory. "Shall we go? The carriage awaits, Cinderella." He glanced down at Chris one last time. "Okay if I keep her out till midnight, sport?"

Christopher nodded solemnly. "Yeah, Mom stays up that late."

Patrick took her hand in his. Mallory hoped he didn't notice she was trembling. His fingertips were rough, the palm was calloused. Her hand felt so small in his. "Let's hit the road, then," Pat suggested and pulled the front door open.

A breath of cold evening air enveloped her as she stepped outside. It didn't make the madness go away. She hoped Patrick would continue to hold her hand. Drat, but she liked it too much. And since Kevin knew her history, she was furious that he had put her in this position, that he had aided and abetted in making her remember what she had, with good reason, renounced.

As Pat held the door of his brother's Oldsmobile open for her, Mallory made a promise. *I'm going to get even with you for this, Kevin Lonergan, if it's the last thing I do.*

Chapter Four

She was more beautiful than her photograph, Patrick thought as he started the car and backed out onto the street. And as skittish as a teenager on her first date.

"You've got a great son," he said, knowing it was the sort of compliment that would put her at ease. Mallory Meyers didn't seem like the type of woman who would appreciate any other sort of compliment. At least not until she knew him better. He bet if he so much as told her she looked nice she would bolt from the car and run back into the house. Yet it was even money that, if Kevin told her she looked beautiful, she wouldn't turn cold or remote. Mallory would probably give Kev one of those dazzling smiles, the kind she gave Rosemary and Chris. The kind he was already craving.

She relaxed about a millimeter's worth. "Thanks. I think Chris is special, too. I understand you've been playing cards with him."

Pat grinned over at her. "Ah, yes. Kid's a real sharp. I think I've won one out of every ten games."

"Go fish?"

"Yep. I'm thinking of teaching him something I might have a better chance at," Pat said. "How's Chris at crazy eights?"

"A killer," Mallory answered.

"Just my luck." Pat noted that Mallory's hands were gripped tightly around her envelope of a purse. The bulk of her coat, and the shadows, hid the long shapely length of her legs, but he had a feeling her knees were held together tightly, her heels set primly next to each other.

"I'm going to need directions to this party," he said. "I can find my way around Greenville blindfolded, but I'm rusty on things in Dayton."

Mallory turned her head to stare out the side window, looking away from Pat. "Take a left at the next light," she directed quietly.

He let the silence stretch between them, wondering if it would make her feel more comfortable or more ill at ease with him.

Mallory continued to watch the passing scenery, the gaily lighted houses, some with Santa Claus figures and reindeer on their lawns, some with nativity scenes, and some with displays of colored and blinking lights flamboyant enough to bring a different type of holiday cheer to the stockholders of the power company. There was no snow on the ground yet. Dayton, with its close buildings and traffic, was too warm for the flurries to stick. The night wind was wickedly cold, biting when it swirled around pedestrians. They passed a group of carolers huddled together as they trilled a holiday chorus.

Pat reached the light and turned. He liked the way his truck handled, but the consensus at the church office had been in favor of Kev's Olds. It would make a better impression among the Rittenhouse crowd. He'd worn his little-seen gray pinstripe suit in an additional effort to blend in. It wasn't often that he unearthed any of his better clothes. Although he spent most of his time on his computer, rather than in the fields, the wardrobe of an entrepreneur differed greatly from that of a corporate man. Hard to believe he'd once thrived in the world of big business. Now it was only his twice-a-year trip to New York that made it necessary to maintain the outward image of a successful man. Would the designer label on his suit impress Mallory Meyers though? Somehow Pat doubted it. Mallory seemed to be a woman who had learned to look deeper than a man's physical appearance.

"So, what is it you do, Mr. Lonergan?" she asked, breaking the silence.

"Call me Pat," he said. "Mr. Lonergan sounds so formal. And it's hard to find a farmer who has a reason to be formal."

A flash of headlights from a turning car allowed him to see her eyes widen slightly in surprise.

Pat's smile was amused. It was the usual response to his claim. "Kev never told you about the family business, huh?"

"He doesn't talk about himself. Probably because he's always so busy listening to everyone else's problems," she explained.

Which, Pat decided, was as good a cover for a parson as any. It saved Kevin from confessing that he'd disliked life on the farm. No, that painted it too tamely. Kev hated the place. It was as much that as Sunshine's presence in the house that had kept his brother and sister-in-law from visiting much. He, on the other hand, had always loved the routine, the sounds in the barnyard, the smell of freshly turned earth, the whisper of the wind through a bountiful wheat crop, and the glow of sunlight on the golden tassels of ripe corn.

His longing for the family homestead had made his years in the Big Apple pure hell. It was another major difference between his brother and himself. Kevin thrived on the activity of a metropolis, rejoiced that attention to his flock of souls kept him within the concrete ramparts. They had completely opposite views of the world, both physical and metaphysical.

Except, possibly, where Mallory Meyers was concerned.

Damn, but she was lovely.

"Yeah, the man's a regular saint," Pat said of his brother. "Anything I should know about the crowd at this party we're headed to?"

Mallory hadn't heard the question, though. Her thoughts were on his casually dropped news. Or perhaps it had been more of a bomb, Pat mused.

"How big is the farm?" she asked.

She tried to hide it, but Pat had learned to recognize nuances. She was wondering how the fact that her escort was a lowly farmer would go over with her boss. Actually he did little more than what needed to be done for upkeep on the property, renting out the land to others. His main operation was managing his clients' farms, planning the crops to be planted, estimating costs, finding the best markets, then investing profits in stocks that built financial security for his neighbors. Nearly all of them were his clients as well. But Mallory didn't need to know that. In fact, he let very few people know the true nature of his work, preferring to let them think he was a simple man of the land rather than a business shark.

"Close to three hundred acres," Pat said. From her expression, he knew the measurement had absolutely no meaning to Mallory. "Big by some standards, small by others. It pays for itself, at least."

"I see."

She hadn't a clue.

"Kev and I grew up there, as did our father and his father. The deed goes back a couple of generations."

"You're going to want to turn right at the third light," Mallory said.

Subject closed. Which was fine with him. He didn't particularly want to talk crop rotation with her. He wanted to pull over to the side of the road and whisper words of love in her pretty little ear.

Instead, he followed her directions, took the turn, and tried another angle. "Kev says you recently received a promotion at Rittenhouse."

Mallory turned toward him and actually chuckled. Well, what the heck! He never would have guessed that *that* would nudge her funny bone. But whatever subject it took to keep the smile on her face, he was willing to keep talking about it.

"They all think I'm hot stuff now," Mallory said. "All it is is a lot more work."

"They?" Pat echoed.

"Kevin, Rosemary, Fran Hutchins."

"So you're what? Assistant manager? Vice president?"

"General manager of the softlines division."

"Like it?"

She was quiet a moment, moved to contemplate the street, the way the headlights made the pavement glow when they approached a damp area. "Most of the time."

"Which means—?"

Mallory shrugged. "I have a child. There are many times when I wish I didn't have to go in to work, that I could spend the day with him."

"I can understand that," Pat said. "I've just spent a couple days in his company. He may be a cardsharp, but he has his moments."

"Yes, he does," she agreed. "And so do you."

"Me?" Now he was puzzled.

"I want to thank you for humoring him, for letting him show you his room. It was very kind of you, Mr. Lonergan."

Damn, now he was a saint, too! The sainted Lonergan twins. Kev would choke on his whiskey over that one.

"The name's Pat. Remember, Mallory? Do we have a story, by the way? Any kind of cover? Are we long lost lovers, or what?"

She blushed at that. He'd probably come down a notch on the sainthood scale, rating only Blessed Lonergan now.

"I think we should keep it simple," Mallory said. "Why don't you just be Kevin's brother?"

"Might be able to handle that," Pat admitted. "When's the next turn?"

Judging by the number of cars parked outside, they were nearly the last of the guests to arrive. Which, as far as Mallory was concerned, was perfect timing. Patrick had to park halfway down the block; he offered her his arm after he opened the door for her. Since the temperature had dropped, creating slick spots on the long Rittenhouse driveway, she accepted, her gloved hand resting lightly in the crook of his elbow. Pat covered it with his hand, his touch sending a warm flush to her otherwise cold face.

The Rittenhouse home was a downsized version of the White House, complete with columned porch and spreading wings. Tiny white twinkle lights flashed in the carefully sculptured evergreens. The soft glow of carriage lamps lined the walk and lighted the massive double-door entryway. Pat ignored the iron door knocker and rapped lightly on the broad panel. It swung open immediately.

"Ah, Merry Christmas, Mallory," Albert Rittenhouse said boisterously. He waved them into the house, gesturing for the waiting attendant to take their wraps. Pat helped Mallory out of her coat, handed it to a silent uniformed man, then stripped off his overcoat. Mallory only got a glimpse of his well-cut suit before Mr. Rittenhouse claimed all her attention. "And how is my favorite new G.M.?" he asked.

"Fine, thank you, sir." She hoped her voice was bright. And, if it was, that it didn't sound forced or phony. Which it was. "Merry Christmas to you, too."

"Wonderful season," Rittenhouse declared. "Makes everyone full of goodwill, don't you agree? Mrs. Rittenhouse just went to check on things in the kitchen. She'll be delighted to find you've brought a guest along this year," he declared heartily.

Mallory suppressed a sigh. Albert Rittenhouse was trying to outjolly Saint Nick. Someone had once likened him to a character in a book by Charles Dickens. She couldn't remember just who, but it certainly hadn't been Scrooge. Unless it was after Ebenezer had been visited by the three Christmas spirits. Maybe a couple of ghosts had done a number on old Rittenhouse once.

"Yes, this year I did have someone to ask along," Mallory said, with a touch of her own false cheer. She

nearly jumped when Pat slipped a possessive arm around
her waist.

"Couldn't have kept me away," he told Rittenhouse.
"I'm Patrick Lonergan."

The men shook hands, while Mallory tried to squirm
unobtrusively away from Pat's touch. He didn't release
her; if anything, his familiar grip tightened, drawing her
nearer.

"Glad to meet you," Rittenhouse said enthusiasti-
cally. Although the look was hooded, he gave Pat a quick
once-over from discreetly patterned tie to highly buffed
shoes. Mallory held her breath, then let it out quietly
when her boss's smile tweaked happily. He approved of
her escort. On looks alone, Mallory had to admit, so did
she.

Mallory wished she knew what Kevin had told Pat
about her. Perhaps nothing. It had been a while since she
had been in the dating game, but Mallory could still recognize the admiring look in a man's eyes. When Pat gazed
at her, she read more than admiration. His emerald eyes
glowed with sheer pleasure.

He wasn't like Kevin, though. Every minute she spent
in his company, she likened him less and less to his
brother. Pat's voice was slightly deeper than Kevin's. The
timbre was the same, but there were times when Pat spoke
that there was a sexual nuance that was definitely missing
in his brother's tone. Patrick's voice caressed.

He was dressed superbly, his executive-cut suit fitting
the broad width of his shoulders as if woven to their specific breadth. The fabric was a soft blend, a smoky char-
coal with fine black stripes running through it. His white
shirt was silk, the French cuffs held in place by cuff links
decorated with an engraved monogram of his initials. His

tie was a geometric pattern in varying, subdued shades of burgundy. Although his dark brown hair was brushed back, the breeze outside had teased one lock forward to curl at his temple.

He didn't look like her idea of a farmer.

But, she remembered, that was exactly what he was.

"What business are you in, Lonergan?" Rittenhouse asked, still the epitome of holiday cheer.

Mallory tensed. Pat's fingers curled slightly at her waist, as if he were trying to reassure her. Or perhaps he was just throwing himself into his role.

How would he respond to Albert Rittenhouse's question?

"Food," Pat said.

The answer didn't faze Rittenhouse. He put it in his own context, that of retailing. "Food. Importer?"

Pat chuckled softly. "No, I leave the caviar alone. My interests lie in supply."

Rittenhouse nodded sagely. "Good business to be in. There are restaurants everywhere. You handle the organic products, too?"

"Absolutely," Pat said.

Rittenhouse nodded toward the archway on their left. The foyer was brightly lighted, but the room he indicated glowed with the soft radiance of candlelight. The murmur of small talk and a background of classical music floated out. "Tell my wife where you'd recommend she lunch," Rittenhouse requested. "The woman's on a new diet kick but doesn't know what the Sam Hill she's looking for, or which restaurants carry the organic stuff. Mallory'll point her out."

"I'll do that, sir," Pat promised, and maneuvered Mallory toward the party.

Mallory stopped holding her breath.

Her escort's laugh was wicked and warm when his breath brushed her ear. "Afraid I'd disgrace you?"

She was on her guard immediately. "No, of course not."

"Worried that I'd blurt it out? Declare I was a farmer, and proud of it?"

"It wasn't that," she insisted, managing to keep from meeting his eyes.

"I am proud of what I do, you know," Pat said quietly. He touched her chin, his touch a caress that forced Mallory to look at him. "There isn't another thing I'd rather be involved in. But I know that not everyone sees farming the same as I do. I'll try not to do or say anything that might embarrass you, Mallory."

"I..."

"Besides," Pat added, his eyes filling with humor once again, "Kev would kill me if I screwed up your evening." He released her and stepped back a pace. "What would you like to drink? Champagne? White wine?"

Oh, he was nothing like Kevin. Kevin was charming, but he didn't make her feel warm and wonderful. She shouldn't let Patrick affect her that way, either. But it was Christmas, and for Christopher's sake, she really should enjoy the short time she and Patrick Lonergan would spend together.

Mallory grinned at him. "Actually, just a cola. I have to be on my best behavior at the boss's house."

"Gotcha," he agreed. "Be right back."

Patrick was barely out of earshot before two of the other managers closed in on her.

"Who was that delicious man?" Gail Tyler asked breathlessly. Her blond hair was gathered up in a wild topknot and secured by a wide, glittering pink bow. Her dress was short, the skirt bouffant, the back nearly nonexistent. Her heels were at least three inches in height, and liberally sprinkled with glitter, as well. Fran would have loved Gail's outfit.

Gail looked longingly at Patrick's broad back as he maneuvered closer to the bar and placed his order.

"Hands off, Tyler," Van Werner snapped. He was a good inch shorter than Gail, in her stiltlike shoes. His black suede sports jacket fit loosely; his slacks were cut full. Instead of a shirt and tie, Van had donned a black turtleneck. His own blond hair was thinning and tended to fly in a halo around his head. He sipped at his gin and tonic languidly. "Mal's had a long dry spell," he reminded Gail.

Mallory laughed, and hugged them both quickly. Although her limited social life revolved around the congregation at St. Edmund's, she spent far more time at Rittenhouse. Gail and Van were her two best friends at the store. They had shared many a meal, but outside of the annual holiday party, they didn't socialize. And, Mallory admitted, that was mostly because she had always shied away from their invitations.

Gail's life was so different from hers. She ran the housewares division and went through boyfriends the way she did panty hose. She was single, intended to stay that way for a good long while yet, and was enjoying every minute of it. When Gail went on vacation, it was to some exotic place, like the Bahamas or Mexico. She drove a sports car, and, although she sold kitchen utensils, Gail bragged that she'd never opened one of the cupboards in her condominium.

There were times when Mallory envied her friend. But she wouldn't have given up her home with Chris for the world. There were limitations when one was a mother, but there were compensations, too.

Van, on the other hand, was a male spinster. He was head of the display department, and as fussy about the way the mannequins looked as he was about the hint of dust on a circle rack. If anyone so much as changed a piece of jewelry on one of his "people," Van made life miserable for everyone in the guilty department. He was a master, an artist. He'd told them all so frequently that there wasn't a soul at Rittenhouse who didn't believe it.

Knowing it was more important to butter up the display manager than to satisfy Gail's curiosity, Mallory began laying on the praise.

"You've outdone yourself, Van," she gushed. "Whatever made you choose to decorate the tree all in silver this year?"

"The mundane features of our gentle hosts," he said. "Really, Mal. With Rittenhouse collecting all those nauseating tributes each year, and his svelte missus draping herself in monotonous granite-toned gowns, it was all I could do to keep the theme from overcoming my impeccably good taste in previous years."

Gail snorted at the mere idea. "So what happened this year?"

"Mrs. R. pleaded, I grew bilious and capitulated."

"Poor Van," Gail purred, and sipped at her glass of champagne. "How much did she offer you?"

He sneered at her. "Philistine. Unfortunately, I received an assistant this year. Their delightful little brat has grown up, or so she says, and insisted upon giving me the benefit of her experience in decking the halls of her high school for the all-important proms and similar debacles. *She* insisted upon adding that little bit of nonsense." Van gestured with his drink toward the archway through which Mallory and Patrick had just entered. Beneath an artistically draped swath of silver lamé and stark white pine branches dangled a bit of greenery with white berries.

"Oh, mistletoe. It sure improves on your bits of tinsel from my standpoint," Gail insisted.

Van let the comment slide off his shoulders. "Now it's your turn," he told Mallory.

"To what? Deride your artistry? Van, I always love what you do," she insisted. As much as he scoffed at the way the Rittenhouse home was decorated, even if he had been the mastermind behind it, Mallory knew that Van would be hurt if she didn't give him his well-deserved compliment.

Indeed, the setting was dazzling, not just with his treatment of sprayed branches and draped cloth, but with the elegant-looking trio of fresh pines that took up one complete corner of the room. The decorations were plentiful but simple. Van had woven ribbons of silver tissue among the branches, used wooden toys—all painted a glossy white—in place of ornaments, and been generous with strands of starlike twinkle lights. He had turned the room into a wonderland.

"This is truly marvelous, Van!" Mallory gushed. "Whatever gave you the idea to—"

He cut her off. "That's not what I mean, Mal. Who's the guy?"

The guy had just been handed two tumblers, Mallory noticed. She had to talk fast before he returned.

"He's Kevin's brother. You know, the pastor at St. Edmund's."

"And you never told us about him?" Gail demanded accusingly.

Patrick eased away from the crowd at the bar. Mallory began to panic. "I just met him. Christopher arranged—"

"Chris?" Gail squeaked in surprise.

"He, uh..."

It was too late. She'd forgotten how fast Patrick could cover distances with his long legs.

"Mal?" Van displayed the same dogged patience he demonstrated when pondering one of his own displays that he was displeased with.

Patrick arrived. "Here you are," he said, giving her a quick smile along with her chilled glass.

Gail moved in closer and offered Pat her hand. "Hi. I'm Mal's friend Gail. Welcome to Rittenhouse, the annex."

"I'm Pat," Patrick responded, squeezing the manager's hand.

Before Mallory had a chance, Van had introduced himself, as well. The display manager ran a practiced eye over Mallory's escort. "You don't look like a man with a brother in the ministry," he allowed.

Patrick's eyes met Mallory's. He grinned and took a swig of his bourbon. "Thanks. I think."

Humor twinkled in his eyes, creating deep creases at the corners. His lips curved upward, etching smile lines in his lean cheeks. Mallory's gaze lingered. She was mesmerized by the shape and texture of his mouth. What would it feel like against hers? How would he taste? It had been so long since her thoughts had turned to carnal matters. But they did now, with a vengeance.

As Pat answered another question, his teeth gleamed brightly, his tongue brushing against them as he said her name.

Mallory came back to earth with a crash. "W-what did you say?"

There was a new light in his eyes, she noticed in dismay. It licked at her hotly, as if he had read her wayward mind.

"What night is the St. Edmund's holiday bazaar?" Patrick repeated.

"Wednesday. This coming Wednesday night," Mallory mumbled, and buried her nose in her tumbler. She didn't even taste the cola as it went down. She was still too tinglingly aware of him. When she gained the courage to look up again, Pat's attention was on Gail.

"Why don't you stop by?" Pat asked the skimpily clad blonde in what Mallory considered a far too seductive drawl. "My brother has great hopes of breaking all previous attendance records this year. The least I could do is round up a few bodies to help out my twin."

This time it was Gail's eyes that brightened. "Mal's pastor is your twin? Identical?" At Pat's nod, she glanced at Van Werner, a strange smile tweaking the corners of her mouth. Gail rolled the stem of her champagne glass back and forth in contemplation. "What do you think? Shall we make an appearance, Van?"

The display manager answered with an odd grimace of his own. "Oh, I think we can both make it."

Mallory's mouth nearly dropped open. She'd asked her friends to stop by the bazaar last year, and had heard every excuse in the book over their absences.

"In fact," Van declared, tossing Mallory a suspiciously arch look, "I wouldn't miss this little show for the world."

Chapter Five

By the time dinner was over, Mallory felt that the only faces that weren't looking at her with renewed interest were those of the host and hostess. It wasn't really surprising, considering that the Rittenhouses had always lived in their own world, descending from the heights of Olympus occasionally to recognize the lowly mortals who slaved for them in the store. However, Mallory could have done without the sly glances she was receiving from the rest of the Rittenhouse crowd.

"How late will this church bazaar run?" the manager from Shoes asked, pausing by her chair. Once desserts had been served and the speeches given, the atmosphere had become casual. Some of the guests had returned to the main room, while others lingered at the table. "I work until closing, but perhaps I can swing by on my way home. Hey, it's a good cause, right?"

The same sentiment had been echoed elsewhere. However, Mallory knew the sudden rush of charity was firmly centered in everyone's curiosity about the Lonergan men.

"His identical twin?" she'd overheard one woman gush to her neighbor. "Well, no wonder our Mallory spends so much time at the church."

At least no one knew that Christopher had arranged her date with Patrick as his Christmas present to her. Of course, they would once they came to the bazaar. If Fran didn't spill the beans, then Chris would himself. He was so proud of his gift.

It was all her own fault, Mallory told herself fatalistically. After Dirk Segal waltzed out of her life, she had gone out of her way to cultivate a reputation for always doing the correct thing, for always behaving as expected. At Rittenhouse, there had never been even a hint of scandal clinging to her record. She'd been perfect. Too perfect. She was a good worker and a loving, caring mother. She was cheerful, punctual, tidy, brave, clean and reverent. A regular Girl Scout. Except that she wasn't any of those things—especially not brave. Now that she had become the favorite topic of gossip for her associates, she was scared stiff.

Find the bright side, Mallory told herself. She had learned that lesson from her aunt Anita, after Dirk returned to his wife and her parents shunned her. Back then, Anita had been the only good thing in her life. Or she had been until the small life within her began moving. At that moment, the center of her world had been realigned around her baby.

Since then, it had only been little things that worried her. Like when the inventory didn't go right or sales were down. Mistakes, Mallory had found, could always be corrected.

As this situation could be. But how? Where was the bright side? She cringed as yet another speculative look was cast her way.

"Your bazaar is Wednesday night, isn't it, Mal?" someone asked. "I'm off that night so..."

Maybe there was a silver lining. Curiosity would pull the Rittenhouse crowd into the church basement. That was a first. So, although it very well might be the last thing she ever did for St. Edmund's, she was going to empty the pockets of her friends at the charity function. Empty them big-time! Until then...

Mallory set her teeth in determination.

"Easy, pet," a deep voice rumbled softly at her shoulder.

Mallory frowned at her handsome escort. Patrick pulled back a chair and settled next to her at the table once more. "You know what they're saying, don't you?" she hissed under her breath. "They think I have the hots for your brother."

He set a champagne glass on the table between them. It was filled with olives he'd pilfered from the bar. "Do you?" Pat asked casually as he chose an olive from the stash.

At Mallory's shocked expression, he popped the olive between her open lips and helped himself to another. "Guess not," he said.

Mallory hastily ate the olive. "How can you think that? You know Kevin would never..."

"I didn't ask how Kevin felt," Pat reminded.

"Well, I wouldn't," she insisted hotly, her voice still lowered so that others wouldn't overhear. "Kevin is a wonderful man. He's..."

"A man, just like any other." He chose another olive, savoring it as a connoisseur would fine caviar. She'd noticed in the course of the evening that he had a passion for olives. Not the ripe black ones. He ignored those. It was the green ones with red pimentos waving from the end that drew Patrick.

"You don't know your brother very well, do you?" Mallory said.

Another olive disappeared, leaving Pat wearing the face of a contented man. "Let's just say I understand the currently rampant suspicion about your relationship with him," he said.

"But—"

Pat shoved an olive in her mouth again. His fingertips lingered on her lips, traced the full curve of the lower edge.

His touch did strange things to her. It had all evening, from the most casual brush of his hand against her back as he guided her through a doorway or seated her at the table, to the more blatant grip of his hand on hers. Now the taste of his skin on her lips sent Mallory's pulse pounding erratically.

"I'm trying to allay those suspicions," Pat said.

His breath was a whisper against her cheek. The heady, woodsy scent of his cologne surrounded her. Seduced her.

Mallory stared into his eyes. They were a dark, passionate green, not the soft, gentle color she associated with Kevin. Pat dipped his head toward her, the single contrary lock of his dark hair falling forward with the movement. Of their own accord, her fingers slid along the luxurious lapels of his jacket.

"Mallory!" a voice called from across the room.

Startled back to reality, Mallory flinched back from Pat.

He sighed loudly and relaxed in his chair. "So much for that ploy." He gave her a self-deprecating grin. "Think enough people noticed?"

Noticed what? That she had forgotten where she was? That she had wanted him to kiss her?

What is the matter with you, Mallory Meyers? she stormed in silent frustration. *Won't you ever learn?*

"Mallory!" someone called again. She glanced quickly over to where her counterpart in hardlines was motioning to her from the doorway. Mallory stood up.

Pat got to his feet, as well, towering over her. "Guess I'll never know now," he said, his voice reflecting regret.

Distracted, Mallory glanced up into his face. "Know what?"

Pat's rakish grin flashed. "If you taste like olives. Then again..." He lifted a hand to her face, traced his fingertips lightly along her jaw. Before she realized his intention, Pat tilted her face up and dropped a light kiss on her lips. "Mmm..." he murmured.

Her feet were rooted to the carpet. Mallory couldn't have moved if lightning had struck. Perhaps it already had.

"And do I?" she whispered. Her voice sounded strange, hoarse, strangled.

"Better," Patrick said.

It was turning into one hell of a holiday, Pat mused as he watched Mallory cross the room. She had a nice walk, not blatantly sexual, like her friend Gail's, but eminently feminine. Her legs were long and shapely. They looked great in those black stockings. But then, everything about Mallory looked great.

Tasted great.

The manager who'd been so insistent that she join his group was a tall, gangly fellow with dishwater-blond hair. His arm was draped over the shoulder of a wide-hipped woman in a shapeless, glittery red dress. At Mallory's arrival the woman immediately launched into a long, involved story that she told with dramatic gestures. Mallory gave every appearance of being very interested.

Pat wondered how she could concentrate enough to maintain a conversation. He certainly couldn't. All he could think about was how right it had felt to kiss her. How much he wanted to do so again. And again.

He moved away from the table, mingling with the crowd, working his way slowly toward the bar in the main room. Various people stopped to chat. Gail sidled up, wrapping her painted fingers around his biceps in an overt invitation. Pat excused himself and ingratiated himself with the Rittenhouses by suggesting various restaurants the newly organic-conscious Mrs. Rittenhouse might try. He knew of them, had arranged the contracts that supplied many of them. But he'd never eaten in one. Outside of the home-cooked meals he had recently enjoyed at Kevin's home, Pat survived on fast food and frozen entrées. He might enjoy dabbling in the business of raising grains and vegetables, but that didn't mean he wanted to mess with them in the kitchen.

His eyes rarely left Mallory's slim form. If people noticed his diligence, so much the better. Rather than dream scenarios that starred his brother, they could conjure Mallory stealing moments alone with him.

He'd lied to her, of course. He wasn't playing a part to defuse the gossip. Mallory probably hadn't heard rumors before, but Pat doubted that her close relationship with his brother had gone without comment in the parish. Just mention Mallory's name at the church, and faces changed. Rosemary Bittner looked for all the world like a proud parent, and Kevin got a besotted look in his eyes.

Well, he could certainly understand their admiration. His own appreciation of Mallory was growing by leaps and bounds.

And if ever there were a woman who needed a heavy dose of male appreciation, it was Mallory Meyers.

She was still smarting from the mistake she'd made in trusting the wrong man, Kevin said.

Mallory wasn't smarting, though. She'd forgotten what life was all about. Pat doubted that even Mallory realized that. But he'd seen a faint dawning in her eyes, felt it in her reaction to his touch. To his kiss.

She had conceived a child, but she was still innocent. Her experience with men was limited, not just by the distance she'd maintained from them since Chris's birth, but by her past.

The idea intrigued him. Intrigued the hell out of him.

So what was he going to do about it? Storm the walls she'd built? Then what? Mallory wasn't like Sunshine St John. Sun saw the mating game as a purely physical pleasure, something to be enjoyed in the same vein as stretching. There had been passion between them, but it hadn't been the tender emotion that Mallory would expect. With Sun, things had been natural, but they'd also been mechanical. Turn a page in a sex manual and try a new position. When they'd dog-eared all the pages, Sun had packed up and moved on.

Kevin had guessed at his relationship with Sun, but had never fully grasped the fact that there was nothing concrete in it. Pat's interest had been in investment brokerage and harvesting farm-related accounts. There had been nothing of love or even close friendship between Sunshine and himself. It was more a case of common sense

In this day and age, it was far safer to have a long-term sexual companion than to flit from one bed to the next. Sun had been a convenience for him, just as he had been one for her.

She'd been gone nearly a whole day before he'd realized she'd left. That was how mundane his life with Sunshine St. John had become.

He'd known Mallory Meyers only for a few short hours, and already could see that she had nothing in common with Sun. Not in looks, thoughts, actions or words.

She was a successful businesswoman, respected by her peers. She was a caring, loving mother. She shared herself openly with the Rittenhouse crowd and with the St. Edmund's parish. Her philosophy might be to avoid romantic liaisons, but she was far from withdrawn. Mallory overflowed with the need to love.

And she was gorgeous to boot.

His mind noted the varied nuances of her personality, the reasons she held part of herself separate. But his hormones didn't recognize them, didn't give credence to them. The more time he spent with Mallory, the more he wanted to lure her from her self-induced slumber. The more he wanted to seduce her.

He might not have the same mystical set of mind that his brother had, but he was still Marie Lonergan's son. Although he enjoyed women—enjoyed them a lot—that didn't mean he didn't respect them. The lessons learned at a mother's apron strings went deep.

Pat nursed a final watered-down bourbon and watched Mallory as she eased her way from one group to another. He'd caught her surreptitious glance at her watch. Earlier she had checked in with Rosemary to see if Chris was all right. That had been nearly two hours ago. Now she was displaying all the signs of a mother who'd been away from her child too long. The thought alone gave him a warm feeling.

And pretty well hobbled his libido.

His conscience was probably in overdrive. Aligned with Mallory's obvious innocence, there was also her delightful son's trust, and Kevin's faith in him.

Talk about tying a man in knots.

Patrick finished his drink. Maybe he couldn't change her mind about men in general. Why would he want to? Let the hordes speak for themselves. He needed only to get Mallory to accept him. Whether she liked it or not, he figured his resemblance to his gentle brother had already paved the way for any move he'd make. As long as he didn't make it too fast.

Mallory glanced up, caught his eye. Ah, the lady was ready to head home.

So was he.

Gail Tyler wore a disgusted look on her face as she let the Rittenhouses' houseman help her on with her coat. "Can you believe the people we've been with this evening?" she demanded of no one in particular. "Someone stole the mistletoe."

She looked accusingly at her escort. Van gave her an angelic smile. "My prayers have been answered," he murmured, and shrugged into his own topcoat.

Pat held Mallory's wrap, his stance close enough that her loose curls fluttered when he chuckled. "I'll bet Kev would envy that connection. He usually doesn't get results quite that fast," he murmured near her ear.

Mallory stepped away from him and turned her collar up. Chills were running down her spine, and they had nothing to do with the freezing temperature outside.

"More likely the Rittenhouses' daughter decided to reclaim it."

Gail sighed. "I suppose so. It wasn't getting much action. I think two married couples paused briefly beneath the branch, but everyone else seemed more intent on avoiding it." She looked directly at Pat.

He smiled an insincere apology and pulled his overcoat on.

So he hadn't been as obtuse as Gail thought, Mallory mused. Her friend was obviously miffed that he hadn't taken the hint when Gail stood beneath the mistletoe. It had appeared that he hadn't noticed, his attention attuned to a conversation nearby.

But, Mallory recalled all too clearly, he had kissed her, without benefit of mistletoe. It had been an hour since then, but she could still feel the butterfly brush of Pat's lips against hers.

"It's early," Gail said. "Why don't we all stop someplace for a drink. Maybe some dancing?"

Van put a weary hand to his temple. "I must make a note to resolve this New Year's not to cave in when this woman nags me," he mumbled.

"I didn't nag you," Gail insisted, then turned a bright smile on Pat. "What do you think? Mal?" she asked, belatedly including her friend.

Dancing. How long had it been since she'd indulged? Other than the turns around the living room with Chris in her arms, that is. She'd danced with her son when he was an infant, to soothe him. She'd used the motion and the music to calm him when he was sick and whining. Had slow-danced by herself when she was low, her partners always imaginary Prince Charmings who had no resemblance to any man she knew.

Mallory glanced at Patrick. He appeared to be waiting for her decision on Gail's suggestion. What would it be like to be held in his arms, to sway against him?

"Not tonight. Christopher's baby-sitter is expecting me," Mallory said.

"More to the point, I promised Chris I'd have his mom back before midnight," Patrick added. "No reason you two can't go, though."

Van Werner scowled at him. "Thanks a lot, Lonergan."

Gail sighed. "It wouldn't be any fun with just Van along. What are you doing for New Year's Eve?"

The question was definitely directed at Pat this time. Gail's gaze didn't dart toward either of her co-workers, didn't include them in the invitation.

Mallory held her breath. She didn't blame Gail for making a pass at Patrick. He was a very attractive man. But there was a part of her, a long-dormant part, that wanted to snarl at her friend. What right did she have to be jealous? It wasn't as if she and Pat had been seeing each other regularly. If Christopher and Kevin hadn't arranged for him to be her escort, she would have come to the Christmas party alone. Wouldn't even have known of Pat's existence.

"Thanks, but I've got plans already," Pat said smoothly.

The answer didn't smooth Mallory's feathers, though. Now she wondered with whom he would be spending New Year's Eve. A man like Pat probably had a number of women panting at his doorstep.

What did she care? Mallory stormed at herself. She already had a very special man in her life. His name was Christopher.

Still, the taste of jealousy remained, though. And why not? In this case, it didn't matter that she and Pat were just acquaintances. The fact was, Gail had horned in on her date. It wasn't really jealousy, just irritation over her friend's action. There was no reason for Gail to think she'd take offense, either. Who knew better than Gail that Mallory had absolutely no interest in men? They'd discussed it often enough when Gail was between men.

Mallory was still seething when she was settled in the car and Pat was backtracking the route to her house.

"It was very kind of you to do this," Mallory said. It was snowing faintly, the merest flurry. The tiny flakes brushed against the windshield and melted immediately. She watched as the wipers brushed the windows clear again. It was better than allowing herself to glance aside at her escort.

Pat tossed her a grin. "I enjoyed it. You've got some very nice friends at Rittenhouse."

"Nosy friends, you mean," Mallory said. "You must have endured a good deal of the third degree."

"A bit," he agreed. "I think I fielded their questions in a vague enough way to let their interest drop."

Mallory sincerely hoped so. But she doubted it.

"I suppose you had to break plans with your—" Mallory found she couldn't say the word *girlfriend*. It stuck in her throat. "With someone else, to do this."

"You mean with another woman. Don't worry, Mal," Pat said soothingly. "I didn't break anyone's heart tonight."

He hadn't used the shortened version of her name before. The fact that he did so now seemed awfully intimate. Mallory gripped her hands tightly together in her lap.

She stared out at the falling snow. "I wonder if we'll have snow for Christmas," she said. "Chris has been anxious to build snowmen."

The weather ought to be a safe subject for conversation. It would be mundane enough to calm her jittery nerves. They had been bad enough before she ever met Patrick Lonergan. Now that she'd spent time with him, had felt warmth in even his casual touch, had experienced the jolt of awareness his brief kiss had sent racing through her body...well, now her nerves were worse than before.

Of course, he hadn't meant anything by that kiss. He'd been trying to disarm the innuendos that had blossomed about her and Kevin. Had been trying to make everyone think that if Mallory Meyers was having an affair with anyone, it was with the minister's brother. From the looks in her associates' eyes, Pat had convinced nearly every single one of them. Only Van and Gail knew her better than to believe either rumor.

Relax, Mallory counseled herself. The evening was nearly over. She would never see Patrick Lonergan again. He wasn't a member of the parish, and he rarely visited his brother. For twins, they didn't seem terribly close.

Twins—identical ones—and yet Mallory was sure she'd be able to tell the men apart. She'd stared deep into Patrick's eyes. The passion that swirled in those depths had never even flitted across Kevin's eyes. Never would.

"Snowmen," Patrick mused. "It's been a long time since I even thought about building one of those. Does Chris go in for snow forts, as well? Kev and I specialized in them when we were his age. Of course, we were at war with each other constantly, so that might have had something to do with it."

The picture of Kevin and Patrick as tousled boys enchanted Mallory. It was easy to see the boy in the man. Pat's nonchalant acceptance of Christopher's friendship was part of it. The male bonding had been so...

Mallory sat up a bit straighter. Bonding. That was exactly what Christopher had been doing with Patrick. He'd always spent a good deal of time around Kevin, but the attention the pastor had given him was different. For all the hours Christopher spent at the church, he was under Rosemary Bittner's eye. The minister and his late wife had remained nothing more than fond adults, listening to her son's elementary school jokes, occasionally giving a few minutes' aid on homework, but still maintaining a distance.

That hadn't been the way Patrick treated Chris. Rosemary herself had mentioned it. Pat and Chris had spent the past few days together playing endless games of cards. Chris treated him more like a friend than as an adult. And Pat had let him, encouraged him. She remembered the byplay at her home earlier. Chris dragging his new friend off to show him his room. Pat asking for Chris's judgment call concerning the time his mother should be back home.

Bonding!

Oh, why hadn't she seen it? And what would it do to Chris to have Pat go away? Her son would feel crushed.

Get a hold of yourself, Mallory! Chris wasn't that stupid. He had known all along that Patrick would be leaving, that he was just visiting his brother. It would be nothing more than the temporary sadness Chris had experienced when Rosemary's grandson had come to visit for two weeks the previous summer. The two boys had been inseparable during the stay, but had survived their separation.

She was worrying over nothing. Everything would be fine.

Pat pulled the car into her driveway. Got out of the car, held her door open. Mallory looked up at him, at the way the snow drifted around his broad shoulders, at the way the porch light picked up a faint touch of copper in his dark brown hair.

Who was she kidding? Nothing was going to seem right ever again.

Chapter Six

She had the biggest eyes he'd ever seen. Or perhaps they just appeared so as Mallory looked up at him. Her up-swept hair was a soft shade of brown. A darker shade would have been too deep, a lighter shade too pale. Her lashes were chestnut, and curved like delicate fans, dipping to disguise the confusion in her eyes.

He knew they were gray, a gray that resembled storm clouds when she grew angry or apprehensive. In the faint glow of the street lamp, they looked obsidian, glistening and black.

Mallory swiveled in her seat, stretching forth first one luscious leg, then the other. Her coat fell open, her skirt rising a fraction.

If Kevin had gone looking for the perfect woman to test his twin's self-control, he'd found her. Pat felt his reserves strained to the max to resist the sweet glimmer of passion that resided deep within Mallory's eyes.

Patience. Rein in the lust, he counseled himself. She was as shy as a fawn when it came to men. She had been more at ease around him in the crowd and had withdrawn again once they were alone in the car. What had she expected? That he'd pull over to the side of the road and ravish her? In his brother's car?

That was exactly what he'd wanted to do.

But he hadn't.

Pat held out his hand to her, assisting Mallory to her feet. The snow had begun to stick to the ground, to cover the pavement. His tracks were the only ones to be seen.

Mallory put her hand in his reluctantly. Pat tried not to hold it too tight. Maybe he'd be lucky and she'd slip; then he could catch her, hold her near. But Mallory's step was as unfaltering as that of a mountain goat. She moved quickly. To escape the cold? Or to get away from him?

Rosemary Bittner opened the door before Mallory could use her key. Warmth and light crept from the house to envelop them.

"You're early," Rosemary declared. "I didn't expect you until much later."

"It's been a long day," Mallory murmured as she entered the house. She hesitated and glanced at Pat as he followed her through the door.

Sensing Mallory's quandary from her movements, Rosemary took the social reins in hand. "You both must be frozen," she said, blithely ignoring the probability that with the dip in temperature the heater in the Oldsmobile had been running full-blast. "I was just making hot chocolate. There are still some cookies. Chris managed to leave you a few."

"Ah, the magic word," Pat said, and shut the front door firmly behind himself. When he turned back, Mallory was five feet away and easing out of her coat without his assistance. Winning her trust wasn't going to be easy. Frankly, Pat admitted, he hadn't the least idea of how to go about it. With luck, Mallory would find her own way through that tricky maze. She was already attracted to him. She'd been as enthralled as he when he briefly played that sensuous game with her at the dinner table.

Maybe it hadn't been just him, though. Some jerk had given her a child, but Pat had a feeling Mallory had never experienced any of the delightful sensations he'd drawn in that teasing touch of his fingers against her lips, the sort of sensations that could and should precede consummation.

And he, Patrick decided, was just the fellow to show her that whole world of wonders.

If she'd let him.

He needed staying power. Starting now. So, before Mallory could refuse the baby-sitter's offer, Pat stripped off his overcoat and tossed it over the back of an armchair. "You know my weaknesses too well, Rosie."

"Yes, I do," Rosemary declared with a chuckle, giving Pat the distinct feeling that she'd read his mind. "The cookies are on the table," she added, and led the way into Mallory's kitchen.

Mallory's back was stiff as she followed the older woman; her shoulders were squared, as if she were going into battle. That didn't stop her hips from moving in what Pat considered an erotic manner, the slight sway from side to side so subtle, so feminine. Pat dwelled happily on each movement as she walked ahead of him. She probably didn't even realize he loved the way she moved.

Rosemary Bittner noticed, though. Her smile combined amusement with a motherly approval before she returned to the stove and added more milk to the pan already steaming on the burner.

Mallory went straight to the cupboard and took down mugs. She stretched a bit, moving up on her toes to reach the upper shelf.

Pat dropped into a chair at the table and continued to admire the view. It was probably as close to heaven as he was likely to get tonight. As platonic matters went, it was pretty close.

"Was Chris a problem tonight?" Mallory asked, placing three earthenware mugs on the table.

Rosemary stirred her concoction complacently. "He never is. I read him a story, and he went right to sleep."

Pat noticed the woman didn't meet Mallory's eyes when she answered. That meant Chris had gobbled up more than the number of cookies his mother had allowed. There was still a fairly hefty pile on the plate Rosemary had placed in the center of the table. Chocolate chip, he noted with pleasure. Patrick loosened his tie, selected a cookie and savored it.

Rosemary tested the hot chocolate, raising her spoon to her lips tentatively. "How was the party?" she asked.

"Fine," Mallory said. "I got a bigger bonus this year from Rittenhouse. Maybe now I can afford to get those new video games Chris wants."

"He'll lose interest in them by the time school is back in session," Rosemary commented. "Trust me. I reared enough children of my own to know. Get something for yourself, instead. You deserve it."

Slipping her hand into a cheery red-and-green kitchen mitt, Rosemary carried the cocoa over to the table and poured equal portions into each mug. Pat was amazed that there wasn't a drop wasted.

Mallory smiled at the baby-sitter. "Isn't that like the pot calling the kettle black? When did you ever splurge on yourself, Rosemary?"

The older woman carried the now empty pan to the sink and ran water in it before joining them at the table. "I had occasions," she said. "Like Mother's Day. We always ate out."

"Mmm..." Mallory mumbled around a cookie. "That's an idea. Chris and I could do it up in style Christmas Day."

Pat stretched his legs out beneath the table and leaned back in his chair. He had a cookie in one hand and the steaming mug of hot chocolate in the other. "That is the most pathetic thing I have ever heard," he announced.

Mallory's eyes widened for just a moment before her brow furrowed in suspicion. "In what way?" she growled.

It was a definite growl, Pat decided. And he liked every purring nuance of it.

"It's Christmas," he said. "That calls for a noisy group of people around a table, sparring over who gets a turkey leg."

Rosemary reached for a cookie. "Pat's right. It's a day for family. You shouldn't be alone."

"Usually it is," Mallory said. She sounded as if she were defending herself. "But this year Aunt Anita is in California, getting to know her new stepdaughter's family. Chris and I will be fine."

Pat snorted in disgust. "Sure you will be. I know exactly the kind of day you'll have. I've had them every holiday for years, and they are the pits, Mal."

Mallory's eyes kindled with anger. "I don't care what you—"

To rile her more, Pat turned to Rosemary. "I think they should join us, don't you?"

Kevin's housekeeper was a wonderful coconspirator. Her smile widened with delight. "Of course! Why didn't I think of it?" she declared. "Since I couldn't be with my children this year, Kevin suggested that I share Christmas with him and Patrick. We'd all be so pleased if you and Christopher came, as well, Mallory."

Mallory took a careful sip of her chocolate. "That's all very nice, but I don't think—"

"Nonsense. It's settled. We will be eating about two. I expect you and Chris to be there." Rosemary's tone brooked no refusal. Her face softened as she reached across the table to cover Mallory's hand with her own. "Please, dear. It would mean so much to me. And I wouldn't have to be the only woman at the table."

"More hands to do the dishes afterward," Pat agreed, knowing the comment would make it easier for Mallory to accept the invitation.

"Dishes!" Her elegantly curved brows rose in exaggerated surprise. "The restaurant looks better and better."

"Oh, all right. If you grace us with your presence for Christmas dinner, I will handle KP detail," he said, as if disgruntled.

"Done!" Mallory announced brightly, and leaned over the table, her hand outstretched. "Shake on it, so the deal is legal. Rosemary is our witness."

His fingers closed around hers and lingered just long enough to bring the wary flutter of awareness back into her eyes. "It's a deal," Pat said, and reluctantly let her go.

He was content to just listen as the two women discussed the menu after that. Considering she had been reluctant to even accept the invitation, Mallory was now determined to help the housekeeper with preparation of the meal.

"Oh, gracious! Look at the time!" Rosemary said, jumping to her feet. "I'd better be on my way home."

Pat helped himself to a last cookie and got up. "It's snowing, Rosie. I'll follow you to make sure you get there all right."

"You needn't bother."

"I insist."

Mallory slid out of her chair as Rosemary left the room to get her coat. "Thank you," she said. "I would have worried about her if you hadn't offered."

And, Pat thought in amusement, *you were worried about how to get rid of me.*

"No problem," he assured her. "I hope you enjoyed your evening."

"You were a wonderful present," Mallory said, "and a very nice man to go out of your way at a little boy's request."

Damn, but she was sweet. "Maybe I didn't do it for Chris," Pat murmured.

"For Kevin, then."

She was determined to ignore the compliment. She probably didn't know that her son had provided that sexy photograph to lure him into the trap. For a trap it was. And Kevin had known exactly how to bait it.

"I'd better pay Rosemary," Mallory said, and left the room.

Pat dipped his hand in his jacket pocket. Yeah, the prop was still there. Now he just needed the opportunity.

"Oh, my, it is snowing, isn't it!" Rosemary exclaimed upon opening the front door.

The flurry had picked up speed during the cookiefest. Nearly an inch had already accumulated on the walkway, blanketing the footsteps that led from the Oldsmobile in the driveway to the front stoop.

"It's so pretty." The housekeeper sighed. "Makes me think about other winter evenings, when my husband and I would build up a fire and sit together while it burned." She pushed away the melancholy and wound a scarf around her neck. "Nasty stuff to drive in though," Rosemary added.

Mallory hugged her friend. They brushed cheeks. "Thank you again for staying with Chris."

"I enjoy it."

Pat was beginning to believe they would exchange nonsensical remarks forever if he didn't hustle things along. He stepped past the housekeeper and took her arm.

"I'll see you tomorrow," she called back to Mallory.

Pat heard the door close behind them, followed closely by Rosemary's chuckle. "It will take a while for my old car to warm up," she said.

"I thought it might," he answered, guiding her around the Olds and opening the door of her own car for her. "Lock your door and sit tight."

He waited just long enough for Rosemary to turn the key in the ignition before retracing his steps to Mallory's front door.

She answered at his first knock, as if she had known he would be back. Her surprised expression told him she hadn't.

"Oh, did you forget something?"

Her voice gave her away. It was breathless.

He took a step inside, leaving the door open behind him. Cold air swept into the house, but neither of them noticed.

"Yes," Pat said. He brushed back his overcoat and pulled a piece of greenery from his jacket pocket. "This."

Her eyes widened. "You stole the mistletoe!"

"Damn right," Pat murmured. He held it over her head; his other hand slid to the nape of her neck, cupping her head, pulling her close. "Remember," he said, "it's traditional." Then he kissed her.

Mallory's hands pushed against his chest in protest for the space of a heartbeat, then slid over his shoulders in surrender.

There was no time for words. There was little time for much of anything. Pat held her still, his fingers buried in the sweet smelling softness of her hair. He moved his mouth against hers, savoring the moment. Her lips were soft, full, and as inexperienced as he had guessed. "Mal," he whispered, and ran his tongue across her bottom lip, pushed inward to lick along her teeth. Mallory shivered and turned her head, slanting her mouth over his in a hungry invitation. Patrick groaned; his hands slid downward and molded her body to his.

Outside, the engine of Rosemary Bittner's car continued to purr contentedly. It took a moment for Pat to remember where he was, that there was no chance of progressing beyond a kiss. Yet. Patience was a virtue at which he excelled. Probably the only one he possessed.

Mallory shivered again, this time from a gust of wind that blew snow into the hallway. She moved back, disentangling herself from his arms. "Merry Christmas, Pat," she whispered.

Which was his cue to leave. "Merry Christmas, Mal." He pressed her hands together, raised them to his lips for a final caress, then stepped back onto the porch.

Gently she closed the door, placing him out in the cold. But not for long, Patrick vowed. He shoved his hands in his pockets, and was whistling happily as he headed back to the driveway. He had wanted Mallory Meyers before.

Now he was more determined than ever to win her over. No matter how long it took.

The whistled strains of "God Rest Ye Merry Gentlemen" drifted back to Mallory as she leaned weakly against the door. A slightly mangled piece of mistletoe rested in her hand. She wondered briefly how she'd come to hold it, when it had changed hands.

When he had decided to steal it.

Had it been earlier, before they went in to dinner? Or had it been afterward, after he drove her slightly insane by touching her as a lover would? The rough texture of his fingers had been amazingly soft, the brief brush of his lips so tender.

This last kiss had been neither brief nor tender. It had been determined. And, Mallory thought dreamily, it had ended far too soon.

No, it hadn't. She had been the one to break the embrace, fighting off the resurgence of long-buried feelings. Self-preservation demanded she keep her longings under control. A tight control. It had been so easy to live in her narrow little world. She didn't need to be reminded of what she had chosen to give up. When she'd given in to her passions before, she had emerged the loser.

Except for Christopher. He was the one joy of her life. Given the chance to change the nightmarish period that she'd endured before his birth, Mallory knew that she would gladly accept all the heartache and pain again.

Rosemary's old station wagon eased out of the driveway and moved down the street slowly, followed by Patrick's borrowed Oldsmobile. Mallory watched until both cars were out of sight before turning off the porch light and kicking off her shoes.

The night-light glowed softly in Christopher's room. He was curled on his side, one small hand buried beneath the pillow, the other outflung. He'd kicked off the covers, just as he always did when first settling in for the night, claiming he was too hot.

Just as Dirk had.

Thank goodness Chris seemed to have inherited very few traits from his biological father. Would other similarities surface in the future? She prayed they wouldn't, worried that they would.

How did a woman combat such fears?

Chris would be seven years old in a few months. It hardly seemed possible that he was growing up so fast, leaving her behind in so many ways. She tried, but there was only so much a mother could do for her son.

Mallory sat on the side of the bed and ran a tender hand through Christopher's soft, tousled brown hair. It was still very like hers in color and texture. Dirk's had been a darker tone. Would Chris's deepen with the years? Dirk had been interested in sports, baseball in particular. The game had always left her cold. But last summer Chris had developed a passion for it, had pestered her mercilessly until she agreed to let him play in one of the city park leagues for children.

There was no reason to think Chris's love for baseball had any connection to Dirk's parentage. Many boys were sports enthusiasts. Chris's best friend, Jeff, had been just as gung ho, as had Jeff's father.

Was it merely the interest of an adult male that had piqued Chris's own interest in baseball? That question led her down the mental lane she had been avoiding for so long. Did a boy reach a certain age when he no longer needed his mother as much as he needed a man's guidance?

Had she been foolish to think that friendship with Kevin Lonergan would give Christopher the role model he needed? Or had she just been thinking of herself, fearing that she might repeat the whole episode with another Dirk, would be attracted only to the type of man who would break her heart?

Chris stirred in his sleep. His eyelids fluttered.

Her little man, Mallory thought tenderly. *I only want what's best for you, Chris. You're my whole life.*

"Mommy?" he murmured.

The nights she worked late, Chris nearly always woke briefly when she returned home and checked on him. "I'm back, safe and sound," Mallory soothed, her fingers brushing his hair back from his face again.

Christopher rolled over on his back. His eyes were still more closed than open. "Did you have a good time?" His voice was slurred and sleep-laden.

"A very nice time," she assured him, and tucked the covers around him.

Christopher was fighting drowsiness. He blinked his eyes in the effort to wake sufficiently. "Did you like my present, then?"

Her present. Patrick Lonergan.

"He seemed like a very nice man," Mallory answered. He had been that. And more. But she didn't want to think about her reaction to him, about the longings he had stirred to life with casual touches and careless kisses. A man like Pat Lonergan took it for granted that a woman would accept his attentions. He hadn't realized how they would affect a woman like her.

Christopher smiled softly, pleased with her answer. "I like him," he mumbled, and yawned. "A lot."

"Hush now," Mallory whispered, and brushed a kiss against her son's temple. "Go back to sleep."

He was deep in slumber a moment later. Mallory crept out of the room, retracing her steps down the hall. She turned off the living room lights and went into the kitchen to clear away the mugs of hot chocolate.

At least that was her intention.

Mallory sank into her accustomed chair, folded her hands on top of the table, and stared at the mug Pat had used. Pictured how his long, masculine fingers had looked as he cradled it. How his eyes had gleamed with mischief as he teased Rosemary Bittner. How they had warmed when he gazed at her. She recalled the easy way he'd conversed with the Rittenhouse crowd. How he'd adroitly avoided Gail's heavy-handed hints.

How it had felt when he kissed her.

Christopher wasn't the only one who liked Patrick, Mallory admitted. She liked him, as well. Liked him a lot.

Chapter Seven

The phone call caught Mallory in the middle of a tussle with an irate customer the next day.

A young sales associate in infant wear sidled up next to her and waited for an appropriate opening. When the customer turned to her daughter to discuss the inadequacies of the store's refund policy, the clerk bumped Mallory's shoulder.

"Er...Mal? Your son's on the phone. Wants to know if he can go to lunch and then shopping for Christmas presents with one of his little friends," she mumbled.

Since the customers' discussion was turning into a debate that didn't—at the moment—involve her, Mallory turned her attention to the message-bearer. "With Jeff? I thought he was bound for the dentist today. I can't come to the phone right now, so tell Chris that if Mrs. Bittner approves, *and* Jeff's mother is taking them, then it's okay. Oh, and I need to know when they'll be back."

The sales associate eased back to the phone just as the customer caved in. "All right. We'll take an exchange, but only if you've got this playsuit in the same size and color. But if this one is as poorly made as the last one, I'm talking to Mr. Rittenhouse personally," the woman said threateningly.

Mallory forced a smile. "As long as you follow the washing instructions to the letter, there should be no problem," she said, and, after scribbling her initials on the sales slip as authorization, handed the paperwork back to a member of the floor staff.

The associate who'd passed along her message to Chris was off the phone and industriously refolding a group of receiving blankets on a table nearby. "So what was the verdict?" Mallory asked, stopping next to the display briefly.

"Verdict?" The girl looked at her blankly for a moment. "Oh, you mean on your son's call. Well, he said Mrs. Bittner said it was okay 'cause she and someone else were going to start setting up tables for your whatcha-macallit on Wednesday."

Which meant that Rosemary and Fran were pitching in early to get the church basement ready for the bazaar. Since they'd been involved in other years, both women knew that it took time to set up the various booths.

Mallory nodded, pleased that her friends had begun a day earlier than planned. It would make things go very smoothly the actual day of the big event. "Great! Then what time will Jeff's mother drop Chris at home?"

"Jeff? Oh, it wasn't Jeff he was going with," the clerk said, and shook out another tiny blanket.

Mallory got a knot of dread in her stomach. She could almost guess what was coming.

"Chris said he was going with somebody named Pat and that you already knew that Pat didn't have a mother and that it would be all right with you anyway since Mrs. Bittner gave it the go-ahead."

Mallory sighed. More male bonding in progress, when she wasn't around to do anything about it.

"They'll be home by six," the girl continued, unaware that Mallory was unhappy with her report. "And they're bringing pizza with them." She grinned widely. "Bet you'll be glad you don't have to cook tonight, huh, Mal?"

Glad didn't exactly describe how she felt, Mallory thought, and ground her teeth in frustration.

Patrick leaned back in his chair at the fast-food restaurant his young guest had chosen for lunch, and watched as Chris wolfed down the last of his chicken nuggets. With barely a break in his stride, the boy dug into his milk shake, all the while playing with the toy that was the real reason he'd asked for a kid's meal.

"Then what happened?" Chris asked, his mouth full, a chocolate mustache already forming above his upper lip.

"Then? Well, it wasn't exactly the kind of party where you play pin the tail on the donkey," Pat said. "After Mr. Rittenhouse opened his present—"

"What was it?"

"A dumb-looking silver bowl."

"Yuck!" Chris shoveled more dessert in his mouth.

"Well, after that, people stood around and talked." *And I tried my hand at seducing your mother.*

"Just talked?" Christopher was agog.

"Yep. So after a while your mom started missing you, and we left," Pat ended.

"And then what?"

Wasn't that enough? The kid was an expert at giving the third degree. "It was snowing, so I drove carefully."

"Yeah, there was lots of snow this morning. Think maybe we could build one of those snow forts you and Pastor Kev told me about?"

Ah, finally. Chris was off the subject. Though why he wanted a minute-by-minute account of the Rittenhouse holiday party was beyond Pat.

"Depends. You want to do that or get a pizza?"

"Both," Christopher declared, and returned to the original topic under discussion. "Did you stay at our house for a while after you brought Mom home?"

Determined little imp. "What are you planning to be when you grow up?" Pat demanded. "A lawyer? You've got enough questions to be a regular legal eagle."

Chris giggled and stuck a straw in his shake to slurp noisily at the melted section. "Did ya?"

There was no escaping. "Yes, I stayed for a while. Mrs. Bittner made hot chocolate and we ate cookies."

"Then what?"

Pat was beginning to hate that phrase. He sighed loudly. "Let's go at this another way. What is it you want to know about, sport?"

Christopher kept his eyes downcast, studying the inch or so of shake that remained in the tall cup. "Did you kiss Mom?" he asked, in a far too casual voice.

Time to go on the defensive here, Pat thought. "Did you want me to kiss her? 'Cause, remember, you didn't give me instructions on that, Chris."

"Did you?"

The kid was going to be the next Oliver Wendell Holmes. "I give up," Pat said. "Yes, I plead guilty. I kissed your mom. I can't help it. She's a pretty lady, and I like kissing pretty ladies. Don't you?"

Christopher's face lightened in a wide smile. "Yeah, I like kissing Mom."

"I rest my case. You're as much a ladies' man as I am. Knew it the moment I met you, Chris. We think alike. Who else have you been kissing?"

"Nobody."

Patrick held his breath. What next?

"Did ya kiss her in the kitchen?" Christopher asked.

"Kiss who?" Pat countered.

"Mom!"

"Oh, her." Now it was Patrick's turn to play with the leftovers on the table. He picked up a cold french fry, contemplated it a moment, then dropped it back on the littered tray. "Not in the kitchen, no."

"Oh." Christopher sounded disappointed.

"I did the same thing you do," Pat said. "I kissed her goodbye at the front door." Of course, he'd done it for a lot longer, and with little intention of making it a good-bye kiss, but what the heck!

"Could you kiss her in the kitchen?"

In the kitchen, in the bedroom, in the boardroom at Rittenhouse. Wherever, whenever.

"What's so special about the kitchen?" Pat demanded.

The last of Christopher's dessert was slurped up through his straw. "That's how Jeff got his baby sister," he announced. "His mom and dad kissed in the kitchen. I really like babies, and I thought maybe we could get one. So could you kiss Mom in the kitchen?"

Pat let his breath out very slowly. This was certainly a twist on the old found-under-a-cabbage-leaf story. "Sport," he announced, getting to his feet, "I think we need to have a talk. You see, Jeff's only got things half-right."

Christopher slid from his chair readily and trotted after the tall man. "Which half?" he asked.

Now how had he gotten involved in an explanation of the birds and the bees? Chris was looking up at him, those wide gray eyes the spitting image of his gorgeous mother's. Only, in the child's eyes, trust and love shone as brightly as a Christmas star.

Chris was precocious, but it was his tenacity that impressed Pat. The kid sank his teeth into a subject and hung on, no matter how you tried to shake his interest from it. He was going to be a real handful in the future. At the moment, though, he was still only a six-year-old. He wasn't going to be interested in the clinical details. *Keep it casual,* Pat told himself. Besides, it was more than likely that Mallory would blow her stack when she learned what he and Chris had discussed that afternoon.

"You ever ask your mom about how you get babies?" Pat asked the boy and dumped the remains of their meal in a trash receptacle.

Chris's hand slipped readily in his as they pushed through the door and back out into the cold. The child had been overjoyed at the idea of riding in Pat's truck. With all the slush on the slick streets, Pat was glad he was behind a familiar wheel.

"No. 'Cause Jeff told me how," Chris answered, skipping happily at Patrick's side. "But he was wrong, huh?"

"'Fraid so." How the heck was he suppose to get out of this one? Pat wondered.

Chris skidded in the muck. Still pondering his dilemma, Pat pulled him up one-handed. Chris giggled in excitement and made every effort to slide again. When they were settled in the wide cab of the aging three-quarter-ton flatbed, the questions started again.

"So how do you get babies?"

Patrick started the truck engine, still searching for the right path. Maybe he could make the whole deal sound impossible, like a machine that was missing parts. "First you have to have a mother and a father," he said.

"I've got a mom," Christopher offered hopefully.

Pat tromped down on his clutch and wrestled the vehicle into gear, stretched his arm across the banquet seat and twisted to look back as the truck began to roll out of the parking spot. He eased up on the clutch, letting the gear engage. "You're half-there then, sport."

"I don't have a dad, though," the boy admitted, a thoughtful look on his face. "Maybe you could be my dad," he suggested.

The truck jerked to a halt and stalled. "Ah, yeah..." Pat murmured, and concentrated on restarting the truck. "Your mother might have other ideas about that, Chris." This time he managed to get all the way out of the parking lot and into traffic before attacking the problem again.

"You just start with a mother and a father. You know," Pat said, "married people, like your friend Jeff's parents."

Christopher nodded sagely, as if he understood.

"That means two people who are in love," Pat added.

"Oh. So you can't be my dad, because you and Mommy aren't in love." Christopher pondered a moment. "You could be if ya wanted, couldn't you?"

Pat felt as if he were digging himself deeper and deeper into a hole. "Hey, I just met her! It usually takes a while to fall in love with anyone." Now, lust... that could happen like a bolt of lightning. A man could be complacent, comfortable, with lust. Or his insides could be twisted in knots. Sort of like his were now, and had been ever since he'd left Mallory Meyers in her doorway the evening before, her mouth damp and still trembling from his kiss.

If there was one thing he didn't want to talk about anymore, it was the subject of babies. Just thinking about the enticing preliminary work involved brought Mallory too clearly to mind.

"Say, wasn't there a toy store around here somewhere?" Pat demanded. "That's one place I'll bet you can direct me to. Which way do I turn at the light?"

Christopher bounced forward in his seat as far as the seat belt allowed. "Cool!" he shouted. A short while later, Pat was deep in a discussion about the latest action figures.

A miracle happened. Mallory managed to leave Rittenhouse when she was scheduled to do so. There were many times during the year when she was held up with various and sundry things at the store, but during the holiday season it was only through divine intervention that she was ever able to slip out the door a spare hour later than expected.

She had finished dealing with the fourth major catastrophe of the day—at least it was a catastrophe from the customer's standpoint—and was heading for her office when another call came through the switchboard requesting a manager's assistance.

The operator gave Mallory an apologetic look. "Sorry, Mal. It's Housewares this time, and since this is Stan's day off..." She let the sentence hang unfinished in the air. Stan was Mallory's counterpart in hardlines.

Fleetingly, Mallory wondered how he'd managed to get time off with the season counting down the final days to Christmas. Well, at least she was reaping a beneficial reward for her diligence this year. She might be stuck slaving a straight fourteen days in a row, but she would be able to take four days off at New Year's. A respite before inventory. She'd already promised Chris that he could call the shots for those days. If he suddenly announced he wanted to go to Disney World, she was more than ready to plunk her year-end bonus down on plane tickets and lose herself in the Magic Kingdom.

However, the stolen time was still a week away. Until then, Christmas Day had to suffice as the lone break in her schedule.

Mallory glanced at her watch. Perhaps she could console the customer quickly and—

"Scram," a dry female voice ordered. "You heard me. Get out of here while you've got a chance, Mal."

Mallory turned with a relieved smile. "That is one suggestion I don't need to hear twice," she told her friend Gail.

"Yeah, well, I'm not always this nice," Gail reminded her. "But since I'm back from dinner, and it is my department, what the hell?"

Mallory fled, giving both Gail and the switchboard operator a cheerful wave of her hand.

Despite the fact that she was heading home at the height of rush hour, the traffic moved smoothly. She hit all the lights right and didn't run into any snarls due to accidents on the slippery streets. On the radio a singer was crooning that it was "beginning to look a lot like Christmas." Mallory agreed wholeheartedly. Not only was the store a continual bustle of activity, but with the snowfall the night before, the yards in her subdivision were cloaked in a lovely winter mantle. The plastic Santas and reindeer no longer looked out of place. The cheerfully colored lights that outlined both roofs and windows seemed to glow even brighter.

It was going to be a busy week, what with the church bazaar, Christmas Eve and Christmas Day all grouped closely together. There would be a number of nights that she worked late, too. Tomorrow she would have the evening shift, working until ten, when the store closed, followed by an early day so that she could escape Rittenhouse for her duties at the St. Edmund's bazaar.

Keeping busy kept her mind from dwelling too often on Patrick Lonergan. Or it did most of the time.

"It's 5:20, and traffic on interstate 75 is at a crawl," the announcer on the radio said.

Thank goodness she lived close enough to the mall to weave her way along surface streets, Mallory thought. She'd be home earlier than expected, and—

And Patrick would be waiting for her.

The idea was strange and pleasant at the same time. Mallory wasn't sure she liked it either way. She didn't want to sort out her feelings, not at this point. Chances were that the attraction was due more to her long celibacy than to anything else. He was a nice man, a very handsome man, and her son liked him. That was it. Just because her pulse raced out of control when he was around, that didn't mean that she should pitch her carefully thought-out guidelines for her life out the window.

To delay the moment when she would be forced to face him again, Mallory took a quick turn and headed for St. Edmund's Church rather than straight home.

She could hear the racket of a hammer when she opened the side door that led to the basement activity room. Fran's voice floated up the stairwell. "No, a little more to the right," she instructed.

"Like this?" a man answered.

Mallory froze, her foot suspended between two steps before realization clicked in. Although the timbre was similar, it wasn't Patrick Lonergan helping Fran. It was his brother.

"Mal!" Fran called. "We didn't expect to see you."

Mallory let the fire door swing shut behind her. She stripped off her gloves and let the scarf that covered her head slip back to lay on her shoulders. "After hearing that you'd begun construction early, I couldn't resist seeing how you were progressing."

"It went faster before Kevin took Rosemary's place," Fran said. "She had to go start his dinner. Trouble is, this man's all thumbs."

"Sore ones, at that," Kevin put in as he climbed down off a stepladder. "How's it look so far?"

Tables had been arranged to form U-shaped areas six feet apart from one another along the sides of the long room. Streamers of red, green, and white crepe paper were draped halfway up the walls. There were already two banners fastened just below them, identifying the goods available at the booth beneath.

When setup was finished, there would also be an area to accommodate families taking advantage of the fish fry, a soft drink stand in a corner, and a tall artificial tree on the stage at the far end of the room. There was still a lot to be done.

"Looks great so far. I wish I could stay to help," Mallory said. "But Chris is expecting me back."

Fran stretched, her hands placed in the small of her back as she arched backward. "Time for me to knock off here, too. Larry's probably combing the freezer, looking for TV dinners."

"We're stopping for the day? I've never heard sweeter words," Kevin mumbled, sucking on the thumb he'd most recently smashed with the hammer. "I'll see if Pat can't help tomorrow. Unlike me, he's quite handy with his hands."

Is he ever. Mallory tried to brush the memory of how Patrick's large hands had eased over her body, shaping hers to his. A telltale flush crept into her cheeks. She hoped that neither of her friends noticed it.

"Speaking of Patrick," Fran said, "how was the big date last night?"

Mallory was sure her face was bright red now. "It wasn't a 'big date.' Mr. Lonergan went to the Rittenhouses' home with me, ate dinner, and then drove me home."

"And?" Fran insisted.

"That's it."

Fran looked totally disgusted. "What did you wear?" she demanded after a moment's thought.

"My black suit."

Fran closed her eyes, shook her head sadly. "You are hopeless," she said mournfully. "Here we line you up with one of the most gorgeous men I've ever seen . . ."

"Come now," Mallory said. "He looks a lot like Kevin, here."

The pastor took his injured thumb out of his mouth and straightened his shoulders. "Why, thank you, ladies. These compliments will surely go to my head," he warned them.

"As if you haven't heard them before," Fran said. "Anyway, where was I?"

"Leaving to fix your husband dinner," Mallory said. "You and Rosemary . . . and Kevin . . . did a great job today."

Fran hefted her purse and quilted coat from beneath one of the tables. "Yeah, well, we couldn't have done it if you hadn't let Pat whisk Chris off for the day. I know you're working tomorrow, so we'll finish arranging this joint without you. What time will you be able to get away on Wednesday?''

Relieved to be discussing the bazaar, Mallory explained the trades she had worked out with various other managers that would enable her to leave early. Within minutes, all three were trooping up the stairs to the parking lot.

Fran was off in a flash, the back tires of her car spinning out a spray of slush. Mallory lingered while Kevin locked the church door once more.

''You know it won't work,'' she said quietly.

''What do you mean? The tables are all lined up exactly as they were last year, and the flow pattern moved easily,'' Kevin replied.

Mallory frowned at him. ''That's not what I'm talking about, and you know it.''

Kevin ran a hand back through his dark hair, brushing it back from his brow. ''It isn't?'' he asked innocently, and concentrated on pulling on his gloves.

Patrick, Mallory remembered, hadn't worn gloves the evening before, yet his hand had been warm when it wrapped possessively around hers.

''You think I don't know what you're doing?'' Mallory demanded. ''Come on, Kevin. You've been hinting that I should take another look at things for a long time now. The suggestion being that just because Dirk was a creep, that doesn't mean all men are.''

''Well, they aren't,'' he said simply.

Mallory glared at him. ''Maybe they just are in different ways.''

Kevin grinned down at her. ''Now why do I get the feeling I've just been reclassified with the scum?''

''Probably because you deserve it,'' Mallory snapped. ''Stop trying to play matchmaker.''

"Too many of us around, I take it?" he said. "It's only because Rosemary, Fran and I care about you, Mal."

Indignation kept Mallory's backbone stiff. If it hadn't, she was sure, she would have wilted, the wind taken out of her sails by the sincerity of Kevin's statement.

"I know, but knock it off, will you?" Mallory concentrated on rewrapping her scarf around her throat. "None of you seem to understand that my life is perfect just the way it is."

"Is it?" the pastor asked in a soft voice.

She hated it when he did that, when he made her doubt her own decisions. But he was wrong. Dead wrong. Her life was going along just fine, peachy-keen. She was too busy to be lonely. Most of the time. She had Christopher, and her child supplied all the love any woman needed.

Now, if she could squelch the nagging longing that Kevin's brother had stirred in her soul, everything would be just fine.

It wasn't going to be easy.

Chapter Eight

There was a faded red pickup truck in her driveway and a snow fort in her front yard, Mallory discovered. The fort had three sides, the front wall built up to a height of two feet, with the bracketing sides sloping away like reclining obtuse triangles. Fortunately, there wasn't a horde of ready-made ammunition within the fort. If there was one thing she could do without, it was snowballs that would turn into ice overnight. She didn't want to think about anything concerning the truck or the man who drove it.

Since nearly all the snow in her yard had been mobilized in the creation of the fort, the lawn appeared denuded compared to her neighbors' yards. There were a couple of lopsided snowmen standing guard before various homes down the street. The neighborhood was one of young families with children all of a similar age. This was the first time a snow fort had ever appeared on the street.

Mallory would have preferred to see a simple snow-man in her yard again.

Christopher was sprawled on his stomach on the floor, watching cartoons, when she let herself in the door. Patrick was stretched out on the sofa, his shoes off, his eyes closed, his breathing soft and regular.

Chris rolled on his side, gave her a wide grin, then pressed his finger to his lips. "Shhh..." he cautioned her. "Pat's asleep."

It was a day for firsts. Ones she didn't particularly like. As if the snow fort hadn't been enough! In the past, Chris had always rushed across the room to give her a quick hug of welcome. Today he stayed sprawled in front of the television, content to toss her a casual grin.

And there was a long, lean grown man sacked out on her couch.

Well, she wasn't giving up one of the highlights of her day. Mallory shrugged out of her coat and tossed it over the back of a chair. Scarf, gloves, and boots were quickly dispensed with. Once free, Mallory padded in stocking feet to where Christopher lay. She knelt and gathered her tolerant son into her arms. His eyes stayed on the TV screen until a commercial replaced the animated figures.

"Have fun today?" she asked.

Temporarily free of distractions, Chris gave her a fierce hug. "Yep," he whispered loudly. "I had chicken nuggets for lunch and got this neat prize." He fished in the pockets of his jeans, at last unearthing a plastic figure. She had barely glanced at it before Chris launched into speech again. "Then we went to the toy store and checked things out."

Checked things out. The phrase sounded so grown-up. Probably because he had never used it before. It was clearly something he had picked up from Pat. How had this stranger managed to gain a niche of his own in Christopher's heart so quickly?

"After that we came home and built my fort. Did you see it, Mommy? Isn't it cool?"

It certainly was. Along with everything else. Too much was happening, all of it apparently beyond her control, and she was helpless to stop any of it.

"Did you get wet building the fort?" Mallory asked, brushing Christopher's soft brown hair back into place.

"Yeah," he said, his eyes shining with excitement. "But Pat made me change clothes when we came in. Just like you do."

Mallory wondered if Chris had complained as bitterly to his new hero as he did to her. She doubted it. At the moment, Patrick Lonergan could do nothing wrong in her son's eyes.

"That's good," Mallory said with quiet approval. "I wouldn't want you to catch a chill."

"I won't," Chris promised, and squirmed out of her clutch as the familiar cartoon returned to the screen. Mallory had barely gotten to her feet when the boy rolled over again. "Oh, Pat said to wake him up when you got home, so we could go get pizza."

Mallory glanced at the sofa, at the sleeping form of the man whom she resented for his entrance into hers and Christopher's lives and to whom she, as much as her son, was inexplicably drawn.

The more she saw of Patrick, the less she felt he resembled Kevin. Kevin had never looked this rugged. This sexy.

Pat's hair looked both wind-tossed and finger-combed. His face was relaxed in sleep, and minus the heart-stopping grin, although his mouth still curved slightly, as if even his dreams amused him. His skin carried the year-round tan of a man who spent most of his time outdoors.

The shadow of a beard darkened the masculine line of his jaw.

Just watching him sleep made her blood race. *Get a grip, Mallory.* She was acting like some ditzy teenager in the throes of her first crush.

Only this wasn't a crush. It was unadulterated, grown-up lust.

She should stop observing him. At the moment, that simple action was beyond her. He looked so good.

To combat the cold temperatures, Patrick had worn a turtleneck pullover under his flannel shirt. Both were a spruce green. Mallory wondered how the deep tone would shade the emerald of his eyes.

Both shirts were tucked inside the waistband of soft, worn jeans. The color might once have been the deep blue associated with brand-new denim, but frequent use had bleached them a pale sky blue. Wear marks showed distinctly at the cuffs, knees, and along his thickly muscled thighs. The fly was even paler, and frayed enticingly, the whole length.

Aghast at herself for noticing that detail, Mallory turned quickly back to her son. "Let him sleep a while longer," she suggested in a strained whisper. "I'll go change clothes."

Christopher grunted in agreement, his eyes glued to the set, his attention on the animated antics, rather than on her.

Thank God for small favors. Whatever would she do if Christopher noticed her odd behavior? There could be no other way to describe the slow perusal she'd given Patrick's sleeping form. Something she would never have done if he'd been awake and conscious of her actions. It was something she would never have believed herself capable of doing under normal circumstances. Why was she so attracted to Kevin's brother?

To Christopher, the man was a newly adopted friend, a masculine ear that listened patiently to his every utterance. Mallory always did her best to pay close attention to Christopher—she listened, but didn't hear half of what her son said. No child could resist a captive ear.

Yet Mallory knew there was more to her son's enchantment with Patrick. She hadn't wanted to admit that she was no longer the center of Chris's universe. He was no longer a baby. He needed more than just a mother's love. He had never said a word to her, but Mallory had seen the envy in Chris's eyes as he watched the interplay between his friends and their fathers.

She had been a fool to believe that the casual friendship she maintained with Kevin Lonergan could take the place of a permanent male adult in Christopher's life.

Kevin couldn't fill the void in Chris's world, any more than he could fulfill the needs in her own. The only difference was that she could tromp down the longings that kept her awake and wanting. Chris couldn't.

The problem had always been there. It was just that the appearance of Patrick Lonergan in their lives had brought it to the fore. He had stepped into the role that Chris had fashioned for him, that of mentor, as well as playmate. And even if Chris didn't see the difference, Mallory was quite sure that Pat did. The amazing thing was that he fit the role so well.

Not just in Chris's scheme either, Mallory thought.

There was something unique, something special, about Pat Lonergan that made it impossible to treat him as nothing more than a passing acquaintance.

Realizing she was still lingering in the living room, watching Pat as he slept, Mallory hustled down the hall to her bedroom to change.

Christopher couldn't help casting Pat as a starring character in his narrow universe, but she wasn't an impressionable child. She wouldn't be a hypocrite, either, spinning impossible dreams about a man who would vanish from her life as surely as Dirk Segal had, only with far less reason to stay. There was nothing she could do about Chris's hurt, but there was a lot she could do about guarding her own heart. Susceptible as it was.

Well, there was nothing she could do about it tonight. There was no way that Chris was going to give up a chance to chomp pizza with his idol. But there was something she could do about her own situation. If she read Patrick correctly, he was attracted to beautiful women. Which she had tried to be the evening before, more for herself than to impress her blind date. He would quickly lose interest if he saw her as she truly was.

The first thing, she decided, glancing at her reflection in the dresser mirror, was to revert to her natural, completely average self, as soon as possible. In short order, she shed suit jacket, skirt, blouse and panty hose, replacing them with a pair of heavy socks, rather baggy, relaxed-fit jeans, and her favorite chocolate-colored sweater. To completely destroy the illusion of beauty, Mallory raked a comb through her hair quickly and pulled it back in a simple ponytail, then wiped away her carefully applied makeup. The woman now reflected in the glass had been successfully reduced to someone who cruised for bargains at the supermarket, nagged about homework and dipped napkins in glasses of water to scrub spots of dirt on a child's face. There was nothing appealing about her.

Fran would be appalled, Mallory decided with a grin of self-congratulation. The thought alone cheered her. Secure in the knowledge that she had done everything possible to appear far from attractive, Mallory pulled open the door of her room and headed back to the living room.

The sound of whispering roused Patrick. Not particularly interested in opening his eyes at the moment, he lay quietly, listening.

The slightly louder noise of a commercial sweep could have made it impossible to understand the hushed murmurs of conversation. Except that Chris Meyers had a whisper that could be heard clearly in the top row of the bleachers at a football stadium.

The other whisper was much softer, the slightest bit husky, and very feminine. *Mallory.* Pat smiled softly as he pictured her as she had looked the evening before, her posture straight and proud, the lines of her classic black suit detailing the delightful curves beneath it, the lacy blouse and loose tendrils of hair making her heartbreakingly fragile. She was a contradiction in terms, both strong and weak.

And she enchanted him as no woman had ever done before.

He heard her leave the room, the soft sound of silky stockings brushing together as she got to her feet, the padding of her footsteps on the carpet. Christopher's feet drummed a bit on the floor as he watched a particularly exciting part of his show, then subsided. The tick of the mantel clock, and the click of the heater turning back on, seemed loud in the early-evening quiet.

Pat snuggled back into the sofa cushions, content with the homey atmosphere. Such simple pleasures, he thought. Ones he hadn't remembered even existed, wouldn't have believed would affect him so if someone had told him about them a week ago.

Mallory had a very nice house. It was neat, but far from perfect. A pile of kids' videocassettes teetered on the floor near the television. Newspapers were dropped haphazardly in a natural-toned wicker laundry basket, advertising flyers from other department stores foremost on the stack. There were fashion magazines and kids' magazines on the end table. The ashes of a forgotten fire were still in the fireplace, and in the kitchen the breakfast dishes awaited attention in the sink.

Not just a house. It was a home. A *real* home.

He liked the no-nonsense furniture, all sturdy and covered in easy care fabrics. There were two armchairs, one a slate gray, the other a tweed with gray, sand and beige. The sofa was six feet long, a fact he'd appreciated when he first stretched out. It was covered in the same neutral tweed, enlivened with toss pillows that picked up the various shades. He'd stacked them behind his head and put his stockinged feet up on the farther arm. Moments later, he'd been out cold.

Now that he was half-awake, Pat drowsily surveyed the rest of the room from beneath drooping eyelids.

Although there were plants hanging at the windows and arranged on tabletops, and tasteful groupings of pictures on the walls, it was the Christmas tree at the far end of the room that drew the eye. It was traditionally decorated, its branches encroaching on the hallway, the star at the top brushing the ceiling. The scent of fresh pine permeated the room. Strands of gold tinsel were draped in crisscross fashion, with linked loops of colored paper and strings of wooden cranberries. Glistening store-bought ornaments fought for prominence with a collection of lopsided handmade ornaments. As soon as they came in the door,

Christopher had plugged in the tree lights so that a kaleidoscope of multicolored lights twinkled on every branch.

It was the same kind of tree he'd grown up with, Pat mused happily. He could still hear the squabbles he and Kevin had had over the placement of the ornaments they'd made at school.

He knew the moment Mallory returned, not from a sound, but from his own heightened awareness of her. Pat was surprised when all she did was join Christopher in front of the television. Obviously she knew how the kid could wear a person out.

Patrick raised his lashes a few more millimeters, so that he could watch her undetected.

"Did I miss anything good?" she whispered to Chris.

"Jest the Roadrunner," the boy answered. "This one is Pepe le Pew, and he thinks this cat is a lady skunk, but she ain't."

"Isn't," Mallory said.

"Isn't," Chris repeated, more from habit than from a conscious effort to correct his grammar. "He's really dumb," Chris added, with boyish contempt.

"Maybe love is blind," Mallory suggested with a grin, and ruffled her son's hair.

Love was anything but blind, from Pat's perspective. He thought she looked more gorgeous in her casual clothes than she had in her evening attire.

She lay on her stomach, her stance identical to that of her son, her knees bent, her ankles crossed, her feet swinging back and forth above the most adorable-looking tush Pat had seen in a while. Her brown hair was gathered back so that the long, graceful curve of her throat was bared. He wanted to bury his mouth against it, to taste the warmth of her skin, to breathe in her scent.

Wanted to savor Mallory Meyers as if she were a fine wine.

The thought alone made the fit of his worn jeans uncomfortable. Pat shifted a bit on the sofa, but to no avail.

Mallory heard his movement. Rolled on her side to look back at him. "Oh, you're awake."

In many more ways than one, and it was getting worse.

Her makeup was nearly nonexistent, just a brush of mascara on already long lashes, a touch of color high on her cheekbones. There was a slight V to the neck of her sweater. It led his eyes in a downward glide that brought him to the rise of her breasts. The sweater pulled slightly across them, molded to each generous curve.

Patrick couldn't tell whether Mallory noted his arousal, but she had certainly taken note of where his eyes had been. When he returned his gaze to her face, the color in her cheeks was brighter.

"Sorry I checked out there," Pat said, and swung his feet to the floor. He leaned forward, forearms on his thighs in an effort to disguise the bulge straining the front of his pants. "Guess I had more exercise than I anticipated."

Christopher got to his knees and crawled over to the television. Without being told, he punched the button, sending the screen to black. "Now we get to have pizza, huh?"

Pat sent Mallory an apologetic look. "I sort of promised."

"You bet you did," she said. "I've been looking forward to it all afternoon."

To spending time with him? he wondered.

"Any time I don't have to cook is a treat, as far as I'm concerned," Mallory added.

"Mom loves pizza," Christopher said. "Only she doesn't like anchovies. What's anchovies?"

"Squirmy little fish," Mallory answered, and tickled her son's ribs with both hands.

The sight of mother and child happily tussling was unexpectedly arousing. Far more erotic than any magazine centerfold or swimsuit calendar. *You are a sick man,* Pat told himself.

With an effort, he pushed to his feet and headed for the kitchen. "Just let me splash some water on my face to wake up more," he called back. It was the closest he was going to get to a cold shower. Fortunately, it was freezing outside. Unfortunately, he was going to be close to Mallory the whole time he was in the cold.

A no-win situation.

Unless he managed to get around her defenses and spend long hours in her bed, buried deep within her softness.

If, that is, he managed to live though this evening. Pat had a feeling that there was nothing cold enough to cool his blood. Not with the way Mallory looked tonight.

Christopher looked after his idol, his small face taking on a sad cast. "I'm sorry, Mommy," he murmured. "You always tell me that I play too rough, but I did anyway."

Totally at a loss, Mallory put an arm around his thin shoulders. "When did you do that, honey?"

"When Pat and I had a snowball fight. I threw as hard as I could and hit his leg. I thought he was just playing when he fell over dead."

The idea of Patrick Lonergan, all six-feet-plus of him, falling down to play dead brought a smile to Mallory's face. "I'm sure he wasn't hurt," she soothed.

"Then why's he limping?" Christopher asked solemnly.

Roses bloomed even brighter in Mallory's cheeks. She wasn't blind. She knew exactly why Pat was walking strangely. She didn't know how her plan had backfired, but it quite obviously had. The thought made her feel warm and womanly. *Idiot!* This was not the way to remove the man from her quietly ordered existence. Not the way to keep her heart safe. "Maybe his foot went to sleep," Mallory suggested. "Now, why don't you go wash your hands and get your coat, so we can go have dinner?"

Christopher was out of the room in a flash.

Mallory got to her feet, as well, drawn to the kitchen as if the sound of running water were akin to the Pied Piper's pipe. She barely noticed that a leather bomber jacket was draped over one of her dinette chairs, or that a damp pair of boots had been discarded near it. Patrick was bent at the waist, splashing water on his face, rubbing his hand at the nape of his neck. Mallory felt like a voyeur, but she couldn't move. She was mesmerized by just the sight of him: the way his shirt pulled across his shoulders, the strength evident in the tendons of his bared forearms. The delightful fit of his jeans, pulled tighter across his buttocks by his bent stance.

He sensed her presence, half turning as he reached for a dish towel to blot the water from his face. "Hope you don't mind me butting in like this," he said, giving her one of his heart-stopping grins. "As heavenly as Rosemary's cooking is, I'm getting a little tired of conversations that center on the appropriate material for a sermon."

As if his words galvanized her into action, Mallory moved quickly into the room, headed for the refrigerator. She pulled it open, with absolutely no idea of why she did so. "Surely your brother has other topics to discuss."

Patrick draped the towel over the outer edge of the sink to dry. "Let's just say he wasn't interested in discussing how the Bengals are playing this season. What are you looking for?"

"Ah, just checking to see if I need to pick up some milk," Mallory said, and quickly closed the refrigerator door, before he could see the untouched gallon on the shelf.

Pat pulled out a chair and bent to pull on a pair of scuffed tan boots. The toes were dark with fresh water stains. "Just say the word, and we can stop on the way back." He glanced up, laughter bubbling in his eyes. "Hope you can handle traveling in a truck. I'm afraid I'm being a bad influence on your son. Chris has decided four-wheel drive is the only way to go."

"Chris is much easier to deal with if he gets his own way," Mallory admitted.

The corners of Pat's eyes crinkled attractively. "So am I," he said, and got to his feet. Mallory had forgotten how large a man he was, how he filled a space with his very presence. "You know," Pat mused, his voice dropping to a seductive level, "I'm very tempted to do what Chris suggested."

It was just that her kitchen was small, Mallory told herself. It wasn't that he had actually moved closer to her. Or she to him.

She tried to keep her tone light. "And what was that?"

His smile did such wonderful things to his face, creasing his lean cheeks, drawing attention to the mischievous curve of his lips.

Pat took Mallory's chin between forefinger and thumb and tilted her face up to his. "He wanted me to kiss you in the kitchen," he said, and followed the words with the action, his mouth brushing quickly against hers.

It was the barest touch, but it left Mallory breathless.

With an effort, she pulled herself together. It took an effort not to take a step back, to put space between them. Pride kept her backbone stiff, her shoulders squared. "Why the kitchen?" she asked.

Pat reached for his bomber jacket and shrugged into it. "Believe me, Mal," he said, "you don't want to know."

Chapter Nine

It really depended upon how you looked at things, Mallory mused on Wednesday evening. Either things were improving, or they were going straight downhill.

Although she hadn't seen Patrick in nearly two days, his name still rang frequently on Christopher's tongue. It was through this medium that she had learned Pat was on hand early, lending a strong back to the remaining work to be done in preparing for the church bazaar.

Mallory had never welcomed the hectic Rittenhouse holiday schedule more. It had kept her from rubbing shoulders with him. At least temporarily.

It hadn't kept him far from her mind, though. And even worse, she couldn't shake the memory of how Chris's face had glowed with pleasure as he snuggled between his idol and his mother at the pizza parlor.

She personally remembered the evening with mixed feelings of longing and disgust. To strangers, they had probably looked like a happy family group. The nuclear family: mother, child . . . and father.

It was foolish of her even to muse on the idea.

Even more foolish to let her heart get involved.

Which was exactly what it was trying to do. At the pizza parlor, Pat had kept the conversation lighthearted, his teasing coaxing reluctant smiles from her and a lot of giggles from Chris. He and Chris had arm-wrestled for the final piece of pizza, Pat losing with a great show of chagrin. With her son crowing in triumph as he shoved his prize into his mouth, Mallory was struck with a poignant longing for the intimate little scenario to be more than just a fleetingly enacted play. How pleasant it would be to share the same type of life-style as the families around them.

She crushed the fantasy immediately, angry at herself for the moment of weakness. Just because it took a man's cooperation to conceive a child did not mean it took one to rear the child. She was doing just great. She had nothing to feel guilty about. She had created a home for Chris, one that was free from conflicts. She would not feel remorse over the fact that her son did not have a father.

Certainly Dirk Segal was no loss.

She couldn't say the same about Patrick Lonergan.

And she knew that she could not avoid him at the Christmas bazaar.

To give Rosemary a breather, Mallory had gratefully accepted Christopher's friend Jeff's mother's invitation for the boys to spend the day of the bazaar together. When she swung by to pick Chris up after work, he'd been bubbling over with details on the astronomical—in Chris's opinion—score he'd run up on his favorite video game. Mallory was entertained with a running commentary that took side adventures into the oddly similar realms of

feeding messy babies and pestering teenage sisters during
their phone calls to boyfriends. Mallory wondered if Jeff's
mother would ever invite Christopher back, despite the
woman's amused assurance that Chris was a well-behaved
delight.

It was a relief not to have his conversation center
around Pat.

He wasn't far from Christopher's mind, though. They
had barely parked in the church lot when the boy announced his intention to find the man and tell him about
the wonderful day he had spent at Jeff's house.

It was hopeless, Mallory admitted to herself. Until
Patrick returned to his farm, there was nothing she could
do to keep the two of them apart. Christopher would
never understand or accept any reason she gave for sepa-
rating him from his hero. And, Mallory admitted, she
couldn't even find reasons to do so that seemed well-
thought-out or logical herself.

Patrick had done nothing to counter the opinions of her
friends. Rosemary frequently said he was a very nice man.
Fran oozed about his willingness to help, no matter what
was required. "You have firsthand experience of that,
Mal," Fran had reminded when she'd called to report on
their progress earlier in the day. Mallory hadn't needed the
heavy-handed hint about his willingness to be her escort
at the Rittenhouse party. Or the memories that had surfaced along with it.

"How's the hunk?" Gail had queried with a leer that
morning. "You know, you'd be a fool to let that man get
away," she'd continued in a more serious vein. "Not only
is he delightfully gorgeous, he is the perfect life's companion for someone on the rise at Rittenhouse. The boss
says his wife followed Pat's advice and is raving about the
restaurants he recommended she try. You made big

brownie points bringing this guy to the party, Mal. Really big points."

Even Van Werner rained praises on Patrick's dark brown crown. "Tell your friend he has my undying devotion," the display manager said, cornering Mallory in the lunchroom. "Stan swears he saw Lonergan make off with that atrocious piece of mistletoe. As a result, my reputation as a decorator is once more intact."

No matter where she turned, Mallory couldn't escape Patrick Lonergan's shadow.

He was more substantial than a mere shade when she and Chris entered the church basement an hour before the holiday bazaar was to open.

Pat was at the far end of the decorated hall, conversing with a man who was fiddling with the tubes that ran from the soft drink canisters to the fountain machine. He looked wonderful, Mallory thought. Tall, broad-shouldered, handsome. He'd donned a ski sweater of holly-berry red and dark green, with a snowy white band, that showed the breadth of his chest to advantage. His jeans were black and fit as closely as a second skin. There wouldn't be a woman in the place able to take her eyes off him.

At Chris's yelled greeting, Pat turned and smiled.

That wickedly intimate grin could have melted the ice in the trees. What it did was turn her knees to mush.

Mallory paused, using the excuse of shrugging out of her coat to keep from flying down the room and into his arms. Chris felt no such compulsion to hide his feelings, and sped toward a boisterous welcome.

A reprieve. Mallory sighed in thanksgiving. It was amazing how her heart was behaving. It refused to listen to all the lectures she gave it, to the memory of the hysteria she had fought at Dirk Segal's abandonment all those years ago. Instead, her rebellious heart acted like a tender bud, longing for and turning toward the sun of Patrick's smile.

She had barely hung her coat on the coatrack before Pat was at her side, a squealing, wiggling, deliriously happy Christopher tucked under his arm.

"Welcome to Panic Central," Pat said. His eyes slid over the creamy white sweater and slacks she wore, lingering a bit at the frosty snowflake design done in crystal beads on her bodice.

Mallory warmed at the approval in his eyes. "That bad, huh?" she asked.

Pat shrugged. "Not so bad, really. The booths are ready and loaded. Fran's off gathering up her family. Rosie's in the kitchen, bossing the chefs around."

The "chefs" were elderly Fred Woods and Kevin Lonergan, who had claimed squatters' rights on the community kitchen, freeing the other men to spend time with their families—and, it was hoped, a good bit of their salary at the many booths.

"So far we've been lucky," Pat continued. "The smoke alarms haven't gone off."

Mallory laughed. "They did last year." She pushed back the sleeves of her sweater. "So, where am I needed most?"

Instead of answering, Pat set Christopher on his feet. "I could use your help, sport," he told the boy. "Knowing my ineptitude at cooking, Kevin put me in charge of the soft drinks. How about if you be my assistant?"

"Cool!" Christopher crowed in delight.

"First matter of business is getting the cups ready. Think you can open the packages and start making handy stacks for us to use? I'll be there in a minute. I need to show your mom something first."

"Okay," the boy caroled happily, and ran at top speed down the hall, toward the soft drink stand.

Pat watched him, a fond grin curving his lips. "He's a great kid, you know that, Mal?"

"Yeah," she agreed softly. "I know. Now, what do you need to show me? A problem area?"

"In a way," Pat said and, taking her elbow in hand, he steered Mallory out of the room and into the stairwell. He backed her into the shadows, placed her back to the cold concrete wall. "The problem is, I'm going to have very little time to do this," he murmured, and bent his lips to hers.

It wasn't the light brushing of mouths she'd experienced in her kitchen a few days earlier. It wasn't the teasing but thorough kiss he'd given her under the mistletoe. This time, his kiss branded her as his for all time.

And, traitors that they were, her lips opened in greedy acceptance under his.

Mallory burrowed against him, her arms around him, her fingers grasping at the tendons of his back as he leaned toward her, his hands braced against the wall on either side of her head. Pat turned his head, allowing the kiss to become even more intimate as his tongue plundered her mouth. Mallory explored his as eagerly, feeding on the desire that his kiss brought flaring to life.

She lost track of time, of the necessity to regain control of her emotions. Of the situation.

How could her body need this man so badly, when her mind raised barriers to such a consummation?

Patrick was stronger than she. He broke the kiss, his hands still not touching her, but holding her prisoner all the same. "Ah, hell, Mal..." he groaned. "The things you do to me."

An imp prompted her response. She slid her arms from around him, let her hands glide over his chest. "Not limping again, are you?"

"Damn right I am," he growled, and dropped a quick, fierce kiss on her lips.

Mallory lowered her lashes coquettishly. "I suppose it's a good thing we didn't plan a kissing booth."

"Would you have manned it?"

"Single-handedly," she teased, glancing up at him again.

Pat grinned wickedly. "Then I would say I'm damn lucky. These kisses didn't cost me a dime."

Mallory gave his chest a playful swat. "Move out of the way, you big ox. I've got work to do."

He pushed off the wall and moved back a pace. His green eyes had darkened to the color of pine needles. The teasing grin faded from his lips. "I want you, Mallory Meyers," Pat murmured quietly. "Very badly."

Damn fool, Patrick raged at himself silently. He knew he'd made a major mistake when the color drained from Mallory's face.

She swallowed, the sound loud in the relative quiet of the stairwell. "I can't," she whispered, and turned hastily to the door.

"Mallory?"

She paused, a bird on the verge of flight. "I'm sorry, Pat." Then she was gone, only the sound of her footsteps on the tiled floor floating back to him.

Well, you blew it big-time, Lonergan. Pat leaned back against the wall, ran a hand that shook faintly through his thick hair. He was an idiot. He knew her history, knew each time she responded to him that she cursed herself afterward. And still she came back, for all the world like a moth fluttering too near a flame.

So what had he done? He'd singed her wings with that stupid declaration.

Maybe he should have said it differently.

Oh, but he did want her. Wanted her so bad it hurt, kept him sleepless night after night. Kept him hanging around town, when common sense told him to head north, to his farm.

The clamor of new arrivals at the upper door galvanized Pat into action. He took the steps two at a time, dashing up the stairs before Frances Hutchins and her family were barely inside the church.

"Hey!" Fran called. "Where are you off to in such a rush?"

"Escaping. Don't let on that you've seen me," Pat said, and gave her a conspirator's wink.

Fran grabbed his arm. "Not so fast, bub. First you've got to meet my better half and the kids."

Patrick shook hands with Larry Hutchins and two gangly teenage boys. He liked Larry immediately. The kids looked as if they wished the earth would swallow them whole, thus disposing of the embarrassment of being seen with their parents at a church function.

"What if someone asks after you?" Fran demanded as Pat pushed the church door open, letting a draft of arctic air into the vestibule.

"Tell Kevin I'll be back soon."

"And if Mallory asks?" Fran asked, her gaze far too knowing for Pat's peace of mind.

Hell. In for a penny, in for a pound, Pat thought. "Tell her I'm cooling off," he said.

Fran's chuckle carried out to him even after the door had swung shut behind him.

* * *

The tantalizing smell of frying fish hadn't filled the church activity room yet. It was strong in the large kitchen area, though. As she let herself through the swinging door, Mallory could hear the sizzle of the grill. Since the church basement also did duty as the attached school's cafeteria, the room was laid out for efficiency, the appliances sized to handle large volume.

Rosemary had moved on to supervising the installation of the soft drink canisters, leaving the room to the offices of the two fry cooks.

Fred Woods stood before the stove, a long-handled utensil in his hand, a drooping white chef's hat perched at a jaunty angle to cover the gleam of his natural tonsure. An industrial-size apron covered his clothing. There were already smears on the bib, where he'd wiped his fingers free of batter.

Mallory stopped to greet him. "How's the culinary business so far?"

The elderly man laughed. "The fish are jumping. I can't vouch for the french fries, though."

"What's wrong with them?"

"They need watching," he said. "You see who's in charge of that detail, don't you?"

On the opposite side of the room, Kevin Lonergan snorted. "I resemble that remark," he called.

Although Kevin had shunned the use of an apron and had donned a fisherman's sweater and black corduroy jeans, Mallory once again found herself wondering how she had ever mistaken Pat for his brother.

"Hi, Mal," Kevin greeted, turning from the vats where baskets of french fries toasted in a caldron of bubbling fat. "Come for the early-bird serving?"

Oh, yes. She'd know the difference immediately. Boy, would she know the difference!

It was possible to be just friends with Kevin. Never with Patrick.

Who knew better than she?

To give herself something to do, Mallory reached for a bag of precut vegetables and began shaking them into a waiting bowl. "I'm always ready for food someone else fixes," she said. "When's the first batch ready?"

Kevin glanced at his timer. "Five minutes, max." He reached over and helped himself to a carrot stick as she spilled them into another bowl. "So, how's it all look?"

"Great!" Mallory forced excitement into her voice. She'd barely glanced at the decorations or the booths. "You all did a fantastic job!" If there was one thing she'd learned as a manager, it was to give effusive praise to her staff. Not all the Rittenhouse upper echelon did, and Mallory felt their departments had suffered for the lack. At least when she sang someone's praises at St. Edmund's, she rarely had to follow it up with a suggestion for improvement.

Kevin chuckled and gave the basket of fries a shake. "Don't thank me. Fran claims I was more of a hindrance."

Mallory felt obliged to ask the question to which she already knew the answer. "Who helped, then? Fran and Rosemary couldn't have done it all single-handed."

"Oh, Pat did."

As if Kevin didn't already know she was quite aware of that fact. "Well, tell him we all appreciate his help," Mallory said. She nibbled on a celery stick. "If the food isn't quite done yet, I'll do a swing around the room to see if anyone needs any last-minute help."

Kevin wasn't done with her, though. "Rosemary says you and Chris will be joining us for Christmas dinner."

"If it's not an imposition," Mallory said.

"None at all. We're all very pleased to have you both join us. Since her daughter moved away from the area, this is the first year Rosemary is all alone for the holidays. She's too valuable to the parish for us to let her pine for her loved ones alone. Having Chris there will ease the sadness of not sharing the day with her grandchildren." Kevin tossed Mallory a casual smile, his real attention divided between the timer and the cooking fries. "You know she loves you as if you were one of her daughters, Mal."

Mallory nodded. "I—"

"We all want what's best for you," Kevin continued.

Then why were they all pushing her into a relationship with Patrick?

She had the answer before she'd finished the question. It was because they cared for her that they had all gone out of their way to promote a romance between Kevin's brother and herself.

The timer buzzed. Kevin went into action, his movements as smooth as if he held down a second job at a fast-food restaurant. The basket of fries came out of the boiling fat; a second batch went in.

"Of course," he continued, "no one would see anything amiss if you decided to bring something to the dinner. Say that gelatin with the little marshmallows?"

After the serious bent of their conversation, the suggestion took Mallory by surprise. She chuckled, the sound low and husky. "Always thinking about your stomach, huh, Kev? I'll see what I can do," she promised, and headed back out to the long, open room.

Chapter Ten

Christopher and two of his first-grade cronies dodged around shoppers, running at top speed down the hall.

"Hey!" Mallory snapped as they whizzed by the booth she was manning. "No running!"

Christopher screeched to a halt, his sneakers squeaking on the tiled flooring. "'Kay!" he called, and took off again, his speed little diminished.

Mallory sighed. "Boys," she said, her voice resigned to the perverseness of nature in giving children far more energy than their parents.

"Bit wound up, aren't they?" Phil Williams, her current customer, remarked. "Too many sweets."

Mallory bristled silently and handed him his change without bothering to count it out. At least he hadn't used catch phrases like "lack of discipline" or "too little supervision." As if he were an authority. His teenage daughters weren't running wild in the hall. They had long since disappeared from the church basement, as had a couple of their male admirers, and were most likely acting wild in the back seat of a car.

Behind Mallory, Mrs. Haber's rocking chair creaked in a constant rhythm. "It's just an abundance of Christmas spirit," she said. "We had it when I was a girl, as no doubt you had it when you were a boy, Dr. Williams."

Mallory had her doubts about Phil Williams ever having been a little boy. He'd obviously popped full-grown and opinionated from thin air, having willed himself into existence.

"I know your patients at the nursing home will appreciate these lovely gifts," Mallory cooed, her voice pitched a shade shy of sarcasm, her best retailing smile pasted to her lips. She handed him a plastic grocery bag wherein lay a dozen of Mrs. Haber's delicate hand-crocheted doilies, and sent him on his way.

"Merry Christmas," Mrs. Haber added cheerily, her chair never stopping its constant rocking movement.

At eighty-six, Mrs. Haber was the oldest of Mallory's volunteers. Not to mention the most prolific. While it took a number of craftspeople to fill the other booths, Mrs. Haber's crochet hook stocked a single booth without help. Mallory had never seen the elderly woman without a tote bag of various materials and tools at her side. Her gnarled, arthritic hands moved constantly, lovingly working threads into nostalgic treasures. Her work transcended time, in Mallory's opinion, and anyone would be crazy to pass up the minimal prices asked for the handworked doilies, decorated pillowcases, and crocheted tablecloths. Mrs. Haber never complained of the work involved, never promised a specific quantity and thus never had to apologize for falling short of it. She was a favorite with the children, as well as the adults, always having time to listen to stories or tell some of her own.

"I like that young man," Mrs. Haber announced during a break in the shoppers.

"Phil Williams?" Mallory was clearly flabbergasted at the mere suggestion.

"Don't be ridiculous," the elderly woman said. "I may be old, but I'm not feebleminded. No, I mean Kevin Lonergan's brother." She nodded, directing Mallory's attention to the end of the room, where Patrick stood talking to Larry Hutchins. Larry had one wiggling boy under his arm, and another held captive by a grip on his collar. Pat was burdened with Christopher, whom he had casually draped over his shoulder, upside down. While Mallory watched, Kevin joined the men and was promptly handed a boy of his own to tote.

Not wanting to be caught observing too closely, Mallory found some busywork to do.

"Those are two of the nicest-looking young men it has been my pleasure to behold," Mrs. Haber continued. "My neighbors were all agog when Kevin visited the house when I was laid up with that weak ankle."

The "weak ankle" had been a nasty fracture that still bothered the frail little woman.

"I believe the Methodist woman next door thought I was carrying on with him, rather than receiving a pleasant visit." Mrs. Haber sounded as if she rather enjoyed the idea of having a lurid reputation. She chuckled softly. "If she has her eye to the draperies later this evening, the poor dear may have a seizure when young Patrick escorts me home."

Mallory rearranged the remaining doilies. She wondered what her own neighbors had thought when they saw Patrick building the snow fort in her front yard.

"What do you think of him?" Mrs. Haber asked.

"Of who?" Mallory countered in an effort to appear unconcerned.

Mrs. Haber grinned. "Who do you think? The man who's holding your son by his ankles."

Christopher's friends were no longer in protective custody, but had been turned over to their parents. That left only Chris with the men, and he was indeed being held by his ankles, his arms dangling toward the floor. Even from a distance, Mallory could see that the boy was loving every minute.

"I hope it's been long enough since he had supper," Mallory said. "If Chris gets sick after this, I'll take you home and Mr. Lonergan can clean him up."

Mrs. Haber's laugh was very appreciative. "So you like him."

"Why wouldn't I? He's Kevin's brother, and he's been very helpful in getting the bazaar set up this year."

It took a moment before Mallory realized that Mrs. Haber's crochet hook had stopped moving. The lacy design of the latest doily lay forgotten in her lap.

"You don't even know, do you?" the elderly woman murmured quietly.

Mallory went on the defensive. "Know what?"

Mrs. Haber's crochet hook went back into action. "I don't think you are ready to admit what is happening."

"You mean the way Christopher is bonding with Pa— Mr. Lonergan."

"Bonding." Mrs. Haber wrinkled her nose. "A modern word to cover an emotion that has no need to be disguised. The boy loves him, Mallory."

The goods in the booth were in perfect order now, awaiting the next wave of shoppers. Deprived of her prop,

Mallory perched on the seat of a folding chair and prayed for the arrival of more customers.

"Christopher is quite taken with Mr. Lonergan," she conceded.

"And why not?" Mrs. Haber asked. "The child is at an age where he needs a father, Mallory."

"I hardly think—"

"Yes, I know." Faded blue eyes twinkled as the rocking chair tipped back and forth. "Patrick's affection for Chris is real and unconditional, just as the boy's is for him. Watch them together, dear. Then watch the interaction between some of the other fathers and sons here tonight."

It wasn't something Mallory wanted to hear, much less do. She stared at the door that led to the vestibule upstairs and the parking lot beyond it. She willed new arrivals to push the door open. "I would say the relationship was more that between an uncle—"

Mrs. Haber sighed. "It isn't just horses that wear blinders."

Mallory's backbone stiffened. "And just what—"

"Oh, look," the elderly woman said. "New arrivals."

Mallory looked up in time to see Gail, Van, and a number of other Rittenhouse employees pile into the hall. Where had they been earlier, when she needed them?

"Hey, Mal!" Gail called and waved. She started toward the booth, caught sight of the Lonergan men, and veered off course. Van and two sales associates from the junior sportswear department followed her lead.

Mrs. Haber's chair picked up speed. "Hmm . . . Competition, dear. You may have to fight for him."

"I have absolutely no interest in Mr. Lonergan," Mallory said from between clenched teeth.

"Of course not, dear."

All the same, Mallory's eyes were now glued to every move Gail made.

Patrick eased Christopher down to the floor, head-first. "Promise?" he demanded.

"Promise," Chris swore. "Cross my heart."

"No more running tonight, then."

"No more running," the boy repeated.

"All right then. Go find your buddies. If it's okay with their parents, I'll treat you all to a round of beer," Pat said.

"Really?" Christopher's eyes were round.

"That's root beer," Pat clarified.

"Cool!" Chris gave him a high five and sped off.

"Walk!" Patrick yelled.

"Oh! Yeah." The boy's steps slowed for five paces and reverted to warp speed.

Pat heaved a great sigh of resignation.

Kevin had moved a few paces away, to chat with some of his congregation. Larry Hutchins and Pat lingered near the soft drink fountain, ensuring that the high-spirited kids didn't decide to help themselves to more sugar.

Larry laughed, his chuckle both rolling and infectious. "Good try, pal. You need more practice."

"Does that help?"

"Dreamer," Larry said. "How do you think I got these gray hairs?"

"After being bossed around for the last few days by your wife, I have a few ideas," Pat answered.

Larry's grin widened. "Ah, the bliss of the single man. Just you wait, Lonergan. Your time's coming."

Patrick's gaze drifted over to where Mallory sat deep in conversation with Mrs. Haber. "Don't be so sure."

Larry followed his new friend's look. "You've got a tough nut to crack there. She's worth it, though."

"So everyone tells me."

"And you don't know it yourself yet?"

"A man could seriously hurt his ego trying to break down the barriers Mallory's raised," Pat said.

"Yeah, you look pretty bruised," Larry agreed, laughter creating creases at the corners of his eyes.

Kevin wished his parishioners a merry Christmas and turned back to his brother. "I heard that," he commented. "Don't believe a word he says, Larry. This guy has got cast-iron armor around his ego."

"Not to mention all the women dropping at his feet," Larry said. "He's all my wife has talked about for days now."

"Speaking of Fran, she is waving at you," Kevin pointed out.

Larry groaned. "Probably ran out of money. See you later."

The Lonergans looked after him silently a moment. "You've got some really nice friends here, Kev," Pat said after a while.

"I've been lucky," the minister agreed. "What about you?"

Pat's smile grew wicked. "You want to know if I've got nice friends, or if I've gotten lucky?" At his brother's frown, Pat sighed and shoved his hands in his jean pockets. "Damned if being a parson hasn't gone and made you lose your sense of humor, Kev."

"Some things don't bear joking about," Kevin insisted.

"Don't go turning into a padre on me. You know what happens when you do. I hightail it."

It was Kevin's turn to sigh. "True. You'd think I'd learn by now, wouldn't you?"

"Naw, not you, Kev. You're hopeless."

"Perhaps just hopeful."

"Always the optimist. Like Mom," Pat said. "Speaking of which, how's the supply of money holding out in the charity foundation we funded in our parents' memory?"

Kevin's smile was soft and rueful. "You never cease to amaze me."

"Why? Because I keep the bases covered? With you praying for me on one side of the veil and Mom on the other, I can't miss, can I?"

"Perhaps we're praying for something different than you think."

Pat shrugged, his eyes straying to the booth where Mallory sat again. "I have a feeling everyone's praying for the same thing," he said.

"Well, you know what was dearest to Mom's heart—" Kevin began, then broke off. "Who in the world—?"

Gail Tyler strode purposefully down the hall, Van Werner and a couple of young girls trailing in her wake. She pulled up short in front of the two men, her gaze turning in confusion from one handsome face to the other. "Okay," she announced, "I give up. Which one's which?"

The Lonergans looked at each other, mischievous grins on their faces. "Haven't heard that one in a long time," Pat said.

"Ten years, at least," Kevin agreed.

"More." Pat dropped an arm around his brother's shoulders. "This, bro, is the Rittenhouse contingent. Gail, Van, and—?" He looked past the familiar faces to two pretty, unfamiliar ones.

"Terry," the tallest one offered. "And this is Suzie. We work for Mallory."

Gail stretched her hand out. "Nice to finally meet you, Pastor. And you'll be pleased to know that we did as you requested, Pat. We brought lots of money with us."

"Just the kind of guests we enjoy here at St. Edmund's," Kevin said, shaking her hand.

Van carefully kept his eyes averted from the decorations around the room. "We wouldn't have missed it for the world," he stated. "There should be more along later, after the store closes."

"I believe we still have a number of wonderful items available." Kevin gestured to the room at large. "Mallory's done a terrific job, hasn't she?"

"Yeah," Terry murmured. "Great," Suzie agreed. Neither girl looked at the hall. They had their eyes glued to the Lonergans, their expressions a bit dazed.

Gail moved in closer. "Why don't you show me around, Pat?" she asked. "Give me the grand tour?"

Kevin surprised his brother by stepping forward and taking her arm. "Now that sounds like something up Mallory's alley," he said, guiding Gail away from Pat's side. "The woman is a wonder. She knows everything that was donated for sale."

"A true saint," Van agreed, sotto voce. "Lead on, MacDuff."

Pat stared after them for a second, amazed at the adroit way Kevin had maneuvered Gail Tyler from his side. That meant he had to deal with the two starry-eyed young ladies left behind. They were at least fifteen years his junior, and both were blondes, albeit from different bottles. Pretty, if you liked the type. Pat found he no longer did.

As if unsure of what they were expected to do now that they were no longer in Gail Tyler's company, Terry and Suzie looked at each other.

Terry seemed to be the more confident. She cleared her throat and launched into the most trite line Pat had heard in a long time.

"Uh, so where are you going when this is over?"

He was definitely getting old, Pat decided. The answer to that one would once have been, *Where do you suggest?* Now it was *Home to bed, alone.* He'd had a pretty strenuous day; he'd dealt with a number of unaccustomed tasks and was feeling the strain. And all of it was his own fault. If he didn't take such pleasure in telling everyone that he was a farmer, they wouldn't expect him to be able to handle all these manual-labor tasks. The truth was, he was rarely in the fields. Most of his three hundred acres was rented out to other farmers. Occasionally he lent a hand at planting and harvesttime, but his true labor was accomplished in front of a computer keyboard, watching a screen of information that was fed from Wall Street. His neighbors joked that he kept a keen eye on pork-belly futures, but his adroit ability to pick a stock on the rise had enabled many of those same men to maintain a comfortable financial cushion.

The farm gave him the perfect excuse to lose the two Rittenhouse women, though.

"After this, I've got to get back to milk the cows," Pat announced, quite sure that neither of them would realize that even if he owned dairy cows, they would not take kindly to being milked in the middle of the night.

Suzie looked stunned, but Terry was still game. "Oh, then you—" She broke off with a squeal as Christopher slid between Suzie and herself. He was on his knees, his velocity rapidly diminishing from the running start he'd taken. On Chris's heels—or perhaps that should be at his toes, Pat thought—followed his buddies with equally dramatic appearances.

Patrick frowned down at the boys. All three grinned up at him, quite pleased with their actions. In his mind, Pat had named Christopher's friends Towhead and Midnight, after their tousled mops of hair. It took a concerted effort to keep evidence of displeasure on his face. He remembered all too well having done the same thing at their age.

"Didn't you promise something?" Pat demanded.

Unfazed, Christopher grinned up at him. "This was sliding, not running," he explained, and climbed to his feet.

The other boys followed his lead. "We're sorry," Towhead said. "Yeah, real sorry," Midnight declared. "Can we still have the root beers, Mr. Lonergan?"

Not a repentant bone in any of their bodies, Pat thought. Had there ever been one in his at their age? Was there now, for that matter?

"On one condition," he said, hoping his voice sounded stern. From the brightness of the boys' eyes, he doubted he was being successful. "You have to not only apologize to these ladies, you have to escort them and carry their packages the rest of the evening."

"Aw, Pat..." Christopher groaned, his chagrin echoed by similar sounds from his two cohorts.

Terry and Suzie didn't look particularly thrilled with the idea, either.

"Then I guess I'll just be buying the ladies a drink," Pat said.

Terry and Suzie perked up a bit. The boys were far more boisterous in their avowals to do as requested, and bombarded the girls with insincere apologies.

"All right, then. Everybody find a table," Pat instructed. It was no surprise to discover the two Rittenhouse clerks chose one a good distance from the first-grade boys.

Pat had just served up the last root beer and was feeling rather proud of the way he'd handled things when he overheard a snatch of conversation between Christopher and his friends. The words froze him in his tracks. Put a lump in his throat.

"Boy, you're lucky," Towhead said wistfully.

"Mr. Lonergan is sure nice," Midnight added.

Chris sipped on his straw, slurping his drink noisily. "Yeah," he agreed. "He's a cool dad. Watch this," he urged, and blew into his straw.

Pat didn't hear the sound of root beer bubbling out of three separate paper cups as the boys proceeded to outdo one another. Chris's voice echoed in his mind, calling him by the name he'd never thought to covet.

Dad.

Damn.

Chapter Eleven

When she awoke the day before Christmas, Mallory knew there was no way of getting around it—she had to buy Patrick Lonergan a present. It would be from Chris, naturally. And it would not come from Rittenhouse. She couldn't bear the knowing looks that would be cast her way, considering that half the store had shown up at the St. Edmund's bazaar to look Pat over.

Fortunately, everyone had come with open pockets. Not only had a good many Rittenhouse paychecks stayed in the church's coffers that evening, but Gail and Van had bought out all of Mrs. Haber's remaining stock. Gail planned to carry the woman's beautifully handcrafted tablecloths in her housewares department. Van was already planning how to use the exquisite doilies as a background on which to display both cosmetics and jewelry. The merchandise had barely been packaged before Patrick gallantly offered his arm to escort Mrs. Haber home. The elderly woman had glowed. Pride in having the most successful booth, and pleasure in the praises Gail and Van had sung over her work, made her appear to float, rather than walk.

Mallory hadn't been nearly as ecstatic, and she had to admit, like it or not, that her mood had had a lot to do with the things Mrs. Haber had said about Chris's relationship with Patrick.

She had been lying to herself, Mallory decided. Her son was not going to be complacent and understanding when Pat walked out of their lives. He was going to be petulant, angry and lost.

Just as she would be.

Only it would be worse for her, because she would know that she had sent Patrick away, with her fear of casual relationships.

He wanted her, he said. Truth be told, Mallory admitted to herself, she wanted him just as badly. A man she barely knew. A man she wouldn't be able to forget.

A man she couldn't have.

Wouldn't allow herself to have.

That was the crux of the matter. When Pat said he wanted her, Mallory understood what he meant, and it was different from what she meant. Only their wording was the same.

It was dangerous to have anything further to do with Patrick. When she was in his arms, she forgot who she was, who she had become, who she had to remain. He made her too aware of her lonely bed, had given her many sleepless nights filled with longing. It wasn't memories of what had transpired between her and Dirk Segal that haunted Mallory anymore, it was fantasies of what might happen if she surrendered to Pat.

If was the key word. She was strong. She could hold out against temptation. She could and would, because what she wanted was more than just physical pleasure. Mallory wanted what she had always longed for, the complete picture, the dream. The one she'd thought she was gaining when she gave herself to Dirk. She would not make that same mistake again. If she ever became a man's lover again, she needed to be his wife, as well. And if she took a husband, he needed to be a father to her son.

It was too much to ask of a man, to take on a ready-made family. She had seen the unhappy results too often. Men and women arranging themselves as if the family were a battlefield and their stepchildren were weapons. Only a few rose above the conflicts. Mallory wasn't sure that she would be numbered among those few. In a showdown, she would always go on the defense for Christopher. Just doing so would put him in the middle, torn between people he loved.

She couldn't subject her son to the prospect. Better never to try than to try and fail, she thought.

At least so her logical mind claimed. Her heart mourned that the chance would never be given.

It wasn't logic that led her to steal time at lunch to shop for a present for Patrick. It was her heart.

On previous Christmas Eves, Chris had spent the day with Mallory's aunt. With the newly wed Anita in California with her husband, a different plan had had to be devised. Rosemary was willing to watch over Chris for the best part of the day, but later in the afternoon she had duties at the church to see to. It was one of Rosemary's joys to prepare St. Edmund's for the Christmas celebration. She would be involved in decorating the pulpit and choir stalls, arranging the colorful pots of poinsettias in the sanctuary and seeing that everything was perfect for the Christmas Eve late-night service.

Thus, a little after four, Rosemary dropped Chris off at Rittenhouse. He came complete with a lunchbox equipped with peanut butter sandwiches, cookies and two boxes of fruit juice. Mallory took time out to settle him in front of the television in the associates' lounge and pop a movie in the VCR.

"If you need me, Chris, you know where the switchboard is. They can page me," Mallory said, stooping to give him a quick squeeze. "You'll be all right here."

"No sweat," Christopher assured, absentmindedly returning her hug. He opened his lunchbox as the FBI warning about pirating the film flashed on the screen.

Now where had he learned that phrase? Mallory decided she didn't want to know. "When the store closes, we'll go out for lasagna, then later tonight, to the church, so we can hear the choir. How's that sound?"

Mouth full of one of Rosemary's cookies, Chris nodded.

"Maybe we can call Aunt Anita and wish her a merry Christmas, too," Mallory offered.

"Okay," Chris agreed. "Mom, you're in the way. I can't see the movie."

Mallory felt as if she'd just been dismissed. Her son was going through some difficult times. Difficult for her, since she hated to see him grow up. Difficult for Chris, because he was trying to take matters into his own hands. Such as giving her a grown man as a Christmas present; such as bonding with that same man behind her back.

The movie soundtrack came up, filling the room. She watched as Chris kicked off his athletic shoes without bothering to untie them and snuggled down in the plump sofa cushions.

"Yo! Chris!" one of the young men from Shoes called. He had frequently fitted Chris over the years, and was an old friend, as far as Chris was concerned. "Whatcha watching? Hey, isn't this that story about the kid named Wart? Boy, I'm glad that's not my name!" the sales associate said, and dropped down on the sofa next to the boy.

The show was one of Chris's favorites, so Mallory was not surprised when he launched into details about Merlin and young Arthur and the legendary sword of kingship. She had never noticed before that the things Chris liked best about the show were not the same things she enjoyed. Was that just the difference between a child and an adult? Or was it the basic difference between a male outlook and a female one?

Was she right in trying to keep Christopher within the walls she had erected to protect them both long ago?

The question was not an easy one to contemplate, much less answer. Especially when there were still nearly two hours remaining until Rittenhouse closed its doors to last-minute shoppers.

Mallory quietly left the room and made her way back to the hectic sales floor, the sounds of Chris's voice merging with those of the animated characters on the screen.

Patrick sat in the back of the church, glad that the lights in the choir stalls didn't reach much beyond the first row of darkly stained pews. The sweetly interwoven strains of "The Carol of the Bells" went through one final rehearsal, men's and women's voices becoming a colorful tapestry of sound.

Because it had been one of his late mother's favorites, Pat waited until the song was finished before continuing with his silent communication with her.

I know it's been a while since I talked to you, Mom. And you are probably quite surprised over the location from which I'm calling. It's been a long time since I was in a church, as you know. I'm sure you've been here frequently since it's Kevin's parish. And I was fairly sure you'd be hanging around tonight.

Pat watched the scurrying figures at the front of the wide hall while he collected his thoughts. Rosemary was busily arranging pots of bright red poinsettias. She passed back and forth frequently, going from one side of the room to the other as she made sure everything was perfect. How many times had he watched his mother doing the same?

I met her last Sunday, Mom. I can just hear you saying that I can't know what I want already. It's only been a week. Well, it will be a week tomorrow. You'd like her, though. She's smart, successful, and feisty. Yeah, and you're right, she's very beautiful. Spectacularly beautiful.

She's got a great son. He's six.

Patrick paused, leery of putting the rest into words, even if they were just in his mind. *He wants me to be his dad, Mom, and the idea scares the hell out of me.* Pat smiled wryly to himself. *Guess you thought nothing could do that, didn't you?*

The choir shuffled around, riffling the pages of their music, and began a softly tender "Silent Night." Pat remembered what it had been like on Christmas Eve when he and Kevin were children. His mother busy in the kitchen, her voice hushed as she sang carols as she cooked. They had always had fried chicken, mashed potatoes and

gravy the night before Christmas, because she claimed she
had made the meal so often she could do it blindfolded.
The delicious scents of fresh-baked pies would still be
hanging in the air, the cooling results tempting both twins
to stay underfoot, rather than play a game in the parlor.

His father would be out in the barnyard, doing mysterious last-minute chores that, for once, didn't include his
sons' help. He would come in from the cold, his nose and
cheeks a bright red, his breath coming in visible vapors.
"Ho, ho, ho!" Michael Lonergan would shout in greeting, drawing a smile from his wife, and an enthusiastic
greeting from Patrick and Kevin. They usually bowled
into him, Pat remembered, nearly staggering their father
on his feet, always jockeying for the first bear hug. And
when he had finished with the twins, his father would slip
off his coat, tossing it over the back of a kitchen chair,
slide his arms around Marie Lonergan's waist from behind and kiss her earlobe.

Funny, Pat mused. He hadn't thought of those happy
moments in years. He lived in the same farm house he'd
grown up in, used the same kitchen, and yet the memories had never surfaced before. Now they seemed to dance
before his eyes. Only, instead of seeing his mother and
father, on this particular stage, he now pictured himself
as the man slipping his arms around the woman at the
stove. The woman who leaned back in contentment in his
dreams was always Mallory Meyers.

They were never alone in the fantasy. Christopher was
there, as well, lying on the floor on his stomach while he
entertained younger children, some with Mallory's soft
brown hair, others with Pat's own darker shock.

It's tantalizing as hell, Mom, but I seem to lack the
courage to attempt it. The responsibility terrifies me. I'm

much more comfortable with a relationship like I had with Sun St. John. No ties, only shared pleasures.

There had been pleasures, hadn't there? If nothing else, he'd shared a bed with Sun for seven years. Why was it he couldn't remember even one special moment that was particularly happy?

Yet just the thought of being with Mallory made him deliriously happy.

Just being with her, Mom, Pat echoed the thought, amazed that such a simple thing could bring contentment. *I don't mean making love to her, either, although I think of little else.*

And why not? She was sexy, a great kisser, and she melted like butter on a hot day when she was in his arms. That wasn't exactly the type of stuff to tell his mother though. Despite the fact that he was fairly sure she already knew the way his hormones reacted to pretty women. She'd said a good number of prayers over the years in which his name had been quite prominent.

I've never felt quite this way about someone before, Mom. I like the sound of her voice, the smell of her hair, the way her lashes dip over those gorgeous gray eyes. I enjoy talking to her, watching her. And I respect her reasoning. I just don't agree with it.

Kevin says she's had some tough times. Christopher's father was a bastard. Excuse my language, but it's the truth. The guy took advantage of her loving nature and left her in the lurch. And despite it all, she's reared a great kid. You'd like him, Mom.

He's a grandson you'd be proud of.

Pat mused on that thought a moment. *Scratch that, Mom. I'm still a coward, afraid to take the next step.*

The choir rustled their papers one last time, stacking everything in order. As they filed out of the church, Patrick joined them, an anonymous man in a leather bomber jacket and jeans. A few blocks away, he melted into the rollicking holiday spirit in a small neighborhood bar. No one paid much attention as he nursed a stiff whiskey alone. There were decisions to be made. For the first time in his life, Pat knew he must seriously consider how the choices he made would affect someone other than just himself.

As usual, it had been nearly impossible to clear Rittenhouse of frantic shoppers. Even after the doors had been locked, there was an irate couple knocking on the window, insisting what they needed would only take a minute. Mallory knew from experience that such would not be the case, and turned them away as politely as possible.

Where, she wondered, did these people come from? The holiday season had been in swing for five weeks. The mall stores had all been open extra hours, especially this past week. Newspapers, radio and television broadcasts all gave a daily countdown of the shopping days till Christmas. Advertising and signs on all the doors shouted that closing time on the twenty-fourth was at 6:00 p.m. And still there was always someone who acted as if it were a personal slight for salespeople to have the evening off on Christmas Eve.

Many of the associates were visibly exhausted, while others got their second wind the moment the doors closed. Cheery shouts of "Merry Christmas!" echoed in the halls near the lockers as coats were bundled on. Feeling a bit as if she'd been through the wringer herself, Mallory gathered her own coat and purse and headed for the lunchroom to pry Christopher away from the television set.

He was holding court. It was the only description that fit the scene, Mallory felt. His face was decorated with peanut butter and jelly; his hands were sticky. Some of the younger associates were gathered around him, listening to a detailed list of toys he expected Santa Claus to bring. A second playing of the King Arthur cartoon ran unnoticed on the screen behind him.

She had never realized it before, but in the past few years the type of things Chris longed for had changed. Once he had been content with any kind of stuffed animal or cartoon-related item. This year his choices were complicated building kits, plastic trucks with monster tires, and a wide variety of video games. The change had been gradual. Was that why it hadn't impressed her as noteworthy?

Was she only noticing now because Chris was going out of his way to show her he wasn't content with just her love?

Mallory dampened a paper towel at the water fountain and joined the crowd around her son. "Here you go, bub," she said, handing him the makeshift washcloth. "Time for this party to hit the road." She hit the eject button on the VCR, then dropped the video in her oversize purse. The movie could be rewound at home.

The teenage associates scrambled into their coats. "Hope you get everything you want, Chris." "Yeah, 'specially that race set!" "Merry Christmas, Christopher." "Have a good one, dude."

"Merry Christmas, Mallory. Hope Santa's good to you," one of them called on the way out the door.

"Thanks. You, too!" she answered brightly. "And rest up! All of you! We've got markdowns and returns on the twenty-sixth."

Their groans echoed in the quickly emptying hall.

Ah, youth... Had she once been that young? Felt that carefree? It was hard to remember. She'd had to be responsible for so long now.

Chris yelled holiday greetings as he scrubbed at his face. Mallory retraced her steps for another dampened towel to complete the job to her satisfaction.

"Doesn't look to me like you're going to be hungry for your favorite meal," she commented, giving his chin a final swipe.

"Um, 'sagna! Then can we open our presents?" Chris demanded.

"One," Mallory said. "That's the deal, remember?"

"Only one?"

It was going to be one fun evening. His voice was the whine of a tired child. At least that hadn't altered.

"But, Mom, I'll have other things to open in the morning. Santa is gonna bring me lots."

"Think so, do you?" Mallory shrugged into her coat and wrapped a scarf around her head.

Christopher struggled with the zipper of his jacket. "I've been real good this year," he told her seriously. "Why can't I open all my other presents?"

The number of packages under the tree had grown as Rosemary and Fran added gifts of their own to the large package Aunt Anita had left. A surprise delivery from California from Anita's new stepfamily had nearly made Mallory weep. She had liked Anita's husband very much. He was kind, thoughtful, and very much in love with Anita. The same qualities appeared to have been passed down to his grown children, who had remembered Christopher this holiday season.

After so many shared Christmases with her aunt, Mallory missed Anita's buoyant spirit this year. But Anita deserved her happiness. She had put her own life on hold for long enough, while Mallory found her feet.

Only a few short weeks ago, they had been showering the newlyweds with rice. "I know you're going to be so happy," Mallory had whispered tearfully, hugging her aunt. "I certainly am," Anita had whispered back. "I only wish you could be just as happy, dear."

"Could I open two packages?" Christopher asked, recalling Mallory to the present. "Just two?"

She looked down at his earnest little face. It took so little to bring a glow of happiness to Chris's face. If only life could be that easy for an adult, as well.

"It depends on how much supper you eat," she said.

"Oh, Mom . . ."

"Any complaints, and we won't open even one."

"But, Mom . . ."

Mallory snapped his lunchbox closed and handed it to him. "If I hear any more arguments, you can take a nap before we go to church, too."

The threat didn't halt his flow of arguments, but there was something soothing about Christopher's complaints. At least he once more sounded like the son she knew.

If only she could roll back time and keep him to herself.

If only the world could stay the complacently narrow one she had built for them seven years ago, when Dirk had left.

If only . . .

Chapter Twelve

Before the night was over, Mallory was forced to resort to threats. Any more displays of poor behavior on Christopher's part, she ruled, and besides his usual cookies and milk treat, Santa Claus was going to receive a note detailing Chris's actions that evening.

What was it about Christmas that turned children into unrecognizable creatures? Her usually well-mannered son was now an alien, one who thought he was a cartoon cat that could tip a plate of lasagna down his throat rather than eat it like a civilized being. Unfortunately, the wielding of Santa's lofty name had not come in time to save Chris's shirtfront from a coating of Italian sauce.

Upon reaching home, Mallory banished him to the bathtub and popped an aspirin to allay the headache that hovered at her temples. She wondered what level of sanity had prompted her to promise Chris the treat of staying up for the special Christmas Eve service. Wondered if

Chris just might fall asleep and thus relieve her of the necessity of dragging herself back out that night.

With the perverse nature of children, Chris not only
behaved the rest of the evening, but appeared to be wide-
awake when nine o'clock arrived.

On the whole, Mallory admitted reluctantly, Christopher was a good-natured child. His spurts of mischief
were short-lived. Emerging from his bath with glowing
cheeks and damply curling hair, Chris agreed to her stip-
ulation that he open only one present that night, and at-
tacked the large box left by Aunt Anita. Since it was the
longed-for action racing set, they placed a call to California to thank Anita and wish the members of her new
family a happy holiday. Within a short time, Chris had
monopolized the conversation, describing everything he'd
done in the past week. Mallory checked her watch, then
started packing things to keep Chris entertained before the
church service. To ensure that they found seats near the
front, they would have to kill at least half an hour before
the choir began. Chris could handle the wait, as long as he
was well supplied. Mallory tucked three of his favorite
books, a pad of paper and a pencil, two rolls of sucking
candies and a personal-size box of fruit juice in a tote bag
and pondered the idea of adding cookies.

"Mom! Aunt E'ta wants to talk to you!" Christopher
hollered from the front room.

Mallory hastily added a dampened washcloth in a
plastic lunch bag for emergency face cleanups, and a
handful of napkins in case the juice spilled, and returned
to the living room. Chris turned the telephone receiver
over to her and his attention to the new race set.

Mallory perched on the arm of the sofa and wound the
phone cord around her finger. "You really outdid your-

self this year," she told her aunt. "Santa's going to have tough competition."

"Santa can handle the heat," Anita said. "What I want to know is, who is this man Chris gave you for Christmas?"

"Uh..."

"The child is quite proud of his gift, but really, darling, how wise is it to encourage him? What do you know about this man?"

Mallory stopped twirling the cord. Of course it wasn't wise to encourage Pat Lonergan. It was insane. But he didn't need encouragement. The man just moved in, sweeping her into a world of sensation. And as for knowing much about him? No, she knew very little about Patrick. Wasn't it bad enough that what she did know was more than enough to keep him on her mind constantly?

"You mean Kevin's brother?" Mallory countered, and hoped her voice sounded far more casual than she felt. "Patrick helped Rosemary and Fran set up the bazaar. It's too bad you missed it, Aunt Anita. It was the most successful one we've ever had. A good number of the Rittenhouse people came by this year and bought out Mrs. Haber's whole booth. I'm afraid I've lost her now. Gail wants to order more crocheted tablecloths from her. Keeping up with that demand will mean no more doilies for St. Edmund's."

"So," Anita murmured, ignoring most of what her niece had said, "he's got you flustered." Even more distressing, to Mallory's mind, was the fact that her aunt sounded quite pleased with the idea.

Mallory tried a comeback. "Pat's just visiting Kevin. He'll be going home after Christmas. It's too bad you aren't here this year, because we've almost got a white Christmas. At least a gray one. It snowed quite a lot this week, but it's all turned to slush now. The roads are a mess."

"Where does this Patrick live?"

It was not going to be easy to defuse her aunt, Mallory realized. "Greenville, I think. All my departments did very well. I was so proud of the associates. They took my talk to heart about being cheerful even if their feet hurt, and—"

"Greenville," Anita mused. "That's not far away. What does he do there?"

"Ah, I believe he told Mr. Rittenhouse he was in the business of food supply. How's the weather out there? I saw on the news that—"

"Food supply." Anita was craftier than Albert Rittenhouse. "So he's a farmer?"

Mallory was feeling trapped. "He said something about three hundred acres, but you know that means nothing to me. Have you been to the beach? I know that Chris would love to have more shells, if you—"

"Hmm…" Anita said. "How does Christopher like this man?"

Mallory sighed deeply. "I give up. You want to talk about Pat Lonergan, we'll talk about Pat Lonergan. How does Chris like him? The man plays endless games of go fish with him, so how do you think he feels?"

"Hmm…" Anita mused. "Kevin's brother appears to be a truly diabolical fellow."

On that, Mallory was quite willing to agree. But certainly not to her aunt. "So how is life with Harvey's daughter and her family?"

"Lovely," Anita answered promptly, at last diverted to a different topic. "I adore them all, just as Harvey promised I would. You know how worried I was, Mallory."

To Mallory, Anita Quillan had always been a rock. The steadfast force who had taken her in when her inflexible parents disowned her; the loving, laughing woman who managed to find a bright lining in the darkest of clouds. Anita was the antithesis of her older sister, Mallory's mother. She had concentrated on a career in fashion, running a very successful modeling agency and charm school. It hadn't been until she was nearing her fiftieth birthday that Anita found a man capable of sweeping her off her feet.

Found? Mallory smiled to herself. Anita had literally stumbled upon Harvey Vinson, tripping over his feet as she hurried through a hotel lobby. It had been love at first catch, according to Harvey. He'd been a widower for three years at the time, and he'd been very persistent in his courtship of Anita. In the end, Anita's determination to remain with Mallory and Christopher had crumbled under Harvey's onslaught.

But then, Anita hadn't really had a chance to refuse. Not only was Harvey a man who didn't understand the word *no*, but Mallory and Christopher had both pushed her to accept the dashing widower's marriage proposal.

Because Anita had always been too busy to consider romance in her life, it had been equally easy for Mallory to shun it in hers. All that had changed when Harvey Vinson came on the scene, Mallory realized. Not only had she and Chris ceased to be the center of Anita's home universe, but she herself had been jealous of her aunt's happiness. She just hadn't recognized the emotion for what it was at the time. She'd thought she was feeling abandoned, replaced in Anita's affection by a man.

Oh, it had been a silly idea. Mallory had thought so at the time, trying to shrug it off. Now she couldn't.

Anita had been absorbed into a separate family, where Mallory had no role, where she was clearly the outsider. As much as she liked Anita's husband, the niggling jealousy remained.

"I'll tell you all about our visit when we get back, darling," Anita insisted. "Right now I'm far more interested in Kevin's brother."

"But, Aunt Anita—"

"Hush, Mallory," Anita said. "Do you remember what I told you the morning of my wedding?"

"You mean that you were making a mistake?"

"Nerves, sweetheart. Nothing more. No, I mean about how I'd only thought I had a full life until I met Harvey?"

"I don't recall—"

"Well, we did get interrupted over the flowers, when it turned out the florist had delivered the wrong ones. Nevertheless, I thought it at the time, even if I didn't get a chance to tell you then."

Mallory could see the pit widening beneath her. She gripped the telephone receiver more tightly. "And what is that?" she asked quietly.

"That I don't want you to follow in my footsteps, darling," Anita said, her voice soft and serious. "I had the agency, you, and then Chris. But it wasn't the whole picture, Mallory, and I didn't even know I was missing out on some of the best things in life. Don't make the same mistake, dearest. It's time to emerge from your protective cocoon."

Mallory was quiet, unsure of how to answer. She watched Christopher as he revved the cars of his new toy over a section of track. So many people were pushing her to make a change in her rules. She knew they all had her best interests at heart, but the memory of her disastrous past dragged like a heavy anchor, holding her back from following their wishes.

Her wishes, for that matter. Over the years she had managed to squash the natural longing to have a mate, a man to share things with, both the good and the bad. She had been successful, and not just because her career and Christopher filled her time. It had only remained dormant for so long because she hadn't met a man who interested her. Who made her aware of what she was missing.

She hadn't met Patrick Lonergan until now.

A long-distance call was not the ideal setting for a heart-to-heart talk with her aunt, though.

"Oh, gosh! Look at the time!" Mallory said, getting to her feet. As if Anita could see her and be convinced she was actually in a rush, Mallory mused ironically. "We're three hours ahead of you, remember? And I promised Chris we'd go hear the music at church this year. We've got to get on the road," Mallory said. "Please thank Harvey's daughter for remembering Christopher with a present, and give Harvey my love. We'll see you when you get back in January."

"Mallory—"

"I'll think about it," Mallory promised hastily. "That's as much as I can say."

She could almost see Anita nod her head in her characteristically brief way. "Fair enough, darling. I'll say an extra prayer for you."

Mallory set the receiver back on the telephone quietly. There were an awful lot of prayers flying around with her name on them.

The parking lot was filling up quickly when Mallory and Christopher arrived at St. Edmund's. Whispered greetings of "Merry Christmas" passed among the congregation as couples and families settled into their seats. There were only a handful of younger children present, but even the older ones fidgeted with a surfeit of energy. To defuse their excitement, parents took turns piloting the small pilgrims past the Nativity scene that was set up in one corner of the church.

During his own trip to the crèche, Chris began his metamorphosis into a stranger again. He sneered at a preschooler who demanded in a stage whisper to know why he couldn't pet the donkey in the stable setting.

"Boy, is he stupid," Chris snarled in derision. "It isn't even a real donkey."

Mallory yanked on his arm, dragging him away from the crowd. "He's also three years old, and—"

"Besides that," a deeper voice added, cutting in, "you're acting like a real creep, sport. If your mom doesn't squeal to Santa, I sure intend to."

Chris's face brightened immediately, all thoughts of superiority wiped from his mind. "Hi, Pat! Did you come to hear the singing?"

"You kidding? I came to see your mom," the man said, and swept the boy up in his arms. He smiled down into Mallory's upraised face, but she could see the questions in his eyes, as if he weren't sure he was welcome. "Hi, Mal," Pat said.

The deep, tender rumble of his voice made her want to melt into his arms, started a frantic fluttering in the pit of her stomach. "Hi," Mallory echoed, her own voice little more than a breathy whisper.

The kiss they'd shared in the basement loomed heavy in her mind as Patrick accompanied them back to the pew and slipped in beside her. He shrugged out of his overcoat, folding it into the semblance of a pillow. "I figure someone is going to need this before very long," Pat murmured, with a glance in Chris's direction.

"Absolutely," Mallory agreed. They hadn't discussed what had happened, and she wondered if he was going to pretend it had never taken place.

His eyes lingered on her face, dropped in an even slower appraisal of the red-and-green-plaid suit visible beneath her camel-hair coat. She had pinned a jaunty batch of holly berries at the neck of her blouse. His appraisal made the collar feel uncommonly tight.

When he reached her all-purpose snow boots, his gaze slid back up to meet hers. "You look great, Mal."

"So do you." He always did to her. Always had. He wore the same suit he'd had on the night of the Rittenhouse party. Mallory doubted there was a woman in the church who could take her eyes off his broad shoulders and wind-tossed hair.

"How about me?" Christopher demanded in a stage whisper, pushing between them. He held his heavy jacket open to display dress slacks and a blue V-necked sweater with snowmen on it, over a white shirt and red necktie.

"Absolutely awesome," Pat allowed.

"That's what Mom said," Chris announced, and wiggled onto the pew seat. "You want to see the books I brought along? There's one about this boy named David and a giant, and there's..."

Mallory moved to slip out of her coat, and found Pat ready to assist her, while Christopher rambled on in a loud whisper.

"Three-to-one odds he'll be out after the fourth carol," Patrick murmured. His wickedly attractive grin curved the corners of his mouth.

Now it was her heart that did strange things. Surely it was thumping loud enough to be heard half a dozen pews away. "He's a stayer," Mallory whispered back, and sank down, perching on the edge of her seat. "He'll make it past more than that."

The smile was in his eyes, luring her deeper into those sparkling green depths. Pat bent over her, arranging Mallory's coat behind her, his every action courteous and solicitous. "Care to wager on it, pet?"

The casual endearment had the blood rushing through her veins even as she ordered herself to remain calm. She felt as revved up as one of Christopher's race cars. "Such as?"

"I win and you give me a chance to redeem myself."

The church was large and drafty, but Mallory felt warm, her face flushed and glowing. "Are you that sure of your bet?" she asked.

Lines crinkled at the corners of Pat's eyes; his grin turned downright deadly. He hitched the knees of his trousers and sat down, Christopher between them in the pew. "Ah, but you see, I have an edge. I listened to the choir practice."

"It should be beautiful," she said.

"Soothing," Pat countered. "Have we got a deal?"

Mallory sank back in her seat. "You're on," she whispered.

Without another word, Patrick turned his attention to Christopher, dropped an arm around the child's thin shoulders, and spent the remainder of the wait letting the boy read to him.

Christopher nodded off before the choir had begun the final stanza of "Silent Night," their third song of the evening. He slept in Pat's arms, his cheek nestled against the breadth of the man's chest.

Mallory felt a slight tightness in her breast at the sight of man and child. They looked so right together.

Patrick glanced over at her, one brow raised in devilish delight. "I win," he mouthed.

"I know," she answered, and gave him a radiant smile. She wondered what he planned to do. What would be involved in giving him a second chance? Giving herself a second chance, Mallory thought. Whatever it was, she no longer had any doubts about how she would respond. Somewhere between the time she had spoken to Anita and Pat's appearance at the manger scene, Mallory had made her decision. It had certainly not been consciously thought out, not with Chris keeping her occupied. Had her subconscious used logic or emotion? Whatever, Mallory knew she had made the right choice. She was going to attempt life again. A full life.

When Pat put his hand over hers, Mallory curled her fingers between his trustingly. His grip tightened in a silent message.

They held hands throughout the service. Like lovers, Mallory thought. She glanced sideways at him, proud that he was so dashing, so masculine, awed that he wanted her, out of all the women in the universe. It seemed the most natural thing in the world for Pat to brush his lips against hers during the greeting, just as she had often seen husbands do to their wives. "Have a very special Christmas, Mal," he said.

Yes, she thought. This year, her Christmas would be very special. Because he was with her.

Her lips clung to his for the space of a breath. Her eyes were as bright as stars. "Merry Christmas, Patrick," Mallory whispered.

It took all his effort to release her, to turn and greet the worshipers who moved to shake his hand, to murmur a greeting in return.

Behind them, Chris was curled on the seat, sound asleep, his hair mussed and tousled, his long-lashed lids fluttering as he dreamed. As the service resumed, Mallory's hand stole back to link with Pat's. He held it tightly, afraid that if he loosened his grip, she would slip from his grasp.

Not just from his physical grasp, but from his dreams, as well.

The scope of those dreams was amazing, considering that these foreign ideas had crept into his mind since meeting Mallory Meyers. Dreams in themselves weren't strange. He'd entertained some damned interesting fantasies concerning her after seeing her photograph. *Those* kinds of fancies he was used to indulging in, the kind that let him plan the exact method of a seduction, the kind that had him wondering how a woman would feel, how she would taste, how she would respond. There had been a good number of those types of dreams lately.

But there had been others, as well. Disturbingly poignant ones.

The congregation moved like a disorganized wave, coming to their feet. Pat moved sluggishly, one step behind even the laggards. It had been too long since he'd been to church for him to remember the responses by heart. Some of the worshipers used pamphlets to follow the service, mouthing the correct refrain in answer to Kevin's chant. Mallory knew it all by rote, her soft voice murmuring each reply.

Patrick stared ahead at the pulpit, where his brother stood. He remembered other times, long-forgotten times, when he'd been a fidgeting boy forced to attend Sunday services. Even back then, Kevin had known what he wanted out of life. He'd been fascinated with the ministry, with the mysteries of religion. His faith had always been strong, unshakable. Piety had held an attraction for Kevin that Patrick had never understood.

Still didn't understand.

For two boys who had looked like mirror images of each other, he and Kevin had always been poles apart in temperament and interests. He was night to Kevin's day, dark to his twin's light.

Nothing had changed. They still were direct opposites.

Except when it came to Mallory and Christopher. On that score, the Lonergan men thought alike. They both cared for the woman and her child.

And that was where these new, rather frightening dreams entered the scene. Pat was no longer fantasizing just about taking Mallory to bed, he was visualizing what it would be like to have her smiling at him across a dinner table every day, to share her joys and her sorrows. He was seeing himself being a father to her son, fathering other children with her.

Mallory had turned his life around. He barely recognized himself anymore. Where was the devil-may-care man who thought only of business? Sunshine St. John had never been able to drag his attention away for more than the time it took for a bit of exercise between the sheets.

Mallory captivated him. She had a successful career, one that she had worked hard to achieve. She had a son to nurture and protect. She was a warm, wonderful woman. Any number of people at both the Rittenhouse Department Store and St. Edmund's Church could sing her praises. She met them on a different level.

As she did Kevin.

But then, his brother wasn't a threat to the security of her heart. He was a friend.

Patrick didn't think he could be *only* a friend to Mallory. He wanted to be her lover far too badly to settle for something as tepid as friendship.

Her hand was warm in his. They stood side by side as the business of the service droned on around them. He was glad that she hadn't pulled away from him. That she had allowed him this little intimacy.

This public intimacy.

Pat stared down at their joined hands, struck by the way the simple action proclaimed his feelings for Mallory in full view of the congregation around them.

And she didn't seem to mind.

A weight lifted inside him at the realization. Perhaps the walls Mallory had built weren't as high or as thick as he had once thought.

Pat squeezed her hand lightly, felt the answering tightening of her fingers on his. He placed his free hand over their linked ones. Mallory responded by covering it with hers.

His fantasy expanded into bright Technicolor detail. *If you're still watching out there tonight, Mom,* Pat communicated silently, *I think you'll be pleased to know I'm not afraid any longer. And I know exactly what I want this year for Christmas. Her name is Mallory. I want her in my life forever.*

Chapter Thirteen

It was uncomfortable, and it was lovely. She, Chris and Patrick looked so much like a real family that Mallory's heart yearned to make it so. Which was impossible.

She stole a glance at Pat as she bundled a still-sleeping Chris into his heavy coat at the conclusion of the service. Pat had waltzed into her life and changed everything. Not just the way she felt, but the way she thought. Suddenly she was daydreaming about how wonderful it would be to have him as a fixture in her life. It seemed incredible, but, although she barely knew him, she was falling in love with Patrick Lonergan.

Once she had the boy's coat fastened, Chris curled back into a ball on the pew seat, still oblivious of everything around him. Mallory envied her son's trusting innocence. If only she could trust like that again, if only she didn't have the past as a reminder that blind trust could be destructive.

Mallory reached for her camel-hair and found Pat before her, holding the coat, ready to assist her. His breath was warm and tantalizing against the nape of her neck. Mallory glanced back over her shoulder at him, savoring the look in his eyes. Warm feelings blossomed inside her, and she knew she could easily fall all the way for this man.

If only he would return the sentiment.

Which he wouldn't.

Patrick had been quite up-front about his feelings. He wanted her. Just as she wanted him. But that was sex, not love. Not a happily-ever-after. The fairy-tale ending. She longed for it, not just for herself, but for Chris as well.

Prince Charming swept her sleeping child up into his arms. He looked so right with Chris's head nestled trustingly against his shoulder. Mallory felt another pang, felt her heart expand with longing. "Boy, talk about a dead weight," Pat mumbled, adjusting the boy's position slightly. "I'll follow you home and help you get him in bed."

As much as her heart hammered in excitement at the suggestion, Mallory refused to take advantage of his good nature. "There's really no need. Chris can wake up enough to walk on his own."

Pat glanced down at the boy and grinned in amusement. "You're dreaming, Mal," he said. "A bomb exploding wouldn't faze this kid."

Although she was inclined to agree, Mallory busied herself gathering up the tote bag of Chris's things, preferring not to read Pat's true feelings in his face. Surely he had better things to be doing than helping her with the sleeping child. "We're imposing..." she insisted.

Around them, parishioners hurried into the aisle, jostling for position as they filed out of the church. By cor parison, Patrick stood tall and motionless, a broad-shouldered man burdened with a child not his own.

Would Christopher be the crux of their relationship? The reason either of them used to slip free of an attraction that should never have been?

She had never expected to be this drawn to a man again. She doubted that Patrick had any intention of changing his own life-style. He was handsome, and charming, and probably had so many women throwing themselves at him that tying himself down to just one—one who already had a child—would be distasteful.

If she was smart, she would stop dreaming of a story-book-cottage life, one in which she was as important to Pat as he was to her, forming a partnership of mind, as well as soul; one in which he stepped into Chris's life, shouldering the responsibility of fatherhood. She should just accept the time she could spend with him. It would be gone so quickly, leaving her more bereft than Dirk's desertion ever had.

Accept and enjoy, Mallory lectured herself as she shouldered her purse and fussed with the scarf at her neck.

"Mal," Pat murmured quietly. His tone stilled her movements. Mallory met his gaze. "Stop reading things into my actions that aren't there. I said I'd help you with Chris, and that's exactly what I'm doing."

She could lose herself in those green eyes. Wanted to do so very much. "Thank you," she whispered.

Patrick's lips curved in the familiarly rakish grin, his playful mood restored by her acceptance. "Think of it as my good deed for the year," he urged, stepping into the aisle and waiting for her to follow.

"Your only one? Since I've known you, you've done nothing but good deeds."

"I had a backlog of years to make up for," Pat said. "Perhaps I should save this one for next year. Start it off with a bang."

Pat threaded his way through the crowd of well-wishers with Mallory tagging along in his wake. Unerringly he found her car in the parking lot, and had Christopher settled in the back seat in moments.

Before sliding behind the wheel, Mallory made one last attempt, offering him a chance to change his mind. She put her gloved hand on Pat's arm, staying his departure. "Patrick..."

He hadn't bothered with gloves, yet even in the freezing temperature his fingers were warm when they brushed against her cheek. "You've got a choice, Mal. You can let me play Galahad and escort you home, or you can be kissed here and now, before an audience of St. Edmund's most devout parishioners."

Her eyes glistened, the gray depths swirling with savored thoughts of her dream. Pat leaned against the roof of the car, bending closer to Mallory. Headlights flashed over them as other vehicles backed out of parking spaces, creating the beginnings of a minor traffic jam.

"It's going to be hot, Mal," Pat whispered, his voice rumbling with a vow to let her explore previously forbidden intimacies. "Hot, wet, and long." Green fire flashed in his eyes, making the promise real and enticing.

Mallory swallowed loudly. Her nerves tingled. Her knees felt weak, just from thinking about such a kiss. "At...at home," she croaked, surprised that her voice was hoarse with longing.

He had such a wicked, wicked smile. And it did wonderful things to her, leaving her feeling light-headed and carefree.

"Maybe I can't wait that long," Pat purred throatily. "Maybe I should..." He leaned closer.

As if caught in an enchantment, Mallory rose up on her toes, her lips parted slightly. "Oh, ye—"

"Merry Christmas!" someone called brightly from a passing car.

Mallory jolted back to reality. Oh, Lord! She'd nearly kissed him herself. And they were still on church property!

His lips were scant inches away; the vapor trails of their breath mingled intimately, entwined in an erotic dance, then dissipated in the night air, just like her dreams.

"I have to get Chris to bed," Mallory said hastily, and ducked beneath his arm, sliding into the driver's seat.

Pat straightened up and stuck his hands in the pockets of his overcoat. "I'll be right behind you." His voice was back to normal, no longer pitched low and provocative. "Drive carefully," he urged. "Looks like we've got our share of nuts behind the wheel right here."

As if to prove his statement, a screech of brakes and the sound of tires sliding on ice preceded the blare of a horn and an expletive yelled out a hastily rolled-down window.

"And lock your door," Pat added. He stood beside her car until Mallory had snapped the lock in place and fastened her seat belt.

He was true to his word. She had barely arrived in her driveway when his red pickup truck pulled in after her. While she opened the door to the house, Pat gathered Chris in his arms once more and carried the boy to his bedroom. Chris mumbled in his sleep, but didn't awaken.

Mallory stooped to take Chris's shoes off as he sprawled across the mattress. "Thanks. I can take it from here."

Pat chuckled softly. "Good try, pet, but you aren't getting rid of me that easily. I'll wait for you in the front room."

How she ever managed to get Christopher undressed, into his pajamas and tucked beneath the covers, Mallory never knew. Her pulse was pounding; she felt breathless with anticipation. And throughout it all, her mind kept chanting a litany: *If only he would love me. If only he would love us.*

In the living room, Pat looked around and laid his plan. He locked the front door, then stripped off both overcoat and suit jacket, tossing them over the back of an armchair. He kicked off his shoes, unbuttoned his vest and loosened his tie. Next step, he mused, and plugged in the lights on the Christmas tree. They blinked, a rainbow of colors that was soft and romantic. It wasn't enough. Pat stood in the center of the room, surveying the materials at hand. His gaze moved from the jumble of track of Christopher's new race set to the two stockings hung from the mantelpiece. It took only moments to build a fire in the fireplace. The flames threw enough light for him to see by, so he switched off the lamp Mallory had left burning.

He'd never plotted a seduction quite like this before, but then, one had never meant this much to him, either. In a couple days' time, he would be back at the farmhouse outside of Greenville. Time was running short.

He had to make Mallory fall in love with him. And if he couldn't do that with all the romantic trappings of Christmas around him, well, he had truly lost the touch that had given him such a hell-bent reputation with the ladies in both Greenville, Ohio, and New York, New York.

Her approach was silent, but he sensed her presence.

"What's all this?" Mallory asked, amusement rippling in the rich, throaty sound of her voice.

Pat sat cross-legged on the floor, continuing his work with the racetrack set, snapping together a fast and action-packed roadway. The pièce de résistance was the double loop-the-loop.

Mallory had gotten rid of her snow boots, so she padded across the room in her stocking feet. She had very sexy ankles, Pat decided, trim and tempting. She had shed her suit jacket, but the neckline of her blouse was still closed tightly, and guarded by a corsage of silk holly berries at her throat.

Pat finished assembling the track and reached for her hand, tugging her down to sit on the carpet next to him. "Just lending Santa a hand," he said, and waved, indicating the low table he'd placed near the fireplace. On it resided an already emptied glass of milk, and a plate of crumbs, evidence that a handful of Christmas cookies had disappeared. "I've left plenty of evidence that the jolly old soul put in an appearance."

"Oh!" Mallory's hand flew to her lips. "I hope I remember where Santa hid all the presents from his sleigh, then." She tried to get to her feet, but Pat held her in place.

"Not just yet," he murmured. "There is the little matter of a kiss."

She smiled at him, dazzling him with her innocence and warmth. "Well, if it's just a *little* kiss, it was hardly worth your drive over, was it?" she said teasingly.

He had her pinned against the floor swiftly, his hands on her wrists imprisoning them on either side of her head. Her soft brown hair swirled out over the carpet. "Not hardly," Pat agreed, and brushed his mouth lightly against hers. Her lips softened and clung, but he was in no hurry.

"You taste very wholesome," Mallory said, and ran her tongue along her top lip, as if she were enjoying the taste of him yet. "Like nice cold milk."

"You can be my very next cookie," Pat offered. "I like them sweet and warm."

Her eyes darkened to the color of rain-washed slate. A reflection of the fire danced in them, hot and hungry. "I could try to be sweet and warm," she whispered. Her gaze dropped to his lips and lingered.

"Well, let's see if you are," he said. Rather than kiss her lips, he set his mouth to the tender, sensitive area just below her ear. He breathed in the scent of her, an unpretentious combination of lavender and soap that he found far more exotic than the heavy, cloying musk perfumes favored by other women.

Mallory gave a light gasp of pleasure. Encouraged, Pat moved on, placing butterfly-light kisses on her temples, her eyelids, her nose. When he returned to her lips, he released her wrists, and was pleased when she slid her hands along the breadth of his chest in a slow, erotic ritual of her own.

Their kiss deepened, becoming all that he had promised her in the church parking lot: hot, wet, and seemingly endless. Pat's mouth stirred restlessly against Mallory's, at once both hungry and tender. He savored the taste of her on his tongue, running the tip along her lips softly before pushing insistently inside her mouth. Mallory welcomed the invasion, her own tongue greeting and caressing his, her body arching against his in a silent message.

"Tell me what you want, little girl," he murmured against her skin. "Santa's always ready to oblige. Especially tonight."

Mallory slid her hands into his hair, her touch driving Pat a bit mad. "I've been a very good girl," she whispered. "Now I'd like to be a teensy bit bad."

"You would, would you?" He grinned down into her face, ran his fingers along the soft curve of her jaw and into the swirling mass of her hair. "First thing to do is get rid of these." He dipped his head to nip at the silk berries, nuzzling her throat.

"It could be arranged." Mallory fumbled with the corsage, finding the metal clasp and freeing it. She tossed the pin away carelessly, her actions reflecting the recklessness Pat read in her eyes.

"Next step," he murmured, and surprised her by pulling at his tie. It followed the direction taken by the holly berries. Bracing himself on his forearm, Pat pulled his shirttail free and with one hand released buttons on his shirt until it hung open.

Mallory watched him through lowered lashes, her lips still parted, her breathing quickening. "I like this step," she said. "Let's see if I can improve on it, though." Her fingers slid along his bare skin, burrowing against the enticing dark hair of his chest. Beneath it, his muscles were hard, tensed, and warm. Mallory continued her exploration, pushing the fabric off his shoulders and down his back, allowing her fingers to glide over the slightly flexed sinews of his biceps.

Pat tossed his shirt and vest aside.

"That's better," Mallory agreed, her hands still tracing each muscular ridge, her touch feather-light, her gaze enthralled.

"Not quite," Pat said. He played idly with a button on her blouse. It lay in the valley between her breasts, allowing him to brush the back of his hand against the soft curves still hidden from view. "Isn't this the age of equality between the sexes?"

"You want equal time?" Mallory raised up enough to lean back on her elbows. "Maybe you'd like to open your present?"

"Ah, and you're it?" In quick succession, the buttons of her blouse were dispensed with. Pat spread the garment wide, his eyes on the quick rise and fall of her breast beneath a silvery satin chemise. The curved neckline dipped low, so that the upper curves of her bosom rose like tempting swells, soft, white and lush. "I like this Christmas gift very much," Patrick murmured. He skimmed his hand over the gleaming fabric, his fingers curving to shape her breast. "Just the right size, too. How clever of you to know."

"Isn't it?" Mallory ran a finger down the center of his chest. "Aren't you going to thank me nicely?"

"Absolutely." His mouth sought hers once more, angling as their tongues performed an ancient mating ritual, sliding, gliding, entwining. His arm slid beneath her shoulders, drawing Mallory up. She clung to Patrick, her hands clutching him to her.

Without ending their kiss, Pat rolled over, pulling Mallory with him so that she straddled his body. Her slim skirt hiked up, displaying a long stretch of silk-stockinged thigh. His hand rested on her knee briefly, then slid upward, following the soft, womanly contour of her body.

She moaned against his lips, and deepened the kiss, her mouth greedy and urgent against his. She rubbed herself along the hard, pulsing length of his manhood as it strained eloquently against the fabric of his trousers. Pat groaned harshly and broke the embrace.

His chest rose and fell rapidly as he gasped for breath. His fingers slid up her arms in a light caress. "I can't remember ever receiving a present I liked quite this much."

"You have lovely manners. I've never been thanked quite as thoroughly before," she murmured.

One of the thin straps of her chemise had fallen, drooping along the upper part of her arm. Patrick tugged it down farther, freeing the other strap, as well. The firelight warmed the satin, giving it a cast of gold. Then the glow was Mallory's skin, blushing and perfect, as her breasts slipped free.

He skimmed the palm of his hand over the eagerly raised tip of one. Mallory arched, thrusting nearer his touch. "You'll be pleased to know that I also like the texture," Pat said. "And the color."

"I'm so glad," she whispered, her eyes closed, her lashes fluttered in a reflection of ecstasy.

"Now, about the taste..."

Mallory shuddered deliciously as his mouth took her nipple and savored it.

"Perfect," Pat said, and moved to favor the other, his beard-roughened cheek scraping across her overly sensitized flesh, his tongue blazing a trail that left her trembling, possessed.

Mallory's fingers curved into his hair, forcing his lips back to her own. "Damn," she panted. "It's been too long since—"

Pat soothed her with his hands and his lips. "Hush, pet." He laid her back against the carpet, resting his own body between her legs, his hardness pressed close to her softness.

"I feel like a silly teenager," Mallory admitted. "Overwhelmed and addicted."

"As long as it's with me, you don't have to worry," Pat said. "Just enjoy."

"Necking and petting on the living room floor?"

"One of the true pleasures of the world that most men and women think they've outgrown."

"Except you," she murmured tenderly. She touched his face, the backs of her fingers tracing the masculine beauty of his bone structure, scraping along the harsh, shadowed stubble of his beard.

"Speaking strictly as Chris's present to you, I thought perhaps you'd enjoy getting more out of the deal than just a dinner partner at a company party," he said. His grin was warm, tantalizingly intimate. Devastatingly rakish.

"That is very self-sacrificing of you," Mallory allowed.

"I aim to please."

"It doesn't matter that Chris didn't have this in mind when he, uh, pinned the gift tag on your lapel?" Mallory twisted a lock of his hair around her finger.

His weight balanced on his forearms, Pat nuzzled her breastbone. "We can't be sure. I'll just cover the bases, so the kid gets his money's worth."

Mallory squirmed delightfully when his mouth closed over her breast again. While one nipple was laved with his tongue, the other was teased by his fingers. "I don't think I've ever had a Christmas quite like this one," she said, her voice breathy and tinged with passion.

"Now wouldn't this," Pat asked, sliding back up to claim her lips, "be a delightful tradition? We could start a trend."

"Making love under the Christmas tree."

Patrick entwined his fingers in her hair again. "The perfect ending to a night begun at a church service."

Mallory's eyes grew wide, her expression chagrined more than shocked at his suggestion. "Oh, dear, that's right! We really shouldn't..."

"Stop now," Pat finished for her, half-afraid he'd lost ground. "I couldn't agree more, Mal." He kissed her long and lovingly, then slid his hand up under her skirt again, intent upon rekindling her passion. "In fact, I think it's time for another exchange of gifts, don't you?"

For answer, she arched her body against his touch. Her hands in his hair, she dragged his mouth back to hers.

Patrick made a silent vow to spend every Christmas Eve in just this manner. Only next year, he promised himself, Mallory would be his wife.

Chapter Fourteen

Christopher bounded into his mother's bedroom a little after dawn, bouncing onto her mattress in his eagerness to wake her. Mallory raised heavy lids, stared through her mussed hair at her rambunctious child and groaned loudly.

"Mom! It's Christmas!" Chris plunked his head down on the pillow next to hers. His gray eyes were as large and shining and silvery as the ornaments on the tree. His lips curved in a wide Cheshire-cat smile that revealed the gaps where he'd recently lost baby teeth. He pushed hair out of her face and peered more closely. "Santa left lots of presents," he added in a singsong voice meant to lure her from the warmth of the bedclothes.

"Now, why would he do a thing like that?" Mallory mumbled, just as she did every Christmas morning, and pulled the blanket over her head.

Chris snuggled under it with her. "'Cause we were good this year," he explained.

"Maybe we weren't, and it's just coal," Mallory said. She wasn't feeling like a particularly *good* girl this morning. No, it was more a sensation of being decadent and wonderful.

Then again, perhaps she had been a good girl. She'd have to ask Patrick how he felt about it.

Just the idea, and the memory of those torrid moments in his arms, sent a bright blush to her cheeks. Mallory was glad that, with the sheets over their heads, Christopher wasn't able to see her clearly.

There was no depressing his spirits on Christmas morning though. "Coal would be cool!" Chris insisted brightly. "I asked Mr. Woods what it was, and he said when he was a little boy that he had to help his dad stick it in the furnace to heat their house, and that it *glows!*"

From the gleam in his eyes, Mallory figured Chris was conjuring up eerie phosphorescent greens, pinks and yellows. Although she'd never actually seen a coal fire, Mallory was pretty sure it would fall far short of Christopher's fantasy.

"Don't worry, Mom," Chris continued, more seriously, "you didn't get any coal. I already looked in your stocking, and it was full of stuff you'll like."

Mallory grinned and tickled his ribs. "And I'll bet you didn't peek at the stuff in your stocking?"

Giggling and squirming, Chris admitted that he had just looked at some of it, but only because a new turtle action figure had been "looking at him" from amid the treats. "Then I came ta get you, Mom. Are you awake now?"

She'd never actually been asleep. At least not for long. And then she'd been dreaming of Patrick Lonergan, anyway, of being in his arms.

She was a totally different woman from the one who had nervously awaited the arrival of Christopher's mysterious Christmas present to her. That other woman would never have engaged in a session of heavy petting on the living room rug. That other woman wouldn't have felt slighted when her partner, instead of consummating their relationship, backed off, hastily dressed, and left her to seek whatever peace remained of the night.

She had been puzzled, insecure at his desertion. What had she done wrong? Mallory wondered. The indecision had lasted barely a moment. As if he could read her soul, Pat had gathered Mallory into his arms for one last, lingeringly erotic kiss at the door.

"If only I had been a better Boy Scout," he'd murmured against her lips.

Mallory blinked up at him, unable to understand his meaning. After all the lovely sensations she'd reexperienced that evening, Mallory had a feeling that her brain had turned to mush.

The pads of his thumbs brushed across her cheeks. His fingers buried themselves in her hair. "I don't suppose you keep any..."

Mallory blushed as she realized what he was talking about. Condoms. Protection. Birth control. Her cheeks burned even brighter. "No, I...I...haven't had..." Her life had been celibate for so long.

"I didn't think so," Pat whispered, and drew her close again. "So, since our opportunities to be alone together are rare, it looks like I'll just have to court you the old-fashioned way for a while." He smiled with that rakish grin that had the ability to turn her bones, as well as her brain, to the consistency of prepared oatmeal. "I think I'll like that," he said.

And then he'd been gone, and she'd moved around the house in a dream, filling the stockings, arranging gifts under the tree. When she'd crawled into bed, sleep had been a long time in coming.

"You look pretty awake, Mom," Christopher insisted, peering at her intently. "Can we open the presents now?"

Continuing her theatrics, Mallory groaned loudly and threw back the covers. "Oh, I suppose we could," she relented. "Get your bathrobe and slippers first."

Christopher was gone in a flash.

Mallory swung her feet to the floor and hunted around for her own slippers. Her silky pajamas whispered with each movement. She pushed her hair back out of her face and stared at her reflection. It wasn't exactly that of a gorgeously sexy woman. The pajamas were more utilitarian than glamorous. Her robe was a fleecy chenille. A bedspread with arms, Mallory thought in disgust. In a few moments she'd be opening boxes that housed twin versions of her current apparel. Perhaps it was time to do more than just okay orders for slinky lingerie. It was time to do a bit of shopping for nightgowns that made her feel beautiful, for underwear that made her feel delectable.

"Mom!"

There was nothing she could do about it now. Mallory belted her suddenly detested robe and headed for Christmas Central. In moments she was buried in scraps of hastily ripped wrapping paper and curls of red, green, gold and silver ribbon.

The tantalizing aroma of baking ham wafted from the house when Kevin opened the door to the Meyerses. "Merry Christmas!" he said. A jovial Santa in a department store would have found it difficult to match the unbounded cheer in the pastor's voice.

"Merry Christmas!" Mallory and Christopher echoed in unison. They'd been practicing the harmony in the car on the way over, much to Chris's delight.

"We brought presents!" Chris added unnecessarily as they stepped into the warm entryway. He was burdened down beneath a hefty box wrapped in green and red.

"Presents!" Kevin echoed, as if surprised, and gave Mallory a fond smile. "You know that wasn't necessary."

"Of course it is," she said. "Chris and I always remember our favorite people at the holidays." She set aside the Rittenhouse shopping bag and the gelatin with marshmallows Kevin had suggested she bring, then slipped out of her coat and hung it on the hall tree. Kevin was busy assisting Christopher with the stubborn zipper of his jacket. In the end, it took Mallory's magical mother's touch to free the boy from his bulky outerwear.

With their wraps disposed of, Kevin led the way into the living room, a tiny space crowded with overstuffed, slip-covered furniture and dominated by a tall live tree. It was simply decorated. A large silver star sat at the crest, traditional strands of popcorn and cranberries encircling it. A great number of candy canes brightened the branches, interspersed with ornaments of colored paper and glitter made by children of the congregation, and cleverly fashioned dried-fruit rings from Rosemary's kitchen. The air was filled with the spicy scents of cinnamon, cloves and pine. Mallory knew that the tree would be stripped of candy canes and nonedible ornaments on New Year's Day. It would then be planted with much ceremony on the church grounds. The dried fruit and popcorn that still decorated it at that point would feed the flocks of winter birds.

On the mantelpiece a line of votivelike candles burned, adding a hint of vanilla to the air, and a number of gaily wrapped packages already sat beneath the tree. However, there was no one in the room. The sound of voices raised in song came from the back of the house, in the kitchen area.

Mallory left Chris under Kevin's watchful eye, letting the child arrange the gifts they'd brought beneath the tree. She took the salad bowl from home, and followed the sound of "We Three Kings" down the hall.

There was nothing sedate about this rendition of the song. Neither was there much to be said for the quality of the voices. Rosemary's warble strained to be heard over an enthusiastic baritone. What surprised Mallory was the sureness with which both sang the third verse of the tune by heart. She would have been lucky to get through the first verse unaided by a songbook.

If their music surprised her, the enterprise they were engaged in left her stunned. Rosemary hovered near the kitchen table, her gaze on Pat's large hands. The sleeves of his dark sweater were pushed above his elbows to display muscular forearms liberally coated with flour as he kneaded dough.

Rosemary broke off her singing to instruct her student in the application of more flour to the pastry. Since she barely came up to his shoulder, the housekeeper looked like a graying elf next to a giant.

Mallory put her tray down on the counter. "Don't tell me," she said. "He's eaten so many cookies, you've got him baking his own now."

Rosemary laughed, her voice warm and motherly. "I wish I'd thought of that. Merry Christmas, dear. I'm so glad you've come." She enveloped Mallory in a fond embrace.

"Hey, Mal!" Pat said, without moving from his task. "I hope you brought the mistletoe, 'cause Kev's neglected to get it."

Despite the fact that he hadn't moved from the table, Mallory felt as if she'd been swept up in a whirlwind of emotion. All he'd done was smile at her.

"Sorry. Kevin said marshmallows, not mistletoe," Mallory said. She thought her voice sounded a bit breathless. She certainly felt breathless when he ran a practiced eye over her, his look telling her how much he approved of the long, full, hunter-green suede skirt and matching vest she'd worn over a white cowl-necked sweater. Her feet were encased in flat-heeled brown boots, a wide brown leather belt cinched her small waist, and the same corsage of holly berries she'd worn the night before was pinned near her heart. Her hair fell in rippling waves around her shoulders.

"Damn—I mean darn," Pat muttered. He took his hands out of the dough, holding them up as if he were a surgeon, freshly scrubbed. In two strides, he was before her. "Just have to do without the mistletoe," he declared, and kissed her.

Mallory felt her cheeks flush hotly. She wondered what Rosemary thought of Patrick's forwardness. He'd kissed her in church last night, before an audience, but that had been little more than a faint touch of their lips. This time he lingered, his mouth savoring hers as if he were a connoisseur appreciating an especially fine vintage.

When he stepped back, floury hands still extended away from her clothing, Mallory was sure she was as bright a red as the berries of her corsage.

Her gaze flew to Rosemary and encountered a complacent, pleased expression on her soft, familiar face. The housekeeper obviously approved of Pat's actions. Well, of course she did! Rosemary had been lauding Patrick's qualities since he'd arrived. But how would Kevin react? Mallory was almost afraid to face the pastor.

She needn't have worried. Coming through the kitchen archway with Chris in tow, Kevin elbowed his brother out of the way and planted a chaste kiss on her cheek. "Merry Christmas, Mallory," he said lightly, ignoring her confusion.

Mallory was nearly speechless. Fortunately, Chris's noisy interest in Pat's project eliminated the need to say anything.

"Wow!" the boy exclaimed, seeing the mound of dough on the table. "Are we going to have homemade bread?"

"Not tonight," Rosemary answered, and returned to the table to inspect the dough. "Patrick is learning to..."

Pat had moved over to the sink, where he was stripping a layer of dough and flour from his hands and forearms. He snorted in disgust at Rosemary's explanation.

"Sh—shucks," he said, once again hastily correcting his language. Because he was in Rosemary's kitchen, or because he was under the minister's roof? Mallory wondered. "I'm just proving that I have a grip on domestic chores," he said.

Christopher looked as wide-eyed as Mallory felt. "Men can bake bread?" he demanded in awe. Apparently the idea had never occurred to him.

"Sure they can," Kevin's voice said soothingly.

"Bakers in bakeries were always men when I was a girl," Rosemary offered.

It was to Patrick, the current idol in Chris's short life, that the boy's eyes turned for clarification though.

"Darn right they can, Chris," he declared in ringing tones. "A man can do any dam—dratted thing he wants to do."

"Within reason," Mallory hastened to add.

Pat grinned at her over Christopher's head. "Spoilsport," he said.

"Cool!" Chris announced. "Can I make bread, too?"

Rosemary hastily wrapped up the lump of dough and stuck it away in the refrigerator. "How about helping me with the rolls, instead?" she countered. "Dinner's almost ready."

After having his hands resanitized at the sink, Chris scrambled up onto a chair, kneeling so that he could accomplish his job efficiently. Mallory was amused to find that Rosemary was using store-bought refrigerator rolls, instead of making her special homemade brand that day. Christopher solemnly took each roll from the bag and carefully placed it on a cookie sheet.

As if they were all members of a large family, Rosemary soon had everyone involved, sending Patrick off to set the table, and ordering Kevin to carve the ham. Mallory was assigned the duty of making coffee, while Rosemary tossed a salad and carried it into the dining room.

Things moved quickly. Soon they were all seated at the table, the soft glow of candlelight softening features, the angelic sound of a recorded Christmas choir gently filling their hearts and the delicious smells of the meal tantalizing their senses. Besides the golden, steaming rolls in a basket, there were bowls heaped with parsley potatoes, green beans, candied carrots and baked apples competing with the platter of honey-roasted ham. Kevin said grace, giving thanks for friends and family, as well as the bountiful feast, then suggested things be passed to the left. Mallory was sure everyone began talking at once.

It was a very special day, an old-fashioned kind of day. Even the holidays she had spent with her aunt Anita paled in comparison. This was the type of companionable celebration she had always felt Christmas should be. It didn't matter that the blood ties were minimal; it was the feeling of affection that bound the pastor to his housekeeper, to Mallory and Christopher. Ten days ago, Patrick's only tie had been to his twin, but in the ensuing time he'd carved his own place in the group. Mallory wondered if he wasn't the catalyst that had drawn them all together.

And soon he would be leaving.

The thought was on Rosemary's mind, as well. "The weather report says we might have snow again tonight. If we do, you should stay in town another day or so, Pat. It wouldn't be so bad if you were returning just to Greenville," she said. "The roads are sure to be cleared off in the city and along the main roads. But will they have done the lesser-used routes, like those to your farm?"

"You don't really have to leave yet, do you, Pat?" Chris added, his face reflecting both hope and sadness.

Mallory was afraid to meet Patrick's eyes across the table. She could feel his gaze on her.

"Have to go sooner or later, sport," he told Chris. "Actually, I've been trying to talk Kevin into coming out for a few days. Sort of visit the old homestead, help me tie up loose ends concerning his share of the place."

Rosemary asked the question about which Mallory was curious about. "I didn't know you owned part of the farm, Pastor. I suppose it is just natural. There were no other children?"

"Just us," Kevin announced cheerfully. "Mother always said Pat caused trouble enough for a houseful of kids."

"It's a talent," Pat said, his tone mischievous rather than modest.

"When the estate was probated, Pat bought me out and arranged to have a trust fund set up, so that the interest is paid to various charities," Kevin continued.

"Since the fiscal year is nearly up, it's time to decide who the recipients are again," Pat reminded. He turned to face his brother at the head of the table. "Would there be any problem in your getting four days away? Say the end of the week?"

The pastor swallowed a bite of food and patted his lips with a linen napkin. "It could be arranged. Rosemary is going to visit her son in Pittsburgh then." He smiled fondly at the housekeeper. "And knowing her kitchen will survive intact without my attempts at cooking to destroy it will make her trip more enjoyable. Besides, it's been a long time since you and I spent time together out there."

He glanced surreptitiously across the table, to where Chris sat poking at his carrots. "Do you still have chickens out there?" Kevin asked.

Both Mallory and Christopher looked up, both sets of gray eyes startled, for different reasons. He couldn't be planning to...

"Chickens? Real chickens?" the boy demanded. "Cool! I wish I could see them."

Mallory frowned at Kevin, trying to make mental contact with him. Trying to discourage him from taking what she knew would be the fatal step. Fatal for her, that is.

"Didn't I hear something about your mom having some time off at Rittenhouse this week?" Kevin continued.

Patrick had picked up his wineglass, but at his brother's comment he leaned forward on his elbows, the goblet balanced between his fingers, and watched Mallory squirm uneasily in her seat. His lips were curved in a smile that was clearly calculating.

"Yeah," Chris announced happily. "Four in a row. She doesn't get them like that, usually. This is special, and because it is, I get to pick what we're going to do the whole time!"

Mallory closed her eyes, resting her forehead on her hand.

"Cool," Patrick murmured, his tone an exact replica of the one Chris always used.

Mallory's eyes snapped open. She glared at him across the table.

"Maybe you could come out to the farm," Pat suggested softly. "See the chickens. Maybe a few pigs, cows and horses, too."

"Wow!" Christopher's eyes were wild with excitement. He bounced in his seat.

"Creep," Mallory mumbled to the man across from her.

"All's fair..." Patrick said.

He didn't have to finish the phrase. She knew what he meant. She also realized that he'd been telling her the truth when he said he was going to court her the old-fashioned way. Things were being manipulated so that she would spend time at his house, sleeping under his roof. But they wouldn't be alone. Kevin would be there, as well. And Mallory doubted that Pat would abuse his brother's calling by making love to her while the minister was sleeping in the next room.

"Can we, Mom?" Christopher asked cajolingly. "I've never been to a real farm before. And you promised me that..."

She didn't need to be reminded. Didn't need to be convinced. For the first time in eight years, Mallory made a snap decision. "Okay."

Four pair of startled eyes stared at her. Rosemary was the first to recover. She beamed happily at Mallory. "Cool," she said.

Chapter Fifteen

Mallory wasn't sure exactly what she expected to find at the Lonergan Farm. Her impressions of Pat himself had undergone so many revisions, she was sure that whatever she fantasized would turn out to be far off the mark. When she did fantasize about him, it was never the farm she had in mind, anyway. Since he'd kissed her good-night on Christmas Day, she'd done quite a lot of dreaming about him, and not just at night.

"Hey! Mal!" Gail had shouted in the open door of her office earlier in the week. "Didn't you hear your page? What's the matter with you? In love or something?"

Well, there were times when she wasn't sure if this was love, but it was certainly *something*.

Christopher operated on a totally new level all week, actually asking to be taken to the library so that he could learn all about chickens, and the rest of the barnyard menagerie. During the drive north, he regaled her with all the details he'd culled. "Do you think I could ride on a tractor, Mom?" he asked hopefully as they followed route 49 into Greenville and turned east on a road that paralleled Greenville Creek.

"You'll have to ask your good buddy," Mallory said, and glanced at the directions Pat had written out for her before he left Kevin's. Greenville wasn't that far from Dayton; the whole trip could be made in about an hour. She wondered why the Lonergan brothers didn't see more of each other. Considering he was native to the area, why was it that in the three years he had been at St. Edmund's, Kevin had never mentioned that his brother lived so close? Why had Patrick never visited his twin before this particular Christmas?

"Look!" Christopher shouted. "Cows!"

"Yep," Mallory agreed, and zipped on past, the speedometer notching a smooth fifty-five on her dashboard. "Which ones give chocolate milk?"

Chris gave her a disgusted look. "Mom," he groaned, his voice already world-weary at six-going-on-seven. "You know cows only make one flavor of milk."

"They do?"

"Yeah."

"What kind? Strawberry?"

Christopher heaved a deep sigh, his thin shoulders rising with the effort. "No," he insisted. "Just vanilla."

"Oh." Mallory nodded wisely, suppressing the urge to grin.

He was silent awhile, his nose pressed to the window as more fields whipped by, the harvested, broken stalks of corn showing through patches of snow here and there.

How different this area was from Dayton, Mallory mused. The three rivers that tumbled toward the city had shaped the geography into rolling hills, meadows and lush woodlands. Greenville offered a completely different vista. The land was flat, planed by glaciers during the Ice Age, a patchwork of fields and small copses stretching toward the horizon in every direction.

More than just geological history took precedence in Greenville, and, Mallory admitted, Chris probably wouldn't care two hoots about any of it at his age. Maybe when he was older he'd be interested in learning about the early Indian wars, of General "Mad" Anthony Wayne's treaty with them at Greenville. She wondered if his interest would be pricked by a mention of the Annie Oakley Museum, but then realized he would probably have no idea that Annie had been a famous sharpshooter from the Greenville area.

"Mom?"

Mallory turned her attention back to her son. "Hmm?"

"Do you like kissing Pat?"

If she hadn't been slowing down, looking for their next turn, Mallory was sure she would have put them in the ditch at the totally unexpected question. She tried to keep her voice calm. "Why do you ask, sweetheart?"

Her son was far more canny that she'd thought. He ignored her evasive counterquestion. "He likes kissing you," Chris said.

"Oh..." What did a mother say to that one? Especially a mother who hadn't had a date in seven long years? Or at least she hadn't, until her precocious son had fixed her up with one.

"So do you?"

Mallory took a deep breath. Time to come clean. With herself, not just with Chris. "Yes, I suppose I do," she admitted.

Chris twisted around in his seat as much as his seat belt allowed. "I like him a lot, Mom. If you like him a bunch, maybe you could marry him?"

Talk about getting a lump in your throat! "Well, you see, honey, I—"

"If you did, then he'd be your husband, see? And he'd be my dad. I think he'd be a cool dad, cause he knows guy things. No offense, Mom, but you just know a lot of girl things."

Mallory resigned herself to her unfortunate biological failings. "When I tried to help you with baseball last summer, I was throwing like a girl, huh?"

"You were bad, Mom. It was 'barrassing."

Where was that turn when she needed it? Why couldn't the farmhouse loom up suddenly, giving her an excuse to end this conversation?

"I'm sorry, Chris. I did my best."

"I know." Christopher was quiet, staring out the front windshield, his minimal height enabling him to see little but a view of the gray winter sky. "So do you think you could marry him?"

The longed-for sign appeared. It wasn't exactly what Mallory had expected. Pat had merely said, "There will be a sign telling you when you're at the turn." Well, there certainly was. It was large, and electric, and had a computer message running across its screen in large letters: This Is It, Mal. Turn Here. A bright red arrow pointing left followed the words.

Mallory maneuvered to the left, down a gravel road, following it between two long fields. Just now, Pat's sense of humor seemed ill-timed. "I'm not the only one involved here, Chris. And just liking the way someone kisses is not enough to make someone want to get married."

Did she sound too stern, as if she were lecturing? She needed to treat Chris like a person, explaining logically, rather than just brushing him off with black-and-whites. He'd obviously been giving the whole situation a great deal of thought.

Mallory glanced quickly at Christopher, then back to the road. Perhaps she wasn't the only one who had feelings for Patrick. He hadn't chosen Pat Lonergan as parent material just because the man could throw a decent pitch.

A twist in the road took them past a stand of trees and the sturdy shape of a large barn; then, as if conjured up by wishes alone, the house was there before them, white, two-storied, and picture-book-perfect. "How about if we talk about all this another time?" Mallory suggested. "We came out here to have fun, right?"

"Yeah." Chris's voice lacked his earlier eagerness.

She pulled the car in next to Kevin's familiar Oldsmobile and turned off the engine. "Then let's have fun," Mallory said, forcing brightness into her voice.

"Okay, but I— Mom! Look! There really are chickens!"

Mallory let her breath out slowly. Ah, the rapid changes in a child's mood. One moment glumness, the next passionate interest. The crisis was avoided. At least for now. What, though, she wondered, would she tell Christopher next time?

"Hi."

The sexy voice was warm, and pitched low. She felt the brush of Pat's lips at her ear a moment before his arms enfolded her, pulling her back against his broad chest.

"Hi," Mallory echoed. She'd been at the farm for the better part of the day now, and this was the first time they'd been alone. It had begun snowing again outside. Mallory had watched it for a while from a window in the front parlor where the three "men" were engaged in a deep game of crazy eights, then roamed out to the kitchen in search of food. She had discovered a couple of pounds of hamburger and a bag of frozen french fries in the icebox, and a large can of baked beans in the cupboard. Otherwise, the pantry had been bare. Well, Patrick was a bachelor who lived alone. Or so she'd thought, until she found the frilly apron in a drawer.

That didn't bear thinking on. She was here for one reason only, and that was to have fun. Regrets came later.

"I thought you were deep in a game of cards," Mallory said, and finished patting another hamburger into shape. Although Chris had been on his best behavior so far, she figured any moment he'd be asking about dinner.

"I was," Pat murmured, still playing with the sensitive lobe of her ear. "You know you gave birth to a sharp, don't you? He actually suggested we play for pennies. Kev's losing steadily, but I'm on to him. I claimed to be broke."

"Very clever," Mallory agreed. Judging by the "toys" she had seen, that claim was far from the truth.

The quick tour of the house that Pat had given earlier had been a little glimpse of heaven. She had always thought there was something romantic about farmhouses, especially ones with wraparound porches, like the Lonergan place. The kitchen was long, and stretched across the back of the house. There were three other rooms on the ground floor, and four bedrooms and a single bath upstairs. Of the two parlors downstairs, one was slightly offset from the other, creating an interesting architectural angle. Both were filled with an eclectic assortment of antique chests and tables and slightly less ancient sofas and armchairs. A fireplace warmed the foremost room, creating a cozy, peaceful retreat on a cold day.

But it was the mysterious room tucked away behind an enclosed staircase that drew both Mallory and Christopher. Here the walls were filled with shelving that held manila folders, all filed sideways, in a way reminiscent of the systems in doctors' offices. A compact photocopier, a fax machine and a laser printer were lined up on a long table before a monster of a desk. There was little evidence of clutter; still, the desk top was filled with the tools of business: a bulging phone book, an adding machine, and a phone with a row of buttons indicating multiple lines, something that seemed quite out of place in a farmhouse. The most incongruous feature, to Mallory's mind, was the top-of-the-line computer.

Personal computers were a common enough feature in many homes. In fact, she'd been contemplating getting one for Christopher. But this wasn't some economy model geared for home usage. It was nearly identical to the desktop computers used in the Rittenhouse offices, a system that tied every aspect of the business into a whole at Albert Rittenhouse's fingertips.

Since Pat had offered Chris the run of the house, with the exception of his study, the importance of this particular "toy" as the keystone to his business was confirmed in Mallory's mind. Although there had been longing in Chris's eyes at his first sight of the computer, he had nodded solemnly and agreed to stay out of the office.

Was running a farm that complicated? she had wondered. At the store, the computer tracked sales, kept a running inventory, even sent merchandise orders electronically to suppliers. Granted, a farmer was no different from any other businessman. Only the amount of planted acreage determined whether his concern was small or large. Which was Patrick's?

Pat's teeth teased Mallory's earlobe, pulling her away from the questions that seeing his home had raised in her mind. "You know, Mal," he said, "there's something about a woman in a kitchen that makes me feel terribly romantic."

"You can take over any time you want," Mallory offered, giving him a teasing grin over her shoulder.

His hands drifted to cup her breasts, shaping them, letting them fill his palms. Teasing, his thumbs brushed over her nipples, winning an instant response. Mallory quivered.

"Perhaps I should warn you. My specialty is charred everything," he said.

Mallory leaned back in contentment, resting her head against his shoulder. "I'd be glad to keep an eye on the smoke alarm for you," she purred huskily.

Pat nibbled a path down her arched throat. "We could go out to eat," he offered. "Actually, that's what I had planned. The hamburger was just emergency rations."

Mallory grinned at him. "Having a six-year-old in residence qualifies as an emergency. Believe me."

"We could let Kevin and Chris have the hamburgers, and I could take you out."

Oh, she could really learn to love this courting business. Pat made it so alluring, so tempting.

"Can't," Mallory said. "These are Christopher's days. I promised him them."

His arms slid away, albeit reluctantly. "Patience is one of my virtues. Okay, okay." Pat leaned back against the kitchen table and held one hand up, as if signaling a halt to any rebuttals. "It's probably my only virtue, if I can even claim to have one. This is Chris's vacation. But, my delightfully skittish young mother, your son is otherwise occupied at the moment. Care to live dangerously?''

He was so damn hard to resist. As if to ward Pat off, she turned to the counter again, filled her hands with more raw hamburger and began shaping another burger. ''In what way?''

Pat's left brow arched provocatively. ''I take it Chris still hasn't explained the dangers inherent in necking in this particular room.''

Mallory looked around. She thought the kitchen delightfully charming. Perhaps it was a bit faded, the flowered wallpaper no longer so colorful, the chintz curtains no longer crisp. It was spotless, though, the linoleum scrubbed and waxed, the appliances glistening. The only discordant note had been that apron. It hadn't looked as if it belonged in this kitchen, even though the room had obviously been decorated by a woman—Marie Lonergan, Pat's mother, most likely. She had been a farmer's wife, a solid, loving individual. However, that stray apron had looked more as if a French maid had pranced around in it. Sans uniform, at that.

What was the matter with her? She was acting like a jealous shrew.

''Just what,'' Mallory asked, her brow crinkling in distrust, ''does Christopher know about kissing in the kitchen?''

''Not as much as I do,'' Pat assured, capturing her once more.

Mallory put her latest hamburger patty down on a plate and turned in the circle of his arms, her fat-slicked hands held carefully away from his clothing. ''Oh? You have extensive experience?''

As if he saw a trap in her words, Pat's arms tightened, drawing Mallory closer, distracting her with the feel of his hard body pressed intimately against her softness. "I'm looking to extend my experience," he said, and dipped his head to hers.

Mallory avoided his kiss. "Pat."

"Relax, Mal," he said soothingly, content to sample other parts of her face. His lips cruised along her cheek, moved down her throat once more.

"Pat. We have to talk."

"About what? Us?" His words themselves were featherlike kisses against her skin. His hands slid down over her hips, lifted her slightly so that they fit closely together, their bodies adjusting, melting, stirring embers best left slumbering.

It wasn't just the longing kindling in the pit of her stomach that caught at Mallory. It was the ecstasy of that single word. *Us.*

What a wonderful word. But there could never be just an *us* for her and Pat. The word implied two people, not three, and Christopher most definitely made three.

"We have to talk about Chris," Mallory said.

"Later." His mouth caught hers this time, covered it with insistent mastery. His fingers bit into the soft curves of her buttocks, raising her even closer, so that as her breasts pressed against his chest, his own arousal strained against the front of his jeans, against the front of her jeans.

Later, Mallory agreed silently. This was just the first of four days she would spend with him. There was plenty of time to talk. About Chris, about her fears. About *us,* she thought happily, and opened the last lock on her heart.

"Mom!"

Christopher's yell from the other room brought them back to reality.

"Mom! I'm hungry. When's dinner?"

Mallory stared dreamily up into Patrick's eyes. "He's hungry," she said.

"So am I."

Mallory didn't think Pat had food in mind. She knew she most definitely did not.

The fire had burned low in the grate, but Kevin made no move toward the basket of firewood in the corner. Instead, he watched the shadow of his brother against the window as Patrick paced the long expanse of the porch.

After dinner, they had scrounged out the dilapidated board game that had seen them through many a winter's evening as children. Christopher had turned out to be a very competitive player, as had his mother, so the night had passed quickly, and boisterously. There had been no mention of a specific bedtime for the boy, but shortly after nine the excitement of the day had caught up with him, and his eyelids had begun to droop. Mallory had said good-night to the Lonergan men, as well, and gone upstairs to her room at the front of the house. The room directly above.

Kevin and Patrick had discussed the charity distributions to be made for the coming year, but the minister doubted that his brother's mind was on the subject. After a while, Pat had pushed out of their father's recliner, saying he needed a breath of fresh air. He'd been pacing for half an hour now, his footfalls hushed but audible on the wood planking of the porch.

Trust a newly bereaved man to recognize repressed desires, Kevin thought ruefully. He saw them in himself every day, as he waited to hear Beverly's step behind him, to hear her voice once more. He stayed busy with his congregation, but there were still so many times, late at night, when he ached for his beloved wife.

The door opened, Patrick's entrance heralded by a swirling blast of freezing air.

Kevin didn't look up. He continued to lean back in his chair, his legs stretched out toward the fire, his fingers steepled together as he stared over them at the dancing flames. "Feeling better?" he asked.

Pat hadn't worn cold-weather gear outside. The tips of his ears and his cheeks were bright red, nipped as the temperature continued to drop. "Hell, no," he growled, and cast a glance ceilingward. "How can I be, with her in a bed up there and you down here? Talk about getting a stranglehold on a man!"

"You look a wreck," Kevin agreed.

"Thanks loads," Pat snarled. He dropped back onto the sofa and glared into the fireplace.

"Guess I should have kept Chris from interrupting you both in the kitchen earlier," Kevin said.

Patrick shrugged. "What the heck! It wouldn't have made any difference. After all, *you're* still here."

"Ah, yes, in my role as chaperon."

"It was the only way she would consent to come out here," Pat reminded. "You know that as well as I do. You make her feel safe."

"And you make her just plain feel," Kevin said.

"Yeah, well, what good does that do me?"

The brothers were silent, each pondering his own thoughts. The fresh log in the fireplace snapped and popped, sending a spray of sparks out. It was the only sound in the house.

"It isn't just lust," Pat said suddenly, "although certainly that's a big part of it."

"And?" Kevin prompted.

Pat scowled darkly at him. *"And?"* he mimicked. "Hell, Kev, you should have eschewed the ministry and gotten yourself a high-priced shrink's couch. Neurotic women would have dropped like flies at your door, anxious to play mind games with you."

"There's Christopher to think of," Kevin said.

"Okay, so you're reading my mind again, looking for those twin vibes. Yeah, Chris is a complication. As if Mallory didn't invent enough of her own without him. Tell me again about this creep that left her."

Kevin got to his feet and stretched. "Not me, sport. I'm calling it a night. If you want to know about her past, ask Mal herself. But..." Kevin paused for dramatic affect. "But if you do, be sure to tell her about Sun St. John."

Pat chuckled, the sound self-derogatory rather than amused. "One bad past deserves another, huh?"

Kevin nodded in agreement and turned toward the stairs.

"You know what Chris wants, don't you?" Pat asked, his voice halting Kevin at the foot of the staircase. "He wants me to be his dad."

Kevin smiled quietly. "Then I think he made an excellent choice."

Chapter Sixteen

The days went by quickly, and the nights oh, so slowly. Mallory knew that was only because she savored every moment she spent with Patrick and abhorred the hours she lay sleepless and alone in her bed, thinking about him.

Kevin's presence kept her from making a mistake. He was a buffer for her emotions. If such a thing really existed. Each evening, when they said good-night and separated, everyone retreating to a separate bedroom, the hunger in Pat's eyes reflected that in her own. Yet they exchanged nothing more than brief kisses and light caresses, more poignant because they were frequently stolen.

Perhaps as a result, she fell further in love with him.

Or perhaps it was the enchanted life they led at the farm that lured her deeper. Early risings were the norm, enabling them to spend every possible minute together. Pat made pancakes and sausages one morning, Mallory countered with French toast and bacon the next. So, on the third morning, Kevin attempted ham-and-cheese omelets, filling the kitchen with smoke and reducing them all to feasting on Christopher's breakfast specialty, heavily sugared cornflakes.

Afternoons varied from walks through the fields and woods to visits to neighboring farms, where Chris played with children his own age or enthused over a variety of animals. When he developed an attachment to a mewling newborn orange kitten, Pat made arrangements for its adoption when it was older. Although not keen on adding a pet to her household, Mallory agreed. Fetching Chris's kitten would give her a reason to see Pat again. She needed that promise to cling to, treasuring it hopefully within herself.

Evenings were old-fashioned wonders. They spent them gathered around the fireplace, the television ignored, the cozy atmosphere enhanced by convivial board games using the well-battered boards and pieces from the Lonergans' boyhood. Chris was thrilled one night when they roasted marshmallows over the crackling logs, and dumbfounded the next when Pat unearthed an ancient popcorn popper, shaking it steadily over the flames until he'd produced a bowl of fluffy corn without using a microwave.

New Year's Eve dawned clear and sunny. Kevin announced his intention of visiting a couple of old friends, and had soon turned his Oldsmobile west, heading back toward Greenville. Christopher voiced his longing to play in the tree house, and had soon enlisted Pat to do safety repairs on it. Mallory nixed the suggestion that she play carpenter's helper and nestled in a comfy armchair with a book. She didn't read, though. She watched the masculine byplay in the yard, the way the man interacted with the boy, teaching him the correct way to hold a hammer, guiding him as together they replaced rotten boards.

It would have been so easy for Pat to brush Chris off, to palm him off with an excuse, rather than make the effort to rebuild the old tree house. He hadn't. And that fact left Mallory simply enchanted.

And afraid.

Time was running out. She didn't know what she wanted, or for what she hoped. Her fantasies were of impossible things. Or, at least, highly improbable things. It was all very well to admit to being in love with Pat Lonergan. Another thing to believe he would return her love, would want her—and Christopher—to be a part of his life.

Even that dream didn't take into consideration the stumbling blocks. Chris wanted a father, had chosen the man he wanted to fill the role and asked his mother to marry the candidate. It was all so easy to her son. At his age, he couldn't see that distance alone was a complication. Although she daydreamed of free-lance work, she still had a career, a position of responsibility, one she had worked hard to achieve. Could she actually give it up? It was time-consuming, demanding flexible hours and easy traveling distance to the store. Rather like the U.S. Mail, Mallory was expected to be available and on hand through sun, rain, sleet, snow, or dark of night. Patrick owned a three-hundred-acre farm an hour's drive from the city. He couldn't leave it, and she didn't favor a two-hour commute every day, sometimes having to travel the route late at night.

When she dreamed, the commonsense aspects vanished. In them there was no desk awaiting her at Rittenhouse. There were only stolen moments, laughter, warmth, love.

And children.

Talk about complications!

How many events in Christopher's life had she missed? She'd agonized over them, torn between her job and home. There had been his first step, practiced and executed under a baby-sitter's casual eye, rather than her loving one. His first word—she'd thought it was *Ma,* until the sitter explained he was calling for a bottle of milk, rather than his mother. If she'd been home with him, Mallory was sure she would have meant more to her son than a bottle of milk.

When she had other children, she didn't want to be tied to a desk miles away. When she—

Mallory jolted to a halt, her mind no longer a fuzzy confusion of dreams. Just a few short weeks ago, her life had been set, running on a smooth track, each step carefully prepared for and executed. Her friendships had been as meticulously chosen and pursued as were the orders for merchandise at Rittenhouse. She had cultivated very few, had held herself distant from those who sought her out. It was only over the past few months that she had moved a step closer to Kevin Lonergan, indulging in a friendship that she knew would remain platonic. She had convinced herself that his influence was all the masculine guidance Christopher would need.

She'd been wrong.

Not only in believing Chris would be content with the few minutes Kevin could give him, but in believing that she herself would be content. That she ever *had* been content in forswearing the needs that had surfaced recently.

Had she been more susceptible to Pat's charm because he was Kevin's brother? Had her guard been down?

Or had she simply been little more than a sexually repressed volcano, so sensitized that she had blown at the first brush of his lips against hers?

It was definitely time to realign her priorities. To decide what she wanted to do with her life.

Again.

Once more, all because of a man.

Mallory stared out at the pleasant countryside, her mind stubbornly refusing to take the next step. It was far too pleasant watching Pat and Christopher working together in the yard.

Her two handsome men.

The call came that evening as they were sitting down to dinner—a bucket of fried chicken that Kevin brought back from Greenville.

Between bites, Chris was excitedly recounting in great detail the adventure of the tree fort. First a snow fort, now a tree fort, Mallory mused. Her son's vocabulary had taken a twist in the past few weeks. One that showed he was definitely male, and proud of it. Building had been only one of his many interests that day. After hammering his share of crooked nails, Chris had moved on to chasing chickens, beating his mother at checkers, attempting unsuccessfully to win entrance to Pat's office and carefully guarded computer and finally drawing a series of pictures of the farm to show to his best friend, Jeff. He had also tried to wheedle permission to stay up until midnight so that he could celebrate the New Year. With his obnoxious behavior of Christmas Eve clear yet in her mind, Mallory prepared to kill that idea when his normal bedtime arrived.

The ringing of the phone caught both the Lonergan men with their mouths full of chicken, so Mallory got to her feet and moved into the office to answer it. She was glad the others were still in the kitchen and thus unable to read her face. Emotions struggled for dominance—sorrow, excitement, fear, desire. Hope.

"I'm sorry to interrupt the fun, Mal," Fran's voice murmured, her tone alone declaring the call was serious, "but I need to talk to Kevin."

"Just let me get him," Mallory said softly, and put the phone down. Out at the table, both the men looked up as she reentered the room. Kevin's face registered mild curiosity, while Pat's juggled concern and fear.

"The store?" he asked.

Mallory shook her head, and was rewarded with a glimpse of relief in his eyes. She turned to Kevin. "It's for you. I don't think it's happy news."

Kevin pushed back his chair and stood up. "Looks like my vacation might be over," he said, and left the table to take the call.

Christopher continued to chatter, detailing the things he wanted to do the next day, before they returned home, but neither of the adults paid him the least heed. Mallory stared at Pat, knowing the thought most prevalent in her mind held center stage in his, as well. If Kevin left, the restraint they had both kept on their relationship would be gone.

Perhaps it would be best if she left, too. It would ensure that their relationship stayed at its current nonthreatening level. They could both return to their normal lives, avoid the entanglements that loomed.

Instead of voicing the suggestion, instead of taking the safest course, Mallory bit into the crispy coating of a chicken wing and kept her counsel.

"I thought I might go pick up some dessert before the stores close," Pat suggested, his voice a bit too casual.

Mallory met his gaze steadily.

Christopher bounced in his chair. "Can I go, too?"

Pat pushed back his plate. "Not this time, sport. Do a few laps in the bathtub, so you're ready for the champagne at midnight." He turned back to Mallory, his manner overly casual. "We probably need more milk for breakfast. I'll get a few other things, as well. That all right with you?"

It was out in the open now. With the nonchalant, albeit coded request, Pat had just asked her to take the next step. The dangerous step. The one from which she couldn't back down. The one she'd been thinking about ever since he first kissed her. Pat had just asked her to sleep with him and, in the same breath, he'd let her know that this time he would provide protection.

Her heart was pumping so loudly she was sure that Kevin would hear it in the next room and decide not to leave. Her mouth was dry, her stomach clenched. It was New Year's Eve, a time for resolutions, a time for new beginnings.

Mallory licked her lips nervously. "Yes," she said, her voice hushed and barely audible. "Why don't you pick up some *things.*"

Kevin left within the hour, headed back to the city to take his place at Fred Woods's hospital bedside. The elderly man had slipped and broken his hip. Kevin intended to stay near the elderly man until his daughter could fly in from California.

Pat was out the door moments later, headed into Greenville for his last-minute shopping. To keep herself busy, Mallory cleaned the remains of dinner away and supervised Christopher's bath. She barely knew what she was doing. All she could think of was the evening yet to come.

Pat was back by the time Chris was dry and dressed in flannel pajamas, robe and slippers. While Mallory lingered upstairs, Chris rushed down to begin the evening's festivities. She brushed her hair, then debated putting on makeup or changing her clothes. In the end, she joined them with just a fresh coat of lip gloss.

The main parlor looked decadent. Was it merely Kevin's absence? Mallory wondered. Most evenings, cushions and floor pillows had been piled before the fireplace. Tonight, the stack looked like something from a Turkish seraglio. Christopher sat upon them like a sultan, a party hat rather than a turban on his head, streamers of narrow adding-machine tape draped around his neck, his legs crossed Indian-fashion. There was a plastic champagne glass in his hand, a slightly amber-tinted liquid bubbling in its bowl.

Pat was seated on the floor, as well, his own neck draped with similar streamers. He held up a bottle of ginger ale, and a second glass. "Ah, at last. I was beginning to think Chris and I would have to drink all this champagne ourselves," he said.

Mallory sank onto a vacant sofa cushion and accepted the plastic goblet of pseudochampagne.

Chris blew heavily into a noisemaker and tossed a handful of shredded computer paper and adding-machine streamers over her head. "Happy New Year!" he shouted.

"Well, not quite yet," Mallory said.

"Almost," Christopher insisted, and pointed to the mantel clock. The hands were nearly touching at the topmost marker, clearly showing that it was just minutes until midnight.

Mallory glanced at her watch. It claimed it was only a quarter after eight. "Well, so it is!" she exclaimed.

"You obviously lost track of time while primping for us," Pat said.

"It happens," Mallory murmured, and slipped yet another notch deeper in love. He thought of everything, making things special for her, for Chris.

"Know what happens at midnight?" Chris demanded after another toot on his noisemaker.

"You grow a foot?" Pat suggested.

The boy's eyes widened, his mouth forming a perfect O. "Do I?" he asked excitedly.

"No, you don't," Mallory said. "It just seems like it." Another year almost finished. Soon he'd have another birthday, would move another step closer to manhood.

"Oh." Chris took another gulp of ginger ale. "Well, I know what happens at midnight. Icky stuff. You have to kiss girls."

Mallory looked sharply at Patrick. He grinned. Wickedly. Wonderfully.

"A man has got to know what he's up against when he stays up until midnight on New Year's Eve," Pat explained. "Fortunately for us all, you're the only girl in sight."

"And I like kissing you, Mom," Christopher assured her seriously.

"Thank you," Mallory said. "I appreciate your sacrifice." She glanced at the adjusted clock. Two minutes to go. "Maybe you'd better fortify yourself with more of this delicious champagne. I know I certainly need more."

Pat poured a bit more ginger ale in her glass. "Wonderful vintage, isn't it?"

"A good year?"

"Absolutely. This year," he said. "I met you, didn't I?"

Mallory's head swam dizzily, as if she were actually sipping champagne. Why was it that Pat Lonergan made her act as if she were a giddy teenager? Why did he make her feel so...so... So very like the girl she'd once been. The one who'd taken chances.

"Let's see," Pat murmured. "Have we got everything covered for this party, Chris? We've got the hats..."

He plunked a pointy silver-colored one on Mallory's head.

"...noisemakers..."

He blew into a whistle, producing a whirling sound that had Chris insisting he had to try it.

"...confetti..."

Mallory contributed by tossing a fresh handful of shredded paper over Pat's head.

"...champagne, and a girl to kiss. Seems like we're missing something." Pat pondered a moment, stroking his chin as he thought. Mallory saw him glance at the clock. "I know! The countdown! Chris! What time is it?"

Christopher leaped to his feet. His hat sat at a tipsy angle; his eyes glowed with excitement. "Almost midnight!" he shouted.

Pat got to his feet, as well, and pulled Mallory up. "Get ready!" he warned.

Mallory was nearly as worked up as Chris, but for an entirely different reason.

"Ten," Pat said. "Nine...eight..." He stared down into Mallory's eyes.

She was barely breathing.

"Seven, six..." Chris continued.

Mallory moved into Pat's arms. "Five, four..." she whispered.

"Hell," he growled under his breath. "It's too long to wait."

There was a wave lapping at her feet, eroding the foundation of the walls she'd built around her heart. "Three . . . t—"

He swallowed the rest of her count, his mouth covering hers hungrily.

"One. Happy New Year!" Christopher crowed as the clock began tolling twelve. "Hey! You cheated!"

Pat broke off the kiss, bent and swept the boy up to their level. "It's allowed. She's your mom, but she's my girl."

The tide was coming in, the waves of love encroaching higher, building within her heart, her mind, her soul.

"Oh," Chris said, easily accepting Pat's statement. "But I get to be next," the child insisted.

Higher and higher the waves built. Mallory hugged her son tightly. "Happy New Year, sweetheart." It felt so right to have Patrick's strong arms encircling them both.

Christopher planted a smacking kiss on her lips.

"Trying to outdo me, are you?" Pat demanded, and let the child slide back to his feet. "Why don't you go get dessert now?"

"Cool!" the boy said and dashed out of the room.

"What is dessert?" Mallory asked.

"For me? You."

The waves lapped, their insistence nearly more than she could bear. Mallory grinned up at him, snuggling into his embrace. "I think I'll like that."

"I intend to make sure you do," Pat said. "Now, where was I before Short Stuff interrupted me?" He pulled her back tightly, slanted his lips over hers.

Lost in sensation, Mallory felt the wave engulf her.

Chapter Seventeen

Patrick paused in the doorway of the room that had once been his, propped his shoulders against the doorjamb as his father had often done on other evenings, and watched as the woman he loved settled her child in his nest of blankets for the night.

Family life was a ritual. The cycle repeated itself with little variation. Different generations, different men, different women, different children. The emotions didn't change. Watching Mallory and Christopher, Pat felt his heart swell with love. Not just for the tender mother, but for her child, as well.

He had never thought to find himself in this cycle again. Having outgrown his original part, he'd thought that there was no longer a place for him in the setting. He had never seen himself as a husband, much less a father, but both roles seemed to appeal to him now.

She looked so right in his house.

Felt so right in his arms.

Watching her with her son in his old room was the final jewel in the crown. Or it would be when he knew she would be repeating the endless cycle beneath his roof, not just with Chris, but with children of their own, a new generation of Lonergans, conceived in boundless love.

He had never felt this way about another woman. Had little memory of any other woman any longer. Mallory had swept them from his mind, replacing them, surpassing them. He was eager to love her with his body, to consummate the emotional passion with the physical need. He had known Sunshine St. John for many long years, and Mallory for just a few short weeks. Yet he knew Mallory intimately, having fallen in love with her spirit, while Sun was still little more than a stranger, after all this time.

Once he had thought Sun one of the most beautiful women he'd ever met. Wherever they went, men had drooled over her, and something in him had swelled, a pride as physical as that of a cock among the hens in his barnyard. He had enjoyed having Sun on his arm, in his bed. But that was all they'd ever had, the physical shell of a relationship.

Ah, Mallory. She was a field of waving grain, acre upon acre of tall, ripening corn. She was Mother Earth, warm, nurturing and loving.

From the brief glimpse of her past that Kevin had allowed him, Pat knew Mallory had built a new life from the ashes of her innocence. Had overcome the snares of rearing a child on her own, of being a woman on her own. Her aunt had been there for her, but it wasn't Anita who had made Mallory the woman he loved. It was her own strength.

She was a remarkable woman. In a situation that could have destroyed her, scarred her for life, Mallory had survived. Although she'd built walls to protect herself, and Christopher, from repeating the past, she hadn't totally cut herself off from the world. She might have avoided romantic involvements, but she hadn't blamed all men for the failings of the one who'd failed to be a true man, the man who'd deserted her. Her friendship with his brother, Kevin, was evidence of that. However, her response to him had been quite different, Pat decided.

No, Pat's relationship with Mallory was special—had been from the first. And who knew what it could become in the future?

For the moment, though, all he wanted to do was to participate in the ritualistic cycle, to play counterpoint to her as Chris was settled for the night.

The last traces of the boy's gastronomic orgy of chocolate cake had been wiped from his face and hands. His teeth had been rescrubbed. His eyelids drooped, and a proud and contented, if sleepy, smile curved his lips, compliments of his mistaken belief that he had weathered the hours, staying up until 2:00 a.m. Despite the diligent efforts of the sandman, Christopher was endeavoring to assert his coming manhood by fighting to stay awake.

"I'm not sleepy yet," he insisted. "Can I have a story?"

"A story?" Mallory echoed in mock surprise.

A warm glow of lamplight spilled over mother and son, highlighting them, while leaving the rest of the room in shadow. Mallory was perched on the side of the bed, her stance and expression so reminiscent of his mother that Pat could almost see Marie Lonergan in her place. Mallory brushed a lock of hair back from the boy's brow, the very gesture a reflection of love and tenderness.

"Haven't you done enough this evening?" she asked the child. "I would think a party animal like you would be worn out by now."

"Not much," Chris murmured, forcing his eyes wide in an effort to convince her.

"Maybe a quick, short story then," Mallory relented. "What would you like it to be about?"

Chris stifled a yawn. "I don't know." His gaze traveled the room, as if he were searching for inspiration. Pat could see it strike as the boy's eyes lit on his lazy stance in the archway. "Could you tell me a story, Pat?"

The request allowed him to take the step forward, to become an intimate part of their close family circle. "I suppose that could be arranged," Patrick said, and strolled toward the bed. There was a cautious look in Mallory's eyes, probably disbelief over his storytelling abilities. He met it with a grin and settled next to her on Chris's bedside. He slid an arm around her, urging her subtly to lean back against his chest. She did so as if it were the most natural thing in the world.

"For a kid like you, I'm sure we need a lot of adventure in the tale," Pat mused. Adventure was the farthest thing from his own mind. At the moment, the comfort and contentment of home life held much more appeal. Pat nuzzled Mallory's hair, breathing in the sweet scent, savoring the silky texture. "And romance," he added. "Every decent adventure story has a damsel to rescue."

Christopher snuggled down into the fluffy softness of his pillow. "Just like in a video game," he said.

"It just so happens that once upon a time there was a beautiful princess who didn't need rescuing," Pat began.

"She already had a handsome young prince to chase dragons from her door."

"What was her name?" Christopher asked.

Pat's arm tightened around Mallory's waist, drawing her closer against him. "Mallory," he said.

"Like Mom."

"I think it's a lovely name for a princess," Mallory said. Her hand slid along Pat's arm until her fingers reached his, entwining intimately with them. "Did the handsome young prince have a name, too?"

"Rover," Pat answered.

"That's a dog's name," Christopher insisted.

Pat nodded. "Well, of course it is. You see, the castle wizard had turned the prince into a guard dog, so he could protect Princess Mallory all the better."

"What kind of dog?"

"Chihuahua."

"What's that?"

"A tiny little dog with a big, loud yap," Pat answered promptly. "Reminds me a lot of you, sport."

Christopher giggled. His eyelids dipped, lingering a moment longer than previously before he forced them upward again. "Then what happened?"

"The inevitable, that's what. You see, word was out among the dragons of the world that Princess Mallory was the most beautiful woman in the universe, and a prize worth capturing."

Mallory's head rolled on Patrick's shoulder. "What does a dragon do with a princess once he's captured her?" she wondered softly.

"Plays checkers with her, of course. Princesses are notoriously good checker players," he said.

Christopher's eyes were closed, his long lashes creating perfect crescents against his cheeks. "Checkers," he mumbled.

"There was this one really crafty dragon who hadn't had a decent checker partner in a long time," Pat continued softly. "When he faced the princely pup, he quivered in fear. This pleased the guardian immensely, and threw him off guard. But he was curious about what the dragon had hidden behind his back. 'Nothing but a magic stick,' said the crafty dragon. 'It can make your favorite dream come true.' Well, Rover had a favorite dream of his own that he wanted with all his heart to come true. 'Give me the magic stick,' he told the quivering dragon. 'Okay,' the dragon said and tossed the stick far out over a field, so that the princely dog had to chase it."

Mallory leaned forward to turn the lamp off, then resettled in the circle of Pat's arms.

Christopher's chest rose in soft, regular breaths, indicating he was asleep.

"The dragon was very crafty indeed," Mallory said. "Then what happened?"

The story was no longer for the boy. Perhaps it always had belonged to her. The room was lit only by a faint spill of moonlight. Her eyes were gleaming as brightly as stars in the winter sky.

Pat's voice dropped to a husky murmur. "The dragon pushed down the castle door and carried the princess off to bed, where he made sweet, passionate love to her all night long."

"What about the checker game?"

"He lied about it," Pat said, and stood up. He pulled her to her feet, swept her up into his arms, cradling her to his chest.

Mallory nestled close, linked one arm around his neck, ran the knuckles of her other hand along his beard-roughened jawline in a tender caress. "There are so many things I want to tell you," Mallory whispered huskily. "I—"

"Hush." The past had made her the woman she was, but it was behind them. Only the future mattered. The immediate future.

Pat kissed her gently. "The dragon had a darn good idea, as far as I'm concerned. And for the past two weeks, I've been thinking about making love with you constantly."

"Constantly?" Her starry eyes were those of Eve, shining with deep secrets, mysterious promises and boundless hope.

Pat carried her across the room. Two steps, and they were in the front bedroom, the one his mother had papered in a soft yellow-and-white pastel flower print, the one room that seemed made with Mallory Meyers specifically in mind.

The bed was wide, the headboard and footboard polished to a gleaming brass. A delicately shaded autumn-gold patchwork spread covered it, enhanced by yellowed antique-lace bolsters and ruffled pillows. It had been Marie Lonergan's retreat.

He laid Mallory tenderly in the center of the welcoming bed. Kicked off his shoes, and tugged his sweater over his head, tossing it aside. When he pressed one knee into the mattress, Mallory opened her arms to him, slid her fingers into his thick hair and drew him down to her waiting lips.

They'd been through the preliminaries before, a week earlier, in the dark hours of Christmas morning. He knew how she responded to his touch, her body arching toward his in an age-old dance of give-and-take.

"I want you," she said, her voice tinged with wonder.

Patrick reveled in the words, but realized that her confession did not mean the future he envisioned was a sure thing. In the past, Mallory had learned not to trust any man. In welcoming him now, she was taking one small step. The larger one was yet to come. When he asked her to join her life to his, would she balk or let his love be the factor that healed past hurts?

"Then I'll make you want me even more," Pat murmured.

Mallory sighed in contentment, swelling his ego nicely. When he reached for the buttons of her blouse, his hands were shaking. His future seemed to hinge on his performance over the next few hours. And the future had never meant so much to him before.

To cover his sudden ineptitude, Pat kissed her, drinking deeply of her sweetness. She tasted of ginger ale and devil's food cake, flavors he had never thought of as particularly carnal before. Her scent was soft and flowery, with overtones of beech smoke, a token from the fire in the parlor fireplace. Pat breathed in, savoring her every scent; teased her, sending his tongue to slowly explore her mouth. Mallory countered with a boldness that surprised and tantalized him. Her nails scored lightly up his bare chest, tracing paths that her mouth soon traveled. She slithered down his body, reacquainting herself with previously explored territory, blazing new and exotic trails when her fingers met his belt and dispensed with it.

He had kept their lovemaking under control on Christmas. It had been almost tepid, giving Mallory a taste of what was to come, without pushing her into total acquiescence. She had given herself before, fully knowing a man in the past. Christopher was the evidence. Pat vowed to himself that he would not let her make that mistake again. Although his hands had frequently strayed below her waist that night, he had caught her own when they tried to claim more intimate knowledge of his own body. So now, when she eased the zipper of his jeans down, freeing his swollen and pulsing shaft, he nearly lost control.

"Mal."

Her name was a gasp that gave her power over him, made her even bolder. She rubbed against him, as content and playful as a kitten. Her fingertips slid along the hot, hard length of him, returned upward in a sensuous glide that skimmed over his sensitized skin. "Yes?" she purred.

"You're rushing things," he said, his voice husky, breathless as he fought to contain his passion.

"Just refamiliarizing myself with the tools available," Mallory whispered. "It's been such a long time for me. Perhaps I've forgotten how...."

His mouth swallowed her words at the same time he captured her wrists and pulled her hands from their tender ministrations. Soon she was the one beyond conscious thought, writhing in pleasure. In short order, he stripped her clothing away, rid himself of his own. Her legs slipped around him, tightened at his waist, drawing him to her in a silent command.

She was many things to him, her roles numerous and varied. The demanding goddess was new, and totally tantalizing.

"Dear Sir Dragon." Her voice was low, the husky growl of a hunting tigress. And he was her prey.

Patrick shifted, fitting himself against her eager, waiting flesh. "Do you wish a boon, my princess?"

She chuckled softly. "Is that what it's called? I was rather hoping for that adventure, the one where a princess gets rescued."

He moved, his body poised for entry and straining as he delayed the moment. "And from what do you need rescuing, Princess?" He pressed forward, teasing her, stretching his own control to the limit.

Mallory gave a very satisfactory noise, part gasp, part moan. "From endless games of checkers," she murmured. "I need a new game to play."

"Or perhaps just a few new moves," Pat suggested. Slowly, he entered her tight canal. Mallory's nails bit into his shoulders, her body arched with pleasure. The pleasure multiplied for him as she closed around him. "Oh, Mal. You feel so good," he ground out, teeth clenched as he held back.

"Ohhh..." She shuddered deliciously beneath him. "I like this."

Her response was nearly his undoing. "Mal?"

Her answer was incoherent. His timing was probably all wrong, but suddenly Pat knew he had to make the leap toward his own dream now.

"I love you, Mal."

Her grip on his shoulders lessened. Mallory blinked up at him, her expression growing puzzled. "Love?" She gulped the word.

"Yes" he insisted harshly, and thrust sharply, burying himself deep within her. "Tell me you love me, too."

She was on the edge, nearly convulsing around him. He could feel the tension in her body, see the clouds of passion that swirled in her eyes. But she was a stubborn woman, a princess who, when in trouble, had always saved herself. "I..."

He needed her to save him now. Save him from the twilight world in which he'd been living for so long. Pat withdrew slightly, then thrust forward again. "I love you, Mal."

He wasn't sure she heard him. Her head was thrown back, her throat arched as she strained toward her peak.

His own body urged him to follow her lead, to seek further pleasure. Pat fell into the rhythm, sliding deep, retreating, riding the building tide. "Tell me you love me," he repeated, his voice pleading hoarsely now.

Mallory shivered, tripping over the precipice, spiraling out of control as passion crested. "Yesss," she moaned.

Pat held himself back, while driving her further. "Not good enough, Mal." Sweat stood out on his brow. The tendons in his back strained. His whole body was stretched taut.

Her body moved with his now, insistent, demanding. Her mouth was hot against his skin, greedy. Urgent.

He claimed her lips again, his hunger for her rapacious, his need to hear her say the words fading as the needs of his body began to spiral out of control. Then they were soaring together, her body quivering around his as his spilled life into hers.

It was only when he lay gasping and spent, still joined with her intimately, that she murmured his name, gave him his answer.

"I love you, Pat."

She fell asleep immediately, cradled where she belonged, in his arms. For the first time in a long time, Pat felt a supreme sense of contentment. Pulling the blankets up around them, he stared into the night, a slight smile curving his lips.

The New Year looked very bright, and oh, so appealing.

Chapter Eighteen

Christopher awoke with a sense that great things were in the air. He'd been dreaming that he lived in a tree, rather like the Lost Boys in *Peter Pan,* and that, also like Peter Pan's men, he could stay up as long as he liked.

His sleep-filled eyes blinked as they focused, not on the branches of a tree and clear blue skies, but on four white walls. They weren't the same as the ones in his room. In place of his cartoon posters were pennants from places he'd never heard of, and framed photographs of teams of people he didn't know.

Oh, yeah, he thought, his fuzzy mind coming back into focus. This was Pat's old room. He was at the farm.

And—this memory cheered him immensely—he had stayed up *really* late last night.

The sad part was, this was also their last day in the country. Tomorrow he would be back in school. Ick!

The house was quiet. That meant his mom was still asleep. Otherwise he would have heard her singing along with the radio while she made coffee. He didn't know what Pat would be doing. Feeding the chickens, maybe. Or playing with his computer. That was what he usually did before everybody else got up. Christopher grinned to himself. He figured it was a secret, because Pat always stopped the second he heard anyone coming downstairs. That made him sort of like Mom, since she always stopped singing when somebody might be able to hear her.

Being at the farm was a lot of fun. Chris liked the kids who lived down the road; he liked their kittens, liked having all this space to run in if he wanted and not have to worry about crossing busy streets. It was quiet in the country, too, which was kind of strange and kind of nice. And he had a tree fort. If he lived here, maybe he could talk his mom into letting him sleep in it in the summer. Then he could have cool adventures, like the Lost Boys.

Maybe he could have one now, before Mom woke up!

Christopher scrambled out of bed and into the bathroom.

The door to his mother's room was closed. Usually it stood open, and sometimes he'd hop on her bed, and wake her up by snuggling under the covers with her. She always looked pretty in the morning, and sometimes funny, when her hair stuck out. She always smelled nice when she cuddled him, all the while grouching about having to get up. She never meant it. It was just a game they played.

The closed door meant she'd worked late and needed extra sleep. At home he'd made her a Do Not Disturb sign with a really mean face on it to scare people away. She'd had to help him spell *Disturb,* but he knew what it meant—wake her only if something was on fire or there was blood involved.

The door to Pat's room was open, but his bed was empty and made. Chris figured that meant his friend was downstairs playing with his computer. It also meant that, if he hurried and got dressed, Pat would probably fix him some pancakes. With that incentive in mind, Chris scrambled into his clothes quickly.

There was no sign of Pat downstairs, though. The office was quiet, the computer not even doing its quiet little humming. Chris walked slowly around the desk, his fingers trailing along the surface and walking wistfully across the keyboard. His friend Jeff's family had a computer, and it played really neat games. He'd used it a few times, and they had some at the school that played learning games. But Pat said his PC wasn't a toy, and not to touch it.

Christopher heaved a big sigh and left the office, his feet dragging.

In the front room, the party stuff was gone. The cushions were back on the sofa, the pillows all piled in a neat row along it. Christopher switched on the TV, clicking the remote, changing channels in search of cartoons. He found a lot of grown-ups talking and laughing as they sat around in chairs, but no cartoons. There was a VCR, but a search through nearby cupboards showed that Pat didn't own any movies. Chris sighed again. As if in answer, his stomach growled, demanding breakfast.

He knew where everything was kept in the kitchen. He pulled one of the kitchen chairs away from the table and climbed up to get a cereal bowl and the package of corn-flakes from the shelf. There was a new carton of milk in the refrigerator, and he only spilled a little of it trying to pour it out. He added two heaping extra spoonfuls of sugar to the cereal, leaving a trail of granules from the sugar bowl to his cereal bowl. This, he had to admit, was the best part of his mom sleeping in. Nobody around to tell him he had enough sugar. Chris stuck his finger in the bowl for good measure and savored the sticky sweetness as he then sucked it clean.

Once breakfast was behind him, and still no adult had put in an appearance, Chris was at a loss as to what to do. Again, the lure of the computer drew him back to Pat's office. It was OFF-LIMITS. The way Pat had told him that had put the words in capital letters, just like the words he'd used on the sign for his mother's door.

So where was Pat?

Christopher went to the window in the office and looked out. There were still some patches of snow on the ground, but they were gray and mushy. He could see the tree with the newly repaired fort in its branches. There were some chickens pecking around on the ground. He hoped they didn't try to get in his fort. It was for boys only, no girls allowed, and he knew that most of the chickens were girl chickens.

There was no sign of Pat, though. Desperate for company, and looking for something to do, Christopher meandered back to the desk. Maybe there was some paper he could draw on. He tried the drawers. They were all locked. There was nothing to do in this stupid house. The only toy was the computer, and Pat was being mean and not sharing it. Christopher punched his fist down in frustration on the alluring keyboard.

The computer hummed to life.

Christopher jumped back in the chair, staring at it fearfully. He glanced quickly around, expecting either Pat to appear or an evil guardian genie to jump him. When neither happened, he was emboldened to lean forward.

Good morning. The words printed themselves across the computer monitor. The computer was talking to him!

What would you like to play with today? it asked.

All right! At least the computer wanted him to have fun. It gave him a selection of pictures in little boxes. Okay, he knew what that meant. He used the little arrow that they called a mouse. Why didn't it look like a mouse, then?

Chris slid the control around, sending the arrow on the screen ricocheting from a tiny smiling cow to a stupid-looking pig to pictures of barns, and some he figured were cities, since there was more than one building. He by-passed a drawing of an egg with a little chicken's head popping out, deciding to see what the snarling dragon was, instead. The arrow glided onto the icon. Chris tapped the button on the mouse twice and waited for the opening screen of a game to appear.

The monitor unrolled column upon column of figures instead.

That wasn't right. There should be a castle and some knights in armor or a pretty princess in a tower who needed rescuing. There should be pathways littered with traps, and demons to disperse for extra bonus points.

Something was definitely wrong. This looked more like the scores of previous players. He didn't care to know what the competition had done. He wanted to play the game.

Chris tapped the mouse again.

Do you want to erase file? it asked.

Yes, he wanted this screen wiped away. Stupid machine. Didn't it know anything? Chris moved the mouse to the square marked *Yes* on the menu.

Are you sure?

Chris smacked the mouse a little more vehemently. *Yes!*

Wah Sung Produce file erased, the computer declared with a cheerful little blip of sound. Chris waited, but the screen did nothing but stare at him. No familiar game setting materialized.

This was really a stupid computer. So, what should he do now? Chris dropped off the chair and wandered over to the window again. Maybe it would snow, and he could make an army of snowmen to guard his tree fort. He checked the sky. There wasn't a cloud in it. Stupid weather. He stared off across the fields, wondering if his new friends at the next farm would have finished their chores and be ready to play yet.

Then he saw it. The invasion. There was a hen strutting around in his fort, surveying the fortifications. Looking for a place to make a nest!

"Hey!" Christopher shouted against the window. The chicken ignored him. She pecked at a board, testing it. Incensed, Chris dashed out of the room, through the kitchen, stopping only long enough to grab his coat, then slammed out the back door, set to repel invaders.

Forgotten, the computer's cursor blinked silently, the pat announcement of Chris's deed glowing on the screen.

Patrick jolted upright at the sound of the door slamming. *What the—* Next to him, Mallory mumbled in her sleep and snuggled closer against his side.

Pat relaxed back against the pillow once more. It was a new year and it was starting off with a bang. He smiled to himself, content with the changes about to occur. Funny how, after all this time, he finally knew exactly what he wanted the future to hold.

What do you think of that, Mom? he mused. *Thought it would never happen, didn't you?*

Marie Lonergan had long despaired of her younger son. He, like all the ten-year-old boys in his school, had been vehement in his announcement that he would never get married, determined to never have anything to do with girls. Since by age twelve Patrick had discovered girls weren't so bad, and by fifteen had gained a reputation at the high school as a stud, no one ever thought that at thirty-five he would still be a bachelor.

His mother had fretted the most about the way women rotated through his life, gaining favor one month and being replaced the next. She'd never met Sunshine St. John, but Pat knew his fond parent would have disliked Sun as much as Kevin had.

"Marriage is a lot like fishing," Michael Lonergan, his father, had once said. "Anybody can throw a line in, but only one special angler is going to take home the ten-pounder." Pat could almost see his father leaning back in one of the kitchen chairs, tilting the front legs up off the floor. It always irritated his mother when his father did that. "Don't you worry, honey," he'd told her soothingly. "When the right woman comes along, she'll reel in that boy of yours just like you did me."

Pat glanced fondly at the woman who slept on at his side. Damned if his father hadn't been right.

She was just as beautiful asleep as she was awake. A warm blush colored her cheeks, the innocent curve of her dark lashes against her creamy skin reminiscent of her son's. He could only see the top half of her face, since the lower was buried under the quilt as she sheltered in its cocoon of warmth.

She was his now, claimed and consummated. And it wasn't nearly enough.

How had this slip of a woman gotten so deep beneath his skin? How had she become so important to him, so necessary to his being, in such a short time? The thought of a future without her was unthinkable, and so, to guarantee that his dream came true, he was going to take the ultimate step. A leap of faith where his happiness and Mallory's was concerned. He was going to ask her to marry him. Just as soon as she opened those gorgeous gray eyes.

Mallory sighed in her sleep and snuggled deeper into the bed, her long legs entwining with his beneath the covers.

Well, maybe he'd make love to her again first, then propose.

Gently, Pat dropped a kiss on Mallory's tousled curls. She smiled in her sleep, nuzzling against his chest, but she didn't awaken. She needed her rest after last night, he mused with a satisfied grin. Patience, Lonergan. From now on, you've got all the time in the world.

He slid from beneath the quilt, careful not to disturb Mallory. The clothes he'd worn the night before lay scattered on the floor. Carelessly he gathered them up and tossed them toward the laundry hamper. Then, naked, he returned to his own room.

There was more than just a beautiful, warm, loving woman in his life now. Since the sun was high in the sky, there was, without a doubt, a hungry boy roaming his house. If he was going to be a father, he had to take care of details like that as well as make love to the child's mother.

As he'd guessed, the room allotted to Christopher was empty, the bedclothes trailing away across the floor as if they'd tried to follow the child out the door. All was quiet downstairs. Pat guessed that the boy had hightailed it to the barn, to chase chickens or look for eggs as the neighbor's kids had shown him to do. Which was the more prudent course? Take a shower or throw clothes on and track Chris down? A glance at his bedside clock told Pat it was well after ten. That meant he would skip the shower. The kid was probably starving by now.

At least Chris hadn't barged in on his mother. The boy had taken to the sight of Pat kissing Mallory, but seeing them in bed together might have been a jolt he wasn't prepared to weather just yet. They'd have to have a talk, Pat decided. Man to man. Because there was no way in hell that he was going to forgo making love to Mallory Meyers while waiting for her to become Mrs. Patrick Lonergan.

Pat pulled on jeans, boots and a heavy sweater, ran a hand through his hair and scratched absently at the dark stubble that covered his jaw. What was there in his limited culinary repertoire that would interest a six-year-old boy? Cinnamon toast? If there was any bread left. It was amazing how much food a kid his size could put away. He'd have to get used to that. Pat smiled as he went down the staircase, a decided spring in his step. There were a lot of things he would be getting used to, and he was going to enjoy every one of them.

The evidence of Christopher's movements was clear and rather sticky in the kitchen. The carton of milk sat on the table, along with the opened box of cereal, the bowl of sugar, and a half-finished serving of cornflakes, with a spoon sinking beneath the soggy mess remaining. The television was off, but the doors of the adjacent cabinets were open, as if a search had been in progress and hastily abandoned. What else had the tyke been up to?

Because it was a normal part of his day, it took a moment for Pat to realize that the quiet humming sound coming from his office was in reality ominous.

Okay, he told himself. The kid was curious. He was on his own, without adult supervision. He was only six years old. A precocious six, but still only six. There were some things a boy that age could not resist. He had only to look back at his own checkered boyhood, count the trips he taken with his father out behind the woodshed, to recognize that truth. So what if Chris had turned the computer on? The Dow-Jones was closed today, and there was no way that Christopher could tamper with his spreadsheets and data bases. The boy had obviously turned the PC on, and then, finding there were no video games available, had simply wandered off as he had done in the front room. They'd have to have a talk about keeping hands off things that didn't belong to you. And to ensure that it never happened again, he'd buy Chris his own computer. A wedding present, he hoped, to his new son.

There was no sense in having the PC on today though. It was the last day of Mallory's visit, and he fully intended to keep her busy with making plans for an immediate wedding date—assuming, of course, she said yes. Which she would. Any of his business associates could tell Mallory, if she asked, that negative responses tended to make him only that much more determined to get his own way.

Pat leaned across the desk to flick the off switch, and found himself staring at a catastrophe.

Wah Sung Produce file erased.

Not Wah Sung. Not his largest account, the one he'd worked on for the past seven years, building it from a small investment into a business worthy of the most profitable portfolios.

"Christopher!"

The boy's name rolled like thunder in the room. Where was he?

Pat shoved to his feet and paced restlessly, trying to clamp down on his anger. *Count to ten,* he advised himself silently. *Make it one hundred. A thousand, if necessary.*

This was part of it, he realized. When he'd thought about marriage to Mallory, he pictured a warm family scene—nights around the kitchen table, before the fireplace, days of Little League, fishing, and lending his expertise to math homework. He hadn't considered the not-so-nice things. Chris was a kid—a great kid, most of the time, but still a kid. He was bound to get into the same kind of trouble he'd always gotten into when he was a boy.

A father had to deal with that, had to guide his son toward the right paths in life. Like his father had done for him, Pat admitted, thinking back fondly on Michael Lonergan's stern talks, ready ear and boundless patience.

Was he ready to walk in his father's shoes? Did he have what it took to be a father—a ready-made father? There was no training ground, no nine-month waiting period in which to prepare himself for this position. In loving and wanting Mallory, he was getting a package deal—mother and son.

Pat's steps took him to the window. The morning was full-blown already, the sky clear, the sun shining. The comical sound of Chris's ferocious roar as he dashed madly after a clutch of hens filled the air.

Had it only been a few weeks ago that he'd realized the old farmhouse was no longer a home? That it was missing a necessary ingredient?

Well, things had changed since then. All because of the woman who slept on in his bed upstairs, and her child.

Pat squared his shoulders. "This is it, Mom," he announced out loud. He had no doubt Marie Lonergan was listening. "Wish me luck. I think I'm going to need it."

Mallory reveled in a feeling of all-over well-being. She stretched beneath the covers, enjoying the feel of the sheets against her naked skin. The touch made her feel decadent and wonderful. The memories of the night before were even better.

Patrick was now her lover, and it was better than she'd ever dreamed. Whatever happened in the future, she would never regret the intimacy they'd shared. For the first time in her life, she felt that she'd done everything right. She also knew exactly what she wanted. The walls she'd raised were gone for good. This time there was nothing to stop her from winning the man she loved.

No matter how long it took, no matter what the obstacles.

Mallory stretched again, running her fingers through her tumbled brown curls, pushing them up and away from her face. She and Pat hadn't talked much. Hadn't wanted to do anything more than explore and enjoy each other. But she'd made a few decisions on her own before dropping off to sleep. Some might surprise him.

They could wait for a while—tomorrow or the next day. Whenever the time was right. For now she just wanted to luxuriate in the memories of making love with Patrick.

She hadn't realized it before, but last night had been the first time she had truly made love with a man. And it had been glorious.

She savored the memory of Pat's voice, husky with words of love. Not just any words, but those three special little words that no man had ever said to her: *I love you.* Hearing them had made her feel that she held the magic stick from the story he had spun last night, for one of her dearest wishes had come true.

Now if she could just wave that stick one more time....

Running footsteps sounded on the stairs. "Mommy, Mommy!"

The bubble burst quickly. Mallory had time only to hastily wrap a sheet around her before Christopher barreled into the room and flung himself on her bed.

"Guess what!" her son exclaimed after giving her a quick hug.

Still disoriented by his boisterous arrival, Mallory pushed a lock of hair out of her eyes. "What?"

"Pat says I'm grounded, except I'm not grounded."

"Not yet, anyway," a deep voice said from the doorway. "Tell her why."

Mallory stared at Pat as he stood in the archway, his shoulders propped against the molding, his face set in stern but calm lines. His hair was a tousled mess, his jaw darkened by a night's growth of beard. Its roughness had scraped along every inch of her body only hours ago, and she'd loved the sensation. He looked wonderful.

But she sensed trouble. "What did you do?" she asked Christopher, her voice pitched at a soft but slightly disapproving tone.

Chris's small shoulders rose and fell in a shrug. "Nothin' much," he said.

Pat cleared his throat.

"Okay. I just looked at his dumb computer," Chris confessed in a rush.

"He wiped out a complete file," Patrick elaborated calmly.

A cold hand seemed to grip Mallory's heart. Wiped out a whole business file? She knew how she would feel if inventory files on her store computer were erased. Happiness and anticipation gave way to a terrible sinking feeling.

She tried to keep her face expressionless as she met Pat's eyes. "Do you keep backup diskettes?"

Pat ran a hand back through his hair in a show of restrained frustration. "The damage has been repaired, but that's not the issue here. Christopher was told not to touch anything in my office. Now he knows that when I say something, I mean it. Don't you, sport?"

Christopher nodded and actually slid off the bed to be nearer the unsmiling man.

"I guess," the boy mumbled. "And I'm only grounded if Mom says I am, right?"

Mallory crushed the hopeful look in her son's eye. "Oh, you're grounded, all right, bub. Count your lucky stars that that's all you are."

She glanced at Pat, but his expression was unreadable. Was their idyllic holiday to end on this note? Was the blossoming of their love to wilt? Pat was a bachelor. He had no idea of the ups and downs, the reality of life, with a curious six-year-old.

"Okay," Chris said, surprising Mallory with his acceptance of the punishment. He'd always tried crying, sulking, and glaring at her to minimize sentences in the past. "But I'm not grounded till we get home," Christopher added, and looked up at Pat. "Right?"

"It's your mom's call, sport. At least for now."

At least for now? A tiny ray of hope gleamed in Mallory's heart.

"Chris and I have something we'd like to discuss with you, Mal," Pat continued.

His voice was so calm and stripped of emotion, Mallory held her breath in anticipation of what was to come, fearing the worst.

Pat's large hand settled on Christopher's thin shoulder. "As you probably know," Pat said, "Chris is very interested in your welfare."

Chris nodded, a happy grin spreading across his face.

"But he is more interested in his own welfare," Pat added. "So he made me a proposition a little while ago."

Mallory found she had to clear her throat before answering. "He did?"

Chris's head bobbed. "I asked Pat if he'd be my dad," he announced proudly.

Mallory swallowed loudly this time. The lump in her throat seemed to be growing larger by the minute. Her eyes misted over. Blinking back the tears, she gulped. "You did?"

"Yep," Chris said. "Only Pat told me there were some con...con...some what?" He looked up trustingly at the man who towered over him.

"Conditions."

"Yeah, conditions to con... con..."

"Consider," Pat supplied. "A good number of conditions."

"What are they?" Mallory asked. Her voice sounded unfamiliar, as if it were tight and forced.

Chris took a deep breath, as if the list were long and laborious. "First, I have to promise to try to remember what I've been told."

"Only try to remember?" Mallory echoed, her eyes searching Pat's for a hint of what was coming. The emerald depths were warm and welcoming. They touched her tenderly, telling her of a love that was deep and abiding.

"I can try," Chris insisted. "'Sides, Pat says a man can't expect too many miracles all at once."

"Just one at a time," Patrick said.

Mallory tingled at the way his voice caressed each word. Was he telling her that she... that they...

"I bet I can already do the second thing," Chris declared proudly.

Pat hunkered down to the boy's level. "Prove it."

Christopher took a deep breath. "Lonergan," he declared. *"L-O-N..."*

Mallory was sure she had forgotten how to breathe, her chest was so tight and she felt so out of breath as her son successfully spelled his hero's surname.

Emerald-green eyes met hers over her son's head. "There's just one more condition to be met," Pat said. "I asked Chris's permission, as man of your house, about this, and he thinks the idea of us all getting married is cool."

"Really cool, Mom," Christopher added. "Can we do it soon?"

"Really soon," Pat said.

"I—"

Without letting Mallory finish, Chris let himself fall against Patrick, giving the man a fierce hug. "That means yes," he translated, before tossing his mother an impish grin. "Can I go visit my kitten now? I won't run, and there's no busy streets to cross."

Feeling suddenly helpless, Mallory gave him a limp wave and collapsed back against her pillows.

It was only after Christopher's footsteps had clattered down the stairs and the back door had slammed shut behind him that she dared to meet the gaze of the man who stood once more in the open doorway.

"He knows how to spell Lonergan," she said.

"I think Christopher Lonergan has a nice sound to it." Pat's raffish smile curled into being. His gaze slid over the covers, working from the foot of the bed slowly upward to where Mallory's ringless fingers clutched the quilt. "Not as nice as Mallory Lonergan, of course," he added.

"You want to adopt Chris?" Why did her voice have to be the veriest of whispers? One that made her sound stunned that he was willing to accept another man's child as his own.

"I love you, Mal," Pat said, although he kept the width of the room between them. "Nothing is going to change that. I want to be a part of your life. I want to be a part of Chris's, too. I want him to be more than just your son. I want him to be our son."

Our son. The simple statement meant more to her than any avowal of love. It meant the past was dead. The hurt she'd lived with was healed. And all because Patrick Lonergan cared deeply for her and her son.

Mallory slid from the bed, a bed sheet draped around her in a sensuous swirl of cloth. "Come here." She purred the request.

Pat closed the door before taking a single long stride into the room. His arms closed around her possessively.

She slid her arms up his chest, and around his neck, her eyes radiating love. "How long do you think *our* son will be gone playing with the kittens at the neighbors'?" Mallory asked.

His grin was downright wicked. "Long enough. But, since I'd rather not take Chris's word for this, answer one question. Will you marry me, Mallory Meyers?"

Mallory's heart swelled with joy. A tear did escape the corner of her eye, rolling over her cheek. Pat caught the drop on the tip of his finger.

Mallory stroked her fingers softly along his rough jawline. She had decided to take a chance with this man, but there was no gamble involved. She trusted him, not only with her life, but with Christopher's, and the lives of all the sons that would follow. It was something she'd once resolved never to do. It was one resolution that was meant to be broken.

Pat grinned down at her, and Mallory's heart relinquished the last of her fears. She loved this man—loved him unconditionally.

"I would do anything to spend the rest of my life with you," she whispered and gave him a tremulous smile. The bed sheet slipped unheeded to the floor. "Even marry you."

"Hardships must be endured," he murmured teasingly. His whiskered cheek branded her as he nuzzled her neck. His hands slid possessively down her naked back.

Mallory gave herself up to the moment. This was where she belonged. Where she had always belonged. In Patrick's arms.

He kissed her lightly, his touch teasing as well as ardent. "You know," Pat murmured softly against her lips, "if we're lucky, Chris might be gone long enough for us to make a start at providing him with a sister."

Mallory drew his lips back to hers. "It sounds like an excellent idea to me," she whispered.

It was.

* * * * *

Get Ready to be Swept Away by
Silhouette's Spring Collection

Abduction
& Seduction

These passion-filled stories explore both the dangerous
desires of men and the seductive powers of women.
Written by three of our most celebrated authors, they are
sure to capture your hearts.

Diana Palmer
Brings us a spin-off of her Long, Tall Texans series

Joan Johnston
Crafts a beguiling Western romance

Rebecca Brandewyne
New York Times bestselling author
makes a smashing contemporary debut

Available in March at your favorite retail outlet.

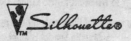

WHAT EVER HAPPENED TO...?

Have you been wondering when much-loved characters will finally get their own stories? Well, have we got a lineup for you! Silhouette Special Edition is proud to present a *Spin-off Spectacular!* Be sure to catch these exciting titles from some of your favorite authors:

HUSBAND: SOME ASSEMBLY REQUIRED (SE #931 January) Shawna Saunders has finally found Mr. Right in the dashing Murphy Pendleton, last seen in *Marie Ferrarella's* BABY IN THE MIDDLE (SE #892).

SAME TIME, NEXT YEAR (SE #937 February) In this tie-in to *Debbie Macomber's* popular series THOSE MANNING MEN and THOSE MANNING SISTERS, a yearly reunion between friends suddenly has them in the marrying mood!

A FAMILY HOME (SE #938 February) Adam Cutler discovers the best reason for staying home is the love he's found with sweet-natured and sexy Lainey Bates in *Celeste Hamilton's* follow-up to WHICH WAY IS HOME? (SE #897).

JAKE'S MOUNTAIN (SE #945 March) Jake Harris never met anyone as stubborn—or as alluring—as Dr. Maggie Matthews in *Christine Flynn's* latest, a spin-off to WHEN MORNING COMES (SE #922).

Don't miss these wonderful titles, only for our readers—only from Silhouette Special Edition!

MONTANA Mavericks

Stories that capture living and loving beneath the Big Sky, where legends live on...and mystery lingers.

This January, the intrigue continues with

OUTLAW LOVERS
by Pat Warren

He was a wanted man. She was the beckoning angel who offered him a hideout. Now their budding passion has put them both in danger. And he'd do anything to protect her.

Don't miss a minute of the loving as the passion continues with:

WAY OF THE WOLF
by Rebecca Daniels (February)

THE LAW IS NO LADY
by Helen R. Myers (March)

FATHER FOUND
by Laurie Paige (April)
and many more!

Only from *Silhouette*® where passion lives.

THE BLACKTHORN BROTHERHOOD

by Diana Whitney

Three men bound by a childhood secret are freed through family, friendship...and love.

Watch for the first book in Diana's Whitney's compelling new miniseries:

THE ADVENTURER
Special Edition #934, January 1995

Devon Monroe had finally come home, home to a haunting memory that made him want to keep running. Home to a woman who made him want to stand still and stare into her eyes. For there was something about Jessica Newcomb that made him forget about his own past and wonder long and hard about hers....

Look for THE AVENGER coming in the fall of 1995.

DWBB1

Silhouette

SPECIAL EDITION™®

The new year brings readers a powerful new trilogy—

by Andrea Edwards

In January, don't miss A RING AND A PROMISE (SE #932).

Just one look at feisty Chicago caterer Kate Mallory made rancher Jake MacNeill forget all about Montana. Could his lonesome-cowboy soul rest as love overcomes unfulfilled promises of the past?

THIS TIME, FOREVER—sometimes a love is so strong, nothing can stand in its way...not even time.

Look for the next installment, A ROSE AND A WEDDING VOW (SE #944), in March 1995. Read along as two *old* friends learn that love is worth taking a chance.

AEMINI-1